PX

Praise for Frank Leslie
and *The Lonely Breed*

"Frank Leslie kicks his story into a gallop right out of the gate . . . raw and gritty as the West itself."
—Mark Henry, author of *The Hell Riders*

"Explodes off the page in an enormously entertaining burst of stay-up-late, read-into-the-night, fast-moving flurry of page-turning action. Leslie spins a yarn that rivals the very best on Western shelves today."
—J. Lee Butts, author of *Lawdog*

"Frank Leslie writes with leathery prose honed sharper than a buffalo skinner's knife, with characters as explosive as forty-rod whiskey, and a plot that slams readers with the impact of a Winchester slug. *The Lonely Breed* is edgy, raw, and irresistible."
—Johnny D. Boggs, Spur Award–winning author of *Camp Ford*

"Hooks you instantly with sympathetic characters and sin-soaked villains. Yakima has a heart of gold and an Arkansas toothpick. If you prefer Peckinpah to Ang Lee, this one's for you."
—Mike Baron, creator of *Nexus* and *The Badger* comic book series

"Big, burly, brawling, and action-packed, *The Lonely Breed* is a testosterone-laced winner from the word 'go,' and Frank Leslie is an author to watch!"
—E. K. Recknor, author of *The Brothers of Junior Doyle*

THE
THUNDER
RIDERS

Frank Leslie

A SIGNET BOOK

SIGNET
Published by New American Library, a division of
Penguin Group (USA) Inc., 375 Hudson Street,
New York, New York 10014, USA
Penguin Group (Canada), 90 Eglinton Avenue East, Suite 700, Toronto,
Ontario M4P 2Y3, Canada (a division of Pearson Penguin Canada Inc.)
Penguin Books Ltd., 80 Strand, London WC2R 0RL, England
Penguin Ireland, 25 St. Stephen's Green, Dublin 2,
Ireland (a division of Penguin Books Ltd.)
Penguin Group (Australia), 250 Camberwell Road, Camberwell, Victoria 3124,
Australia (a division of Pearson Australia Group Pty. Ltd.)
Penguin Books India Pvt. Ltd., 11 Community Centre, Panchsheel Park,
New Delhi - 110 017, India
Penguin Group (NZ), 67 Apollo Drive, Rosedale, North Shore 0745,
Auckland, New Zealand (a division of Pearson New Zealand Ltd.)
Penguin Books (South Africa) (Pty.) Ltd., 24 Sturdee Avenue,
Rosebank, Johannesburg 2196, South Africa

Penguin Books Ltd., Registered Offices:
80 Strand, London WC2R 0RL, England

First published by Signet, an imprint of New American Library,
a division of Penguin Group (USA) Inc.

First Printing, September 2007
10 9 8 7 6 5 4 3 2 1

Chapter 1

Arizona Ranger Wilson Pyle built a quirley with his gnarled, slightly arthritic fingers and snapped a match to life on his belt buckle. As he touched the flickering flame to the end of the twisted cigarette, his partner, Kenny Danaher, kneeling atop the rocky escarpment above Pyle and the rangers' two ground-tied horses, yelled, "I don't see a damn thing down there, Will!"

"Nuthin'?"

"Don't look to me like there's been a soul in that old ghost town since the miners pulled out two years ago."

Letting smoke dribble out from between his wind-burned lips, Pyle glanced around. "Look hard, Kenny. It's late. No doubt quite a few shadows in that canyon."

Pyle was tired. He and Danaher had been on the trail the last five days, brush-popping owlhoots between the White Mountains and the Chiricahuas. Or trying to. Desperadoes holed up like black widows in Mormon tea this time of the year. The old ranger felt as though his saddle had grown into his ass.

"Ah, hell." Danaher lifted his field glasses again, directing the lenses out and down. Long dark red hair fell down from his black-brimmed hat, and his thin red beard was rimed with trail dust. His green duster hung slack on his lean frame, scratched from brambles and cactus thorns.

Young enough to be Pyle's grandson, Danaher had the patience of youth—which is to say, very little patience at all. But then, Pyle didn't have a gal waiting for him back home in Benson like Kenny did. A young wife with a baby on the way. Pyle hadn't had a wife waiting on him in a long time, having outlived two—a half Apache and a pretty blond ex-dance-hall girl from St. Louis by way of Prescott. The old ranger didn't have anything waiting for him back in Benson—except a bottle, a dime novel, and a cord of wood that needed chopping out back of his rented shack near the ranger station.

"Hold on!" Danaher said above the chill winter breeze sighing among the rocks. "I do see something, after all. Holy shit!"

Pyle's heart quickened. He removed the quirley from his lips and straightened, his tired back creaking. "What is it?"

Danaher was turning his head slightly from left to right, following something with the field glasses. "You ain't gonna believe this, Will." His voice was sharp with mockery. "Oh, Lordy, you just ain't gonna believe what I see down there."

Pyle relaxed, and a faint smile shone on his leathery face, all but hidden by his thin gray beard. "What is it?"

"Coyote strollin' down the main street just like he owned the place. Got him a rat hangin' out of his mouth."

Danaher lowered the glasses and turned to stare down

the scarp at Pyle resting on a flat boulder near his paint mustang, one spurred boot propped on a knee. "You want to go down there and arrest him for trespassin' or huntin' on mine company land without a permit?"

Pyle chuckled. He blew out a long plume of cigarette smoke, then stuck the quirley between his teeth and hiked his old Walker Colt higher on his hips. "Come on, kid. We're gonna go down and have a look."

"What for? I told you there ain't nothin' but a coyote down there, Will!"

"Mount up," Pyle said, tightening his paint's saddle cinch. "That bullion's gonna be passin' through here on the old army road, about a mile east. We best go down and have a look up close. Could be owlhoots holed up, sharpening their horns and cleanin' their irons for to-morrow."

Worse still, it could be the Thunder Riders—they'd been raiding along the border for several months now—though a vague dread kept the old ranger from mention-ing their name aloud.

"Ah, shit. I'm gonna be late getting home for supper, ain't I?" They were on the last day of their campaign and had expected to be back in Benson by nightfall.

"Just take a minute."

"It'll take an hour at the least."

Pyle grabbed the apple and swung into the saddle—a task that seemed to get harder every day. "Orders are or-ders, son. Cottonwood Canyon has been a prime owlhoot nest ever since the company pulled out, so we're gonna give it a look-see. Now quit flappin' your lips and mount your horse."

Danaher cursed as he cased his field glasses and began descending the scarp, his duster flapping around his long, denim-clad legs, the afternoon breeze bending his hat brim over his deep blue eyes. "You knew we were gonna ride into that canyon all along, didn't you, you old geezer?"

"Yep." Pyle laughed. "I was just takin' a smoke break and restin' my tired old ass!"

With Pyle leading, the rangers found a game trail angling across the canyon wall and followed it down into the cottonwoods lining a dry riverbed on the canyon floor. As they crossed the riverbed, their horses' shod hooves ringing like cracked bells off the water-polished stones, Pyle scrutinized the shanties—all of them made of adobe or logs and sod—and the falling-down stables huddled in the creosote and mesquite.

The shacks and corrals looked like the ruins of some lost civilization. They gave off the spooky aura that Pyle felt whenever he was around ancient Indian cliff dwellings or the Native kivas he came upon frequently as he patrolled the territory's deepest reaches.

The breeze swept the chaparral, lifting veils of sand. A rough-legged hawk, perched on a splintered gray corral post, stared intently at the approaching riders, lifting one long-taloned foot at a time. Its wings ruffled and spread, the talons pushed off the post, and the hawk rose, screeching, toward the ridge the two rangers had just left.

"Population, two," Danaher drawled, riding off Pyle's paint's right hip. "I missed him from the ridge."

"Let's hope he's all you missed." Pyle checked down

the paint, canted his head left. "You start at the west end. I'll start at the east. We'll meet in the middle."

When the younger ranger had heeled his piebald off toward the west end of the town, weaving around corrals, chicken coops, goat pens, and privy pits, Pyle put the paint forward.

He swung between a couple of tar-paper shacks, the paper having come loose and fluttering in the breeze, and pulled up behind the town's easternmost Main Street dwelling. Remaining mounted, he sidled the paint up to the livery barn's rear double doors and pulled a handle.

The door opened with a soft thud and a scrape. Pyle backed the horse away from the barn as he swung the door open, and the black mouth of the barn expelled the rotten smells of hay, manure, and rodent scat on a vast, musty breath.

He sat the horse to one side of the open door, using the door as a shield, listening for sounds of human movement, one hand resting on the walnut grip of his holstered Colt. Hearing only the faintly creaking timbers and scuttling mice, he booted the paint through the opening.

The horse had taken only two strides along the barn's mashed-earth floor when a great whooshing sounded, and a sudden wind barreled out of the bowels of the rancid-smelling livery. There was a roar like the shuffling of a giant card deck. The paint whinnied and lurched to the side. A flickering black cloud welled up from the shadows.

Pyle lowered his head to the paint's neck, keeping a

firm grip on the reins, feeling the horse's muscles bunch
and leap in fear beneath the saddle.

Several screaming bats bounced off the ranger's
raised left arm and a couple nearly ripped the soiled Stetson from his head. The covey careened through the open
doors behind him, their screeching diminishing gradually until they were gone and a heavy silence fell. Dust
and straw flecks sifted.

Pyle patted the neck of the jittery, snorting paint.
"Easy, boy. They're gone."

The horse shook its head indignantly. Pyle nudged it
on down the barn's central alley, swinging his head from
side to side. When he'd reached the closed front doors
and had seen no sign of anything living in the barn except bats and a couple of kangaroo rats, he kicked the
front right door wide and booted the horse onto the
town's main street.

He looked around at the false-fronted buildings that,
with their dilapidated porches and brush arbors and broken windows, looked like giant tombstones in a forgot-
ten cemetery. Tumbleweeds were basted along the
buildings' stone foundations and boardwalks, and several were hung up in the windows.

Horse tracks were etched in the street's deep dust, but
since the town was still on a secondary trail used by
prospectors and saddle tramps, the tracks didn't mean
much. There was no way to know if the town was being
used as an owlhoots' nest—especially by owlhoots who
intended to go after tomorrow's bullion run—unless Pyle
saw direct evidence.

Namely, the owlhoots themselves.

Pyle dismounted the paint and dropped the reins, then shucked his Henry rifle from the saddle boot. Leaving the horse in the shade of the livery barn, he jacked a shell into the rifle's chamber, off-cocked the hammer, and began angling across the street.

He spied movement out of the corner of his right eye. Danaher rode into the far end of the town, a rifle resting stock down on his thigh. Pyle waved to indicate all clear so far, then mounted a boardwalk and stuck his head through the window of a drugstore.

He walked through three buildings on each side of the street and looked into two more, then gingerly mounted a gap-boarded walk in front of the Bale of Hay Saloon. He turned to see Danaher stride toward him before swerving onto a boardwalk on the same side of the street as Pyle. The kid disappeared into a sporting house—the newest and probably the best-preserved building in town.

Pyle stepped through the saloon doorway, which had long been missing its two louvers, and strode past the long mahogany bar. The backbar and mirror were gone. The dust on the bar and on the few tables left behind by human scavengers was thick and littered with mouse droppings and the tracks of rodents and even birds.

The ceiling creaked over Pyle's head. He stopped and looked up. There was another soft creak, as though someone were moving slowly across the floorboards. Dust sifted from the rafters to tick on the floor in front of Pyle's boots.

The old ranger hefted the Henry repeater and thumbed back the hammer. Holding the barrel straight up, he crossed to the back of the saloon, then slowly climbed the stairs, wincing each time a rotten riser squawked. He stared at the pine-paneled wall growing before him, from which a rusty nail protruded.

A shuffling rose behind the wall on his right, growing louder—something moving toward Pyle fast. He extended the rifle straight out from his right shoulder and aimed at the paneled wall, eyes wide, heart thudding.

A dun gray shape appeared, moving in a blur across the landing at the top of the stairs. Pyle caught only a glimpse of the beast—a scrawny brush wolf with pricked ears and a bushy gray tail—before it bolted off to his left. Footpads thumbing and toenails clicking, it clattered away down the hall.

Pyle lowered the rifle, depressing the hammer. He leaned against the stair rail and sighed. "I'm gettin' too damn old for this."

He suddenly lifted his head. Again he'd heard something. This time it had come from outside, though he couldn't tell from which direction.

He turned, tramped down the stairs and across the saloon's main hall, and outside. Swinging his head from left to right, he stepped gingerly across the boardwalk and into the street.

He looked at his horse. The paint was staring toward the other end of the town, its eyes wide and cautious, ears twitching.

Pyle moved out into the sun-washed street, where a light, cool wind was swinging a shingle chain and stirring the dust and old manure. Up the street, boots thudded and spurs chinged raucously.

Pyle tensed as Kenny Danaher stumbled out the front

door of the sporting house, which sat alone on a wide lot surrounded by sage. The junior ranger's hat was off, and his shoulder-length red hair spilled over his shoulders as he lurched across the house's front porch. Holding both arms across his lower belly, Danaher headed for the steps. He dropped to a knee and lowered his head. Keeping his arms folded taut across his belly, he lifted his chin suddenly and stretched his lips back from his teeth.

His beseeching scream echoed up and down the street. *"Wiillll!"*

He rose to a crouch and bounded down the five porch steps, tripping halfway down and tumbling into the street. He rolled onto his side. Blood glistened across Danaher's belly, welling out between his crossed arms.

"Will!" the kid screamed again.

A high-pitched laugh rose from the sporting house, but no one appeared on the porch. If faces peered through the broken windows, Pyle couldn't see them.

He started toward Danaher, thought better of it, and stopped. Whoever had stabbed Kenny would pink Pyle from the windows or the open door.

The Thunder Riders? Pyle's spine turned to jelly. Could his luck have gone that sour? But why in the hell *wouldn't* the woolliest gang in the Territory and northern Sonora be after that gold? He'd heard there was over fifty thousand dollars' worth.

To his right was an alley. Pyle swung toward it, digging his heels in as he dashed between an old harness shop and the doctor's office. He ran around behind the harness shop, then up the alley, leaping trash heaps and what remained of firewood and weed clumps. By the time he reached the rear of the sporting house, his chest was burning and his heels ached in his boots.

At the rear corner of the general store, he took a quick study of the sporting house sitting just west, thirty yards beyond. No faces or rifles shone in the windows on this side of the house. No gunmen waited on the porch or the roof.

Pyle sucked in a deep breath and, squeezing his Henry in both gloved hands, bolted up toward Main Street along the general store's sun-blistered wall.

His spurs rang softly, occasionally catching in the sage. Ten feet from the street, he angled toward the sporting house's front porch, toward where Kenny now knelt in the street, his head down, shoulders rising and falling sharply. Blood stained the dirt beneath him, and liver-colored cords of gut leaked out from between his arms.

Pyle raked his gaze along the front of the sporting house, then dropped to one knee beside Danaher. "I'm gonna get you to the other side of the street, Kenny."

The young ranger only shook his sagging head. "I'm done, Will. Get outta here."

Pyle kept his eyes on the front of the sporting house. It looked abandoned.

"Try to stand. You gotta help me here, boy."

Pyle wrapped his arms around the young man's bloody waist, tried to heave him to his feet, all the while keeping a sharp eye on the front of the quiet sporting house. Kenny was nearly a deadweight, but when Pyle had hauled him up almost to standing height, the young ranger straightened his knees, took some of his weight off Pyle.

Pyle swung him around and, holding his rifle in his right hand while wrapping his left arm around Kenny's waist, began leading him toward the other side of the street.

Keeping a firm grip on the young ranger's cartridge belt, Pyle jerked frequent looks over his right shoulder, his spine crawling as he expected a bullet at any second. It seemed to take an hour to reach the narrow gap between a blacksmith shop and Herriman's Jewelers. He passed the rain barrel at the mouth of the gap and kicked through dead leaves and rusty cans, heading for the rear of the blacksmith shop. His heart lifted slightly when the jewelry store shielded him and Danaher from the sporting house.

Danaher gave a long, raspy sigh, and his knees buckled. The kid's arm fell from around Pyle's neck, and he hit the alley hard on his knees, then plopped forward on his face.

"Kenny!"

Breathing hard, Pyle knelt beside the young ranger and turned him onto his back. Danaher's eyes were half open, staring glassily. His chest was still. An awful fetor rose from the wide, gut-leaking wound in his belly.

Pyle scrubbed his jaw, cursed, then ran his hand lightly over the dead ranger's face, closing his eyes. He stood heavily, squeezing his rifle as he stared down at Danaher, whose arms rested slack at his sides, his legs crossed at the ankles.

He took a deep breath, walked back to the mouth of

the alley, and shouldering against the jewelry shop on his left, stared at the sporting house on the other side of the street. The west-falling sun gilded the porch posts and upper-story windows.

Pyle gritted his teeth as he jerked the Henry's hammer back. Holding the rifle at port arms, he strode into the street, his jaw hard, eyes boring holes into the house's front wall.

Halfway across the street he raised the Henry's stock to his cheek and glared down the barrel as he shouted, "Show yourselves, you goddamn butchers!"

A bullet tore into his right knee a half second before the rifle report reached his ears and he saw the smoke puff in the window right of the sporting house's open front door. The mocking laugh he'd heard before rose again, and a plump round face appeared in the window.

As Pyle's bullet-blasted knee buckled, the old ranger triggered a shot into the window casing to the right of the laughing face. His knee hit the ground, and he groaned as he shifted his weight to the other knee and rammed a fresh round into the Henry's breech. Trying to ignore the throbbing pain and feeling the blood drain into the street, he raised the Henry and swung the barrel toward the house.

Smoke puffed in the open front door. Searing pain lanced his left shoulder. His shot pulled wide as he screamed and jerked straight back, dropping the Henry.

His back hit the street, and he kicked both legs out before him, pain from the bullet-riddled knee setting his entire leg on fire, while the bullet in his shoulder did the same to his chest and left arm.

He lay faceup in the street, grunting and sighing and flailing around with his right hand, trying to locate his rifle. In the bottom periphery of his vision, figures moved. Boots thudded across floorboards, spurs rattled and twanged. A woman's evil chuckle mingled with men's laughter.

Pyle lifted his head. Two men and a woman filed out of the sporting house and into the street. The first man was a big black hombre with a mustache, a long tan duster, and a sombrero. The other man was an Apache in deerskin leggings, wolf coat, red sash, and matching bandanna, with a matching brace of .44's on his hips. He held a Sharps carbine down low in his right hand. He stopped to Pyle's left and deftly kicked the Winchester out of the ranger's reach. The black eyes bored into Pyle's, and he grinned with recognition, flashing a silver eyetooth.

"Old man, you should have quit while you still had some years left!"

"Yasi." Pyle grunted at the renegade Apache who had once scouted for General Crook in the Sierra Madre, before too much tizwin had driven him loco. Two years ago he'd been rumored to be running with the notorious Thunder Riders—mostly Yanqui rapists and murderers who raised hell on both sides of the border. "You murderin' savage. I figured I'd run into you sooner or later."

The woman between him and the black man cracked a snaggletoothed grin and laughed. She appeared to be half Mexican with some Indian blood. Short and plump, she wore a heavy brown poncho, fringed deerskin leggings, and moccasins. She cackled delightedly, causing the dried-up flower in her hair to nod. "Sooner rather than later, eh, amigo?"

Pyle summoned all his remaining strength to his right arm, jerked his hand to his holstered .44. The woman laughed again, then leapt forward and, lifting one stubby leg, kicked the revolver into the air over the ranger's head. She stooped, pressing the barrel of her Spencer repeater against Pyle's temple. The desert rose in her hair sagged. Tin and bone amulets jostled on her poncho.

She stared down the rifle's forestock from four feet away. Her flat black eyes twinkled in the dying light.

Toots was her name. Her real handle was something long and Spanish.

Toots thumbed back the Spencer's hammer.

Pyle glared back at her. If Considine's bunch was in the country, all hell was about to break loose. He was almost glad he wouldn't be here for it. "Go to hell, *puta* bitch."

"Usted primero," cackled the round-faced, flat-eyed outlaw as she squeezed the trigger. *You first.*

Chapter 2

A horse's terrified scream shot through the night.

Yakima Henry snapped his eyes open. A foot thudded softly on the porch beyond his cabin's front door.

Yakima grabbed the Winchester Yellowboy repeater off the mattress beside him as the door burst open with a thunderous crash accompanied by a high-pitched, ear-numbing devil's whoop.

A short, bulky, long-haired figure leapt into the cabin and crouched just beyond the frame, silhouetted against the stars behind it. Ambient light glinted off white stone as the Apache's right hand, clutching a tomahawk, whipped back behind his head.

Yakima snapped up the Yellowboy and fired twice. The Apache screamed as the bullets punched him straight back through the doorway and into the yard beyond, the tomahawk skidding along the porch and thudding into the dust.

Outside, Yakima's black stallion, Wolf, loosed another terrified whinny amid the squawk and wooden clatter of the corral gate being opened. The Apaches were after the horses.

Yakima leapt out of bed and, clad in only his long underwear, crossed the cabin in three giant strides, bounded through the front door, and hurdled the dead Apache. He'd taken one headlong stride toward the corral when a bullet whistled past his right ear and thumped into the ground. Yakima saw the rifle flash out of the corner of his right eye and heard the ringing report.

There was the quick rasp of a cocking lever. Yakima dove to his left and rolled onto his back as the rifle flashed again up near the peak of his cabin roof. The flash revealed the blue and white calico shirt and red bandanna of the Apache squatting there, rifle extended over the edge of the roof.

Yakima raised his Winchester and fired two quick shots. The Apache grunted. His silhouette jerked back, then sagged forward to tumble over the edge of the roof. The brave hit the porch below with a thud and a crunch of cracking wood. The rifle clattered to the ground beside him.

A shrill Apache war cry rose across the yard, and Yakima rolled onto his belly, ramming a fresh shell into the Yellowboy's breech. Two rifles flashed and thundered near the corral gate, the slugs tearing up sand and gravel in front of Yakima, one clipping a sage branch and tossing it over his head. He returned fire quickly—*Boom-rasp! Boom-rasp! Boom-rasp! Boom!*—and saw through his wafting powder smoke a shadow fall as the open corral gate squawked on its hinges.

Another shadow cut away in the darkness, the quick

footfalls of moccasined feet sounding clear in the sudden silence.

Yakima levered another round into the Yellowboy's chamber as he bolted up and ran, covering the fifty yards between the cabin and the corral in seconds. Near the corral gate, he stopped and angled his Winchester down toward the figure slumped on the ground, but the Apache lay facedown and still, the two holes in his back bright with fresh blood. A Spencer carbine with a lanyard and a brass-riveted stock leaned against the brave's motionless right leg.

Yakima slammed the corral gate closed—relieved to see his black stallion and his paint standing still as statues on the other side of the corral—then dropped to a knee, aimed the Winchester in the direction of the quickly fading footsteps, and emptied the chamber. The smoking shells arced over his shoulder and rattled into the gravel behind him.

He leaned the empty Yellowboy against the corral, then picked up the dead brave's Spencer and shucked the stag-handled, double-edged knife from the oiled sheath thonged low on the Apache's thigh. Bolting forward, mindless of his bare feet, he headed off across the night-cloaked clearing.

Until tonight, the Apaches hadn't discovered him here on the high, pine-studded slopes of Mount Bailey. Now that this small group of night raiders had, Yakima had to make sure they were all dead—or there would be more.

He lunged forward through the darkness, arms and legs pumping, heart racing. The night air was as cool as a knife blade against his sweat-slick face. He traced a course through the sage and bunchgrass, leaping boulders and small piñons. When he'd run a hundred yards, he stopped suddenly and stared into the mixed pines flanking the rocky escarpment rising ahead of him.

The Apaches had probably tied their horses in the rocks, well away from the cabin and Yakima's mounts.

He pricked his ears against the rasping of his own labored breath.

Before him, at the edge of the pines, the darkness shifted slightly. He sucked a sharp breath and dove to his left, hitting the ground on his shoulder as a rifle boomed thirty yards in front of him, the barrel spitting knives of blue-black flame.

Yakima rolled left once, twice, three times, gritting his teeth as the Apache's tracking slugs blew up grass and sand behind him, the lead whining as it bounced off rocks. He rolled a fourth time as a slug burned a furrow across his right shoulder.

He flung himself desperately sideways two more times, then stopped.

The rifle had fallen silent.

He whipped up the Spencer he'd managed to hang on to, worked the trigger-guard cocking mechanism, and fired at the place where the Apache's rifle had flashed. He squeezed off two more shots before the Spencer clicked empty, then tossed the rifle aside. Gripping the knife in his right hand, he dashed toward the pine-studded escarpment.

At the place where the rifle had flashed, he stopped, hunkered down on his heels, holding the knife between his knees so it wouldn't reflect starlight, and pricked his ears, listening. Ahead and to the right, beyond the screening brush and a jumble of black boulders, a horse snorted and thumped a hoof.

Nothing else but the chitter of crickets and the distant screech of a nighthawk.

Yakima rose to a crouch and moved forward, toward where the horses were tied, holding the knife low in his right hand. He set one bare foot down softly, wincing at the occasional scrape of a sharp rock, pine needle, or weed.

The slight whisper of a breeze was behind him. It was suddenly rife with the sour, gamy smell of Apache. Yakima wheeled, instantly swinging the knife up and out.

"Ayeeee!" the Apache screamed as his stocky silhouette leapt straight back and away, starlight gleaming off the blade in his right hand.

He stopped, lunged forward, and swung the knife so quickly it sliced the air before Yakima's belly with a shrill whistle. Yakima thrust his shoulders forward and pulled his belly back so that the tip of the Apache's knife only ripped his undershirt and sliced an icy cut across his stomach.

The Apache loosed another high-pitched yowl as he brought the knife toward Yakima again on the backswing. Yakima ducked, and the knife whistled over his head. He lunged forward before the Apache could leap back and, flipping his own knife so that the curved blade angled up, drove the bowie into the Apache's belly, thrusting so that the blade penetrated beneath the rib cage.

The knife was so sharp it went through the Indian's midsection like a glowing pick through suet.

Hot blood washed over Yakima's wrist and forearm as he twisted the knife tip through the heart. Bracing his left hand on the Indian's right shoulder, he withdrew the blade quickly, blood showering from the Indian's gut. The Apache grunted. He stood before Yakima, swaying like a drunk, knees slightly bent, shoulders slumped, chin dropping toward his chest as he inspected his ruined midsection.

Yakima sucked a deep breath, his sweat chilling in the cool night breeze. "There you go, you thievin' bastard."

As if in response, the Indian rasped, then dropped to his knees, tumbled forward, and lay still.

Yakima used a tarpaulin tied with rope to his paint horse to drag the four dead Apaches to a gorge a good mile from his cabin. He dumped the bodies into the gorge and loosed rocks down on top of them. Not even the buzzards and wolves would find them there.

That job done, he retrieved the braves' four, half-wild mustangs from where they'd tied them on the other side of the scarp. Most settlers in this country would have shot the horses. He should have shot them, too, but he couldn't bring himself to do it. He'd always felt a stronger kinship with horses than with men.

Releasing them from his cabin was out of the question, however. They would return to the Apache encampment, and from there the Apaches would backtrack them to him.

Yakima had intended to make a supply run to Saber

Creek tomorrow. He could lead the Apache mustangs for the first ten miles and release them at Papago Springs.

He would also check on his neighbor, the old desert rat Lars Schimpelfennig, who prospected the barrancas west of Bailey Peak and occasionally holed up in an ancient goatherd's cabin along Torcido Gulch. Yakima had heard that Diablito had jumped the reservation again and had promised to kill every white man between Benson and Lordsburg. Lars had been poking and prodding this country for a good ten years and had never had more than minor run-ins with the Chiricahua, but it wouldn't hurt to check on the old German.

When he'd corralled the Apache horses with his own paint and black stallion, he returned to the cabin, donned his buckskin coat, and slept fitfully on a chair on the front porch, boots crossed on the porch rail, snapping his eyes open at every night sound.

One such sound made him slam his chair down and lower his legs from the porch rail as he jerked his Winchester sharply right, thumbing back the hammer. A coyote stood at the corner of the house, staring at Yakima. The brush wolf's ears were pricked, and its brown eyes were touched with the gray light of the false dawn.

Yakima released the rifle's hammer and loosed a relieved sigh. The coyote had been coming around since Yakima had started building his humble ranch headquarters six months ago, with the intention of catching and breaking wild horses for the cavalry. He'd fed the coyote deer and grouse scraps and had come to enjoy his frequent visits in spite of having found the animal sniffing around on his kitchen table one morning when Yakima had stepped out to fetch water from the creek, leaving the cabin door cracked. "Sorry, fella. No scraps this mornin'."

The coyote put its head down, nose working, then groaned and turned away, padding softly off toward the cabin's rear.

Yakima gave a wry chuff. He'd been here less than a year, having fled trouble in Colorado—trouble and the memory of a pretty whore with the unlikely name of Faith—and he was already talking to coyotes.

Yakima leaned the rifle against the cabin wall, stood, and stretched, feeling the tension leave him. If there'd been any Apaches within three miles, the coyote wouldn't have shown itself.

He glanced east. The sky was lightening above the pine-studded ridge. Turning his gaze toward the corral, he saw the black mustang move up to the gate, hooves thudding softly in the quiet morning, and thrust his blaze face toward the cabin. Wolf loosed a whinny and shook his head, blue-black mane buffeting. A couple of the Apache mounts shook their own heads and milled around with their tails up, edgy.

Yakima stepped off the porch, crossed the yard, and opened the corral gate. Wolf sprang out, putting his head down to gallop, then buck-kicking in frisky circles around the yard.

"Go find yourself some grass," Yakima told the horse, throwing the gate closed and securing the leather latch. "We'll be headin' out soon."

Yakima returned to the cabin to build a fire in the stove and start breakfast. Hooves drummed behind him, the ground trembling beneath his boots. Yakima chuckled to himself but didn't turn around. Then, at the last second, he stepped to one side as Wolf ran by. The horse lowered his head to give Yakima's shoulder a playful nip, missing by inches.

Yakima had had enough shoulder bites and ripped shoulder seams to know when another attempt was coming.

"Keep it up," he scolded, mounting the porch as the self-satisfied black went buck-kicking and snorting across the yard, "and I'll send you to the Apaches with those other four."

After a breakfast of venison sausage, buckwheat cakes, and tea, Yakima shook down the ashes in the sheet-iron stove and secured the cabin. He saddled the black stallion, who'd been eagerly snorting around outside, always seeming to sense when a long ride was imminent. He strapped his packsaddle on the paint horse, strung a lead rope to the four skittish Apache horses, dallied the rope around his saddle horn, and started off down the mountain.

The sun was high when he left the cool, aromatic pine forest for the low, gravelly slopes covered with chaparral. The air was winter-cool, the sky a faultless cobalt bowl, the sun brassy. Occasional roadrunners and kangaroo rats dashed across his trail. Bobwhites and wrens flitted about the greasewood.

He released the Apache horses at Papago Springs, then continued eight miles south, toward Saber Creek, before meandering southeast up Torcido Gulch. Sheer rock scarps jutted along both sides of the gently climbing trail, the slopes covered in greasewood and barrel cactus, which angled their cigar-shaped shadows across the caliche.

It was high noon when Lars Schimpelfennig's cabin appeared among the boulders and cactus about halfway up a rocky bluff—a makeshift hovel of stones and logs, with a narrow porch jutting over the steep slope on the right, supported by posts and boulders and roofed with brush. The dry logs were cracked and weathered, the stone walls bleached and buckling.

Yakima stopped Wolf and the paint a good hundred yards from the cabin, poked his flat-brimmed black hat off his forehead, and stared up the bluff, frowning.

Lars usually kept coffee on the stove all day, while he chipped and picked for gold in the surrounding steeples and knobs, but no smoke rose from the shack's tin chimney pipe. No sign, either, of the mule and the two burros he usually let graze freely on the slopes below the cabin.

The old German wouldn't have pulled out without letting Yakima know. Being two of only a handful of non-Apaches in twenty square miles, they'd become friendly over the past several months, trading game and supplies and showing up periodically at each other's doorstep with a bottle and a poker deck.

Yakima swiveled his head to look around. Nothing moved except the breeze-jostled creosote branches. He swung down from his saddle, looped Wolf's reins over an ironwood shrub, then shucked the Yellowboy repeater from its oiled boot. As he did, a breeze drifted from the direction of the cabin, and both Wolf and the paint snorted and sidestepped nervously, smelling something they didn't like. Holding his gaze on the cabin above, Yakima levered a shell into the rifle's breech, off-cocked the hammer, and began climbing the bluff's steep slope, meandering around the cactus, shrubs, and boulders.

Twenty yards from the sunbaked hovel, he stopped and held the Winchester at port arms. He yelled just loudly enough for anyone in the near distance to hear: "Hello, the cabin. Lars, it's Yakima Henry."

The cabin stood silent beneath the blue sky and the jagged rocks of the ridge crest. A lizard scuttled along the shack's rock wall and disappeared in a crack. The cabin door was open a foot, but Yakima couldn't see inside.

He continued up the slope, climbed the three rotten steps to the porch, then nudged the door with his rifle barrel.

The stench was like a punch. Wincing and holding his breath, hearing flies buzz, he peered inside until his watering eyes adjusted to the darkness. Thick blood was pooled on the floor a few feet from the door, strewn with what could only be hacked-up human limbs and intestines. A blood-soaked boot poked out from beneath the wooden eating table. Something was stuffed inside.

Yakima turned away and dropped to one knee, his gut contracting at the horror.

"Christ!"

A half second later, a bullet barked into the railing a foot left of his head. Another half second after that, the rifle's blast sounded, echoing around the canyon.

Chapter 3

Yakima snapped his head up, staring east of the old prospector's cabin, the direction from which the rifle report had sounded. At the same time, he began raising his Winchester, but before he could get the butt snugged to his shoulder, a man shouted, "Hold it! The next one's goin' through your brisket, you son of a bitch!"

Yakima froze on one knee, letting the rifle barrel sag as he peered up the rocky slope east of the cabin. Amid the creosote, his eyes picked out the man standing in the shade of a large, slab-sided boulder, aiming a rifle straight out from his left shoulder.

He wore a white shirt, black trousers, and suspenders. His sleeves were rolled above his elbows, and a snuff brown slouch hat was tipped back off his forehead. Gray muttonchop whiskers and a mustache showed against the saddle brown of his face. A copper star shone on his shirt pocket.

"Set the rifle down and stand up!" he shouted, still aiming down his Henry's barrel.

Yakima set the rifle on the porch and straightened his

legs slowly, holding his hands up, palms out, an incredulous look on his face. What the hell was a lawman doing way out here?

The lawman lowered the rifle to his side, keeping the barrel aimed at Yakima. Glancing around cautiously, he began moving down the slope toward the cabin, his hat's leather thong swinging beneath his chin, his spurs ringing, boot heels raking gravel.

When he was about halfway to the cabin, he turned his head slightly and whistled. Presently, a blaze-faced dun moved out from behind the boulder and, bridle reins wrapped around its saddle horn, put its head down and doggedly followed the lawman through the chaparral.

The lawman aimed his rifle at Yakima's belly as he leapt onto the porch and stopped, squinting his flinty blue eyes under his hat brim. He was Yakima's height, about six feet, nearly as broad through the shoulders, and narrow-hipped, but a good fifteen or twenty years older. His sun-leathered skin was pockmarked, his shoulders bowed slightly, and deep lines spoked his eyes. Still, he had the look of a tough son of a bitch.

"You're not Apache," he said, canting his head to one side. "What the hell are you?"

Yakima kept his hands raised. "I ain't Apache."

"You live here?"

Yakima shook his head. "Friend of mine did. What's left of him's still inside."

The lawman strode forward and, keeping his Henry's barrel aimed at Yakima's belly, glanced through the cabin's open door. His rugged features pinched up, and, his blue eyes glistening from the stench, he turned back to Yakima. "Chiricahua?"

"That's what I figure."

"You gotta handle?"

Yakima told him his name.

"You wouldn't know anything about two dead Arizona rangers just east of here, would you, Henry?"

"Maybe you better ask the Apaches about dead rangers."

The lawman shook his head. "These weren't killed by Apaches. White men killed 'em—an old friend of mine and a kid. And that gravels me." He strode forward and stopped a few feet in front of Yakima, eyes glazed with unreasoning anger. "Might be you're part of the gang that killed 'em. The gang that's lookin' to bring down that gold shipment passin' through this country tomorrow."

Yakima held the man's stony gaze. "Might be."

The man swung the Henry's barrel sideways while snapping the butt toward Yakima's cheek. Yakima flung his forearm up, blocking the blow.

He leapt straight back, then swung his foot up, planting the heel of his boot against the side of the lawman's face. The lawman screamed as he bounced off the cabin's front wall, dropping the rifle, and piled up on the porch. He rolled onto his back, groaning, his cheek as red as an Arizona sunset, blood trickling from his split lower lip.

"Son of a *bitch*!" he raged, shaking his head as his right hand fumbled for the walnut-gripped Colt Army holstered on his hip.

Yakima stepped down on the man's forearm, clamping his hand against his thigh, then reached down, slipped the Colt from the holster, and tossed it over the railing into the yard a good twenty feet below. The gun hit the gravel and rolled.

Yakima picked up the man's Henry and gave it similar treatment, then scooped his own rifle off the porch, thumbed back the hammer, and snugged the barrel against the man's forehead. The lawman froze, squinting up the barrel at Yakima, his pupils contracting fearfully.

"I said I *might* be one of the killers you're after," Yakima growled. "I didn't say I *was*."

Keeping the rifle aimed at the lawman's head, he backed into the cabin and, holding his breath against the sweet, coppery death stench, pulled a lariat off the wall. He stepped back onto the porch, held the Winchester's maw an inch from the lawman's right eye. "On your belly."

The man glared up at him, then cursed and slowly did as he'd been told. Yakima dropped to a knee, set the rifle down, and quickly wrapped the rawhide around the man's wrists. When he'd tied a square knot, leaving a good five feet of the rawhide hanging free, he ordered the man to his feet and shoved him toward his horse.

In a minute, he had the lawman lying belly down across his saddle and was tying his ankles together. When he'd looped the end of the lariat around the man's wrists for one finishing dally, he led the horse back out toward the boulder from which the man had fired the warning shot.

In the shade of the boulder, Yakima stopped, wrapped

the reins around the saddle horn, then walked back past the man's head, which hung down behind the stirrup fender. He stopped at the horse's right hip and held his rifle out like a club.

The lawman turned his red, enraged face at Yakima. His hat was back on the porch, and his pewter hair hung toward the ground. The blood from his split lip had switched direction and was trickling into his eye socket. "You'll rue this day, you son of a bitch."

Yakima rammed the Winchester's barrel against the dun's hip. The horse lunged off its rear hooves and galloped down the rise and into the chaparral beyond, weaving around barrel cactus and ironwood shrubs, scaring a wren out of its cactus burrow, and kicking up a fine curtain of cinnamon dust.

"Not half as much as you," he said when the hoof thuds had dwindled into the distance.

Yakima returned to the cabin and, wrapping his bandanna around his nose and mouth, stepped inside.

He didn't look at what was left of the old German's hacked up body on the floor. He knew where the old man kept his coal oil, so, sidestepping the massive pools of congealed blood and viscera, he grabbed the oilcan off its shelf, popped the cork, and doused the room. Stepping outside, he dribbled the remaining oil on the porch, then tossed the can back into the cabin. He struck a lucifer to life on his thumbnail and tossed the burning match through the door.

The match ignited the oil with a thunderous *whoosh*, and flames instantly filled the cabin's interior and licked out through the door, smoke billowing, the fire roaring and snapping and crackling as it rapidly consumed the dry wood.

Yakima leapt off the porch and, holding his rifle over his shoulder and not looking back at the cabin, strode down the hill to where the black stallion and the paint horse waited in the brush.

He mounted up and, dallying the packhorse's lead rope around his saddle horn, put Wolf into a wind-splitting run. He held his rifle across his saddlebow and kept a sharp eye on the ridges. The smoke would no doubt attract Apaches, and he wanted to be out of the area when it did.

After twenty minutes, he checked Wolf into a trot. He stopped at Ironwood Springs for ten minutes, letting the horses draw water from the murky granite tanks, then headed off again under the brassy sky. He saw no one but a couple of saddle tramps on a distant horse trail until he pulled up on the crest of the low ridge overlooking a vast sunlit valley, broken here and there by rock outcroppings and boulder-strewn knolls.

Amid the sage a mile from the ridge lay Saber Creek—a motley collection of sandstone hovels strewn willy-nilly about the valley floor. The town, once a Mexican village, had grown up haphazardly along the Butterfield Stage line. It still wasn't much, and because its sandstone and adobe buildings and bleached-log corrals blended so well with the sandy valley floor and the chaparral, many folks didn't know it was here.

Yakima didn't care for the town, as it didn't care for him. But it had a nice watering hole and a mercantile, and it would have taken him another day to ride to Benson.

He put the horses down the ridge and followed the trail between the outlying corrals and goat pens and into the town itself, weaving around the heavy traffic—ranch wagons and freight outfits serving the gold and silver mines in the Dragoons and Chiricahuas.

A woman's voice rose behind him. "Look what the cat dragged in!"

He stopped and turned, squinting against the wagon dust. A young woman stood by the stone well coping twenty yards before the best saloon in town—Charlier's Hotel and Tavern. Anjanette Charlier smiled at him boldly from beneath the hand shading her eyes, her long jet-black hair dancing in the chill breeze. She was a tall, dark, regally beautiful young woman, with what appeared to be a small knife scar on the right side of her dimpled chin.

She wore a simple brown skirt with a wide black belt, men's black stockman's boots, and a red bandanna. A cream blouse stretched taut across her full breasts, the top two buttons undone to expose deep cleavage. Half French, Anjanette had been raised by her French grandfather, who had prospected nearly every mountain range in Arizona before buying a saloon here in Saber Creek and putting his granddaughter to work renting rooms and slinging drinks to miners, drovers, and mule skinners while he cooked and tended bar.

Yakima pinched his hat brim, feeling the old male pull. Old Antoine's granddaughter was not the kind of exquisite beauty a man saw every day on the Arizona frontier. "Miss Anjanette."

"It's been a while," she said, placing her free hand on her hip, her bosom swelling till a good half of her cleavage pushed up from the V-necked blouse. "What's kept you up in those hills so long, Yakima Henry?"

He'd met her last time he was in town, when he'd gotten thrown out of the Saguaro Inn and had had nowhere else to drink. She'd served him several relatively cold beers, a hot supper, and, since it had been a slow evening, had sat down to chat and play a game of red dog. No whore, this girl. A pretty tavern owner's granddaughter who served only the liquor, not herself, though Yakima didn't doubt that plenty of men had tried to change her and her grandfather's mind about that.

"I've been working my shotgun ranch," he said, savoring every moment of the girl's beauty. "Had no time for town—till I saw my tea tin was empty."

"Stop by for a drink later." She grinned and thrust a hip out, let her eyes flicker across his chest and shoulders. She tossed her straight black hair back. "First one's on the house, and Old Antoine's got soup on the stove, though I won't vouch for how good it is. I didn't *see* him throw any rats in it."

"Don't mind if I do. Sounds right delicious."

He turned forward and gigged the black down the dusty, bustling street, moving through wagons, horseback riders, and the occasional mining rig drawn by donkeys. Dogs and goats ran loose in the streets, and chickens scratched in front of the old brush-thatched dwellings owned by members of the original Mexican families.

He wanted to visit the sheriff's office about as much as he wanted to run barefoot across hot coals, but it wouldn't be right not to inform the lawman about the Apaches running wild. Crossing to the far side of town, he pulled up before the small sandstone building housing the sheriff's office and jail. A brush arbor shaded a six-foot patch of hard-packed dirt in front of the building.

Yakima wrapped Wolf's and the packhorse's reins over the hitchrack, before which three saddle horses stood hanging their heads. He mounted the stoop and knocked once on the stout cottonwood door, then tripped the metal latch and stepped inside.

He stopped just over the threshold. The sheriff sat behind his desk on the room's right side while three other men sat to his left, in spool-back chairs. The three men— all dressed in dusty trail garb and battered Stetsons, with six-shooters on their hips and Winchester carbines resting across their laps—turned to Yakima suddenly, surprised by the interruption.

The sheriff turned also, ridging his shaggy sand-colored brows. Mitch Speares was big and rangy, in his mid-thirties, and wore two Remingtons, positioned for the cross draw, on his narrow hips. His thick silver-blond hair hung over his collar, his bangs combed low across his right eye. His brushy mustache and sideburns were a couple of shades darker than his hair, and his dung-brown eyes were set close to his wedge-shaped, sun-blistered nose.

Yakima kept his left hand on the door handle. "Sorry for intrudin', Sheriff."

"What's the matter with you, breed? Can't you see I'm in a meetin' here?"

Yakima shrugged and stepped back, pulling the door closed. "Have it your way, Sheriff."

Speares scowled. His swivel chair squawked as he stood and shouted, "Well, what the hell you *want*?"

Yakima opened the door again, but remained outside. "Just thought you might wanna know about the Apaches who paid me a visit last night. I think it was the same bunch that killed Lars Schempelfennig yesterday."

"Schempelfennig? Who the hell cares? That crazy desert rat's been pushin' his luck far longer than it would have held for most folks in 'Pache country."

"Just thought I'd mention it." Yakima's gaze was blank, but his lips twisted in a smile. "If I recollect, there's a few shotgun ranches in that area. I figured it might be your job to warn them if you heard Chiricahuas had jumped the reserve and taken to the warpath."

As Yakima began drawing the door closed again, Speares said, "Hold on, goddamn it. Get your ass in here, breed."

Feigning a guileless look, Yakima moved into the sheriff's small, dim office, leaving the door half open behind him. Small gaps between the rocks of the building's wall shone with brassy daylight. Dust motes slanted through the light shafts. A couple of prisoners slumped on the jail cots at the back of the room. One, who had one foot on the floor, was loudly sawing logs while a rat nibbled off the tin plate near his boot.

Speares looked at Yakima distastefully. "Where was Schempelfennig's place exactly?"

"Torcido Gulch."

"How far up?"

"Three miles after the red cliffs."

Speares looked at one of the men seated to his right. "Doesn't Rack Lewis have a place up that way?"

One of the men—stocky, unshaven, and wearing hemp suspenders—nodded. "Bill Larsen has a horse ranch just east of Rack's. Have 'em about ten kids between the two of 'em."

One of the other deputies turned to Yakima, scowling as he said, "Yeah, but Larsen's kids are all half-breeds."

The deputies chuckled, shoulders jerking.

Speares glanced at the man who'd spoken last. "Leo, you better ride out an' warn 'em."

Leo frowned. "What about the gold shipme—" He cut himself off, glanced at Yakima, then returned his gaze to the sheriff. "You didn't deputize us fellas to be errand boys, Mitch. Besides, I won't get back before—"

He stopped again when the sheriff turned his stony eyes on him. "You'll get full pay whether you're here or not." Speares's tone was at once reasonable and sharp-edged. "Now ride on out an' warn Lewis and Larsen about the Apache trouble. In addition to your regular pay, there'll be a bottle in it for you. Maybe I'll even be able to coax one of the whores over to the Mexican's place to spread her legs for ya—if'n you finally take a bath."

The other deputies chuckled as Leo's face turned red behind his three-day growth of beard. With an injured expression, he stood, donned his hat, and hefted his rifle. As he brushed past Yakima, he cut a hard glance to the half-breed, then strode out the door and spat loudly under the brush arbor.

Yakima looked at the sheriff, then turned toward the door.

"Henry."

Yakima swung back to Speares, who stood facing him, thumbs hooked behind his cartridge belt as he rose up and down on his boot toes. "Make sure you're out of town by sundown. I don't want you breakin' up any more saloons."

One of the remaining deputies chuckled and gave one corner of his waxed mustache a twist. "I heard him and some Mex really tore apart the Saguaro Inn. Left a good bit of blood on the floor, too."

Yakima kept his eyes on the sheriff. "I'll be leavin' first thing in the morning—after I've bought the supplies I need."

Speares slitted his left eye. "Think so, do ya?"

Yakima splayed his fingers on his thigh, in front of the holstered, stag-butted Colt, and held the lawman's hard gaze. The deputies shuttled glances between Yakima and the sheriff. It was suddenly so quiet that the rat could be heard making soft *snick-snick* sounds as it nibbled bread from the tin plate in the cell.

Speares smiled. "I reckon it *is* gettin' a mite late to be headin' back through 'Pache country. I'll relax my rules just this once. Just make sure you stay away from Charlier's. Understand?"

Yakima kept his expression neutral, but he felt a devilish tingle. Normally, to avoid trouble, he would have done what the sheriff ordered. But he wasn't much in the mood for following orders. He shook his head.

"Can't do that neither, Sheriff. Miss Anjanette already offered me a drink. Standin' her up wouldn't be polite."

One of the sitting deputies said slowly, "Why, that smart-ass—"

"Now, now, Charlie," Speares said, lifting the corners of his mouth once more as he continued locking gazes with Yakima. "No point in gettin' our fur up. Ain't healthy." He reached into the breast pocket of his collar-less pin-striped shirt and flipped a coin to Yakima, who grabbed it out of the air. "First drink's on me, breed. We'll be seein' you later."

Yakima flipped the nickel in his hand. "Obliged." Pocketing the coin, he stepped straight back out the door, then grabbed both sets of reins off the hitchrack and, keeping an eye on the sheriff in the jailhouse's dim interior, swung onto the black and pulled the two horses into the street.

In the jailhouse office, Speares watched the half-breed ride away, his heart thudding, his gut burning, then turned to the two deputies sitting tensely, staring at him curiously.

"Get the hell out of here!" he barked. "Be back at first light with those rifles loaded. We'll head from here to the bank. Do not—I repeat, *do not*—be late!"

The two men whom Speares had deputized an hour ago to help make sure the gold shipment made it from to-morrow's stage safely into the bank vault, lurched to their feet and filed quickly out the door.

When they were gone, Speares sagged into his chair. He continued staring at the empty doorway, his eyes stony, his lips bunched with fury, and slipped one of his long-barreled Remingtons from its cross-draw holster. He flicked open the Remy's loading gate, took a cartridge from a leather loop on his belt, and filled the chamber he normally kept empty beneath the hammer.

Speares cursed and spun the cylinder, then snapped around in his chair to face the cell directly behind him. Inside, the mule skinner, Kirby Yates, whom Speares had arrested for drunk and disorderly conduct at four o'clock in the morning, continued snoring loudly. Thumbing the Remington's hammer back, Speares extended the pistol straight out from his shoulder and fired through the bars of Yates's cell door.

The pistol report sounded like a cannon blast in the close quarters.

Both prisoners leapt up on their cots with startled grunts and groans. "What the hell was *that*?" bellowed Yates, jerking his foot off the floor and craning his head toward his blood-splattered plate.

Speares lowered the smoking revolver and turned toward the door, holding the Remy in both hands as though weighing it.

"Rat," Speares said as he flicked open the loading gate and removed the spent shell.

Chapter 4

Yakima cut a look over his left shoulder as he angled across the street toward the Arizona Livery and Feed Barn. Mitch Speares had been an outlaw longer than he'd been a sheriff—it was widely known that the man had been a regulator in Wyoming and Colorado and was probably still wanted up that way—and Yakima knew he wasn't above trying to backshoot an adversary.

The sheriff did not appear in his open doorway, so Yakima rode the black up the livery barn's hay-covered ramp. He ducked under the heavy freight hook hanging from the loft and clomped on into the barn's shadows, which were thick with the smell of hay, manure, and livestock.

A voice rose from the darkness on his left. "Well, I'll be damned. I figured you'd know enough to stay outta town after what happened last time."

The liveryman ambled out of the shadows, a hay stem wedged in his big yellow teeth, his snakeskin galluses bowing over his bulging paunch. He held a worn bridle in his gloved hand. Scowling, he tipped his leather-billed immigrant cap off his freckled forehead.

"What happened last time wasn't my doin'." Yakima slipped his Winchester from his saddle boot and slung his saddlebags over his right shoulder. "Besides, I worked off my bill at the Saguaro Inn. Split enough wood to last 'em the next three winters."

"That ain't what I'm talkin' about," said the livery-man, whose name was Charlie Suggs. "I'm talkin' about that Mex you fought. He sees you in town, he's gonna want some payback for cuttin' off his finger."

"I'll give him one of mine. Feel better?" Yakima reached into a front pocket and flipped a gold piece in the air. "One dollar in advance. I'll pick up both horses first thing in the morning."

Suggs closed his fist around the coin and continued scowling at Yakima. "You can find yourself an alley tonight, too. I don't want you in here. Damn it, Saber Creek is a civilized town, and uncivilized folk need to stay in the mountains where they belong."

"That free?"

Suggs squinted and cocked his head. "Huh?"

"That advice free?"

The liveryman filled his lungs. His round bearded face turned red. "Yeah, it's free!"

"Good, because I just came to have my horses stabled. Grain 'em and rub 'em down and go easy on the water till they cool."

Yakima headed toward the open door.

"Anything else?"

"Yeah." Yakima glanced over his shoulder. "Clean out their hooves and check their shoes."

As he descended the ramp to the street, casting a cautious glance toward the jailhouse on his right, he heard the liveryman grumbling behind him, "Shore are cheeky for a dirt-worshiper!"

The wind was kicking up as the sun angled behind the distant sawtooth ridges. Yakima squinted his eyes against the blowing dust and straw as he headed west, stepping over fresh horse apples and goat dung.

As he approached Charlier's—a two-story adobe built in the old Spanish style, with a couple of small balconies with wrought-iron railings on the second floor—a tumbleweed flew toward him, and he ducked. The weed continued on past him and pasted itself against the front window of Thaddeus Wilford's undertaking parlor.

Gentle piano music filtered out of the tavern before him, sounding beneath the moaning wind like a spring rain on a tin roof. Half a dozen horses were tied to the hitchrack, and loud male voices spilled over the batwing doors.

Mounting the porch fronting Charlier's, Yakima paused to peer over the scarred batwings. The room was about half full, and tobacco smoke wafted up to the low, herringbone-patterned ceiling. Several Mexican freighters in dusty trail garb sat in the shadows to the left. Most of the other tables were occupied by American cowboys, Mexican vaqueros, mule skinners, drifters, and a few burly, sun-seared prospectors in hobnailed boots. A short, skinny Mexican with a receding hairline and a handlebar mustache was playing the piano.

Anjanette was running drinks from the bar while her pugnacious grandfather, Old Antoine, set them up and served the four men bellied up to the mahogany. Yakima made for a table in the room's far right corner, weaving around the other tables and avoiding outstretched legs and beer pooling on the stone tiles. He set his saddlebags and rifle on the table, kicked out a chair, and was about to sit down when someone poked his back.

He turned. Anjanette smiled up at him, a beer in one hand, a shot in the other. The red bandanna held her coal black hair back from her face. Her voice was raspy. "Something to cut the trail dust?"

"Don't mind if I do. Just the beer. I don't drink the hard stuff in town." He reached for his right hip pocket.

"I told you, first one's on the house." Anjanette set the beer on the table, straightened, and swept her hair behind her shoulder. Her breasts swelled up from the low-cut shirtwaist that she'd donned for the evening trade, and her cheeks were flushed. "You hungry?"

"Maybe later. I'll enjoy the beer first. Been a while since I've had anything to imbibe with."

"Let me know. Antoine has split-pea soup and bacon sandwiches. Gotta cover some ground. Friday night!" The girl turned and strode back through the tables toward the bar, her skirts billowing out from her full hips and thighs.

Yakima sat down and watched her round ass as she swerved around a ceiling joist from which a lantern and *ristra* hung. He wasn't the only one appreciating Anjanette's wares. Nearly every table she passed fell silent while the mule skinners and drovers hung their jaws and stared.

Yakima sipped the beer and grunted ironically. He ought to come to town more often. . . .

He crossed his boots on a chair and settled back in his seat, enjoying Old Antoine's yeasty ale and rolling a cigarette from his makings sack. When he'd finished the drink, Anjanette brought him a bowl of soup, a sandwich of grilled, buttered bread piled with thickly sliced bacon, and a mug of freshly drawn ale.

"That's some kind of service," he told the girl as she collected his empty mug.

"You looked hungry."

Yakima reached into his pocket, but she waved him off. "Your money's no good here, Yakima Henry."

She flashed a smile as she wheeled and headed toward the bar, carrying the tray high on her right shoulder. He felt his pulse in his neck. He didn't know why he was tormenting himself. He had no future with Anjanette, as he'd had no future with Faith, the lovely blond doxie in Colorado.

Really, he had no future with any woman. Having been raised in the tall-and-uncut, he was at home only in the far, lonely reaches. It was no life for a woman—at least no woman he'd met so far.

Still, he entertained a brief fantasy of finally settling down with a woman, of waking up to one every morning, going to bed with one every evening. Sitting down to table with a woman for buttery soup and a thick sandwich like the one he was eating now. Having someone to talk to about what he'd done or was going to do, or about how he felt or what he was thinking about.

That might be a nice way to live. Maybe, when he was older and didn't mind giving up his freedom, he'd give it serious consideration. . . .

He was half done with the soup when he glanced up to see Speares enter the saloon with a dapper little man in a three-piece suit, black bowler, round-rimmed glasses, and gray muttonchops. The pair headed for a table that three mule skinners had just vacated, and they immediately hunkered down in serious discussion.

Given the dapper gent's appearance, he was no doubt the president of the local bank, and he and Speares were no doubt discussing the gold shipment the U.S. marshal had thought Yakima was after. The marshal was another reason Yakima had better get back on the trail first thing in the morning. When the man got free of his bindings, he'd likely track Yakima to Saber Creek. There were laws against assaulting lawmen, even those who deserved it.

As he ate and sipped his beer, enjoying the meal, Yakima kept an eye on the sheriff. He and the banker ordered beer and shots, and Anjanette came back with both, setting the glasses on the table before the men. Speares spoke to the girl, grinning, but the girl stared at him icily, her cheeks drawn in.

When she held her hand out for money, Speares grabbed her wrist, pulled her toward him, and spoke harshly through gritted teeth. He cast a quick glance at Yakima. The girl looked at Yakima then, too, her suntanned cheeks flushing. She pulled her hand from

Speares's grip, wheeled, and headed back to the bar, her jaw set hard.

Yakima held his spoon in front of his mouth, frozen in his chair, shifting his gaze between Anjanette and the sheriff. Something told him that the girl was the reason Speares hadn't wanted Yakima patronizing Charlier's.

Well, he'd be damned. Letting a man know he wouldn't be ordered around was one thing. Getting between the man and his girl was like dancing between a diamondback and a scorpion.

He felt foolish, and that made his gut burn with anger.

Yakima swallowed his last bit of soup and dropped the spoon into the bowl. He glanced up to see Speares staring at him from twenty feet away. The lawman had his back to Yakima, but he'd craned his neck around to stare across his right shoulder. The man's eyes beneath his shaggy bangs were dark, his face flushed.

Yakima lifted his beer glass in salute, and sipped. Speares turned away, jaws moving as he said something to the dapper gent lifting a shot glass to his mustachioed mouth.

Yakima finished his beer and set the mug on the table. He'd best not push his luck tonight—especially since the sheriff had obviously set his sights on Anjanette. Besides, Yakima had made his point. He wouldn't be pushed around. Now he'd better spread his hot roll in the ravine behind the livery barn and lay low until morning, then get the hell out of town as fast as Wolf could carry him.

He grabbed his Winchester and saddlebags, but before he could stand, someone put a hand on his shoulder. Anjanette crouched beside him. She wore a strange smile as she said tightly, only inches from his face, "Please don't go, Yakima."

"Sorry, miss, but it's been a long day and I'm—"

"I think he's going to kill me."

Yakima stared at her. She held a tray full of empty glasses in her right hand. Her half-exposed bosom rose and fell.

"The man's crazy," she said, just loudly enough for Yakima to hear above the din. "He knows I don't want him near me. He says he's going to kill me so no one else can have me."

Yakima stared at her skeptically.

Anjanette opened her mouth to speak, but a voice booming above the din cut her off. "Well, well, I hate to break up this little powwow, but what the hell did I just get done telling you, girl?"

Towering over Yakima's table, Speares grabbed Anjanette's arm and jerked her around behind him so quickly that she dropped the tray of empty glasses, tripped over a chair, and fell with a yelp against the wall.

She gave an enraged scream and, whipping up a razor-edged pearl-handled knife from behind her belt, bolted toward Speares. The sheriff stuck out his hand to grab the knife, and the blade sliced across his palm.

"You little *bitch*!" Speares shouted, glancing down at his bloody hand, then lunging forward and grabbing the girl's right wrist as she swung the knife toward him once more.

He squeezed her wrist until, giving a defiant scream,

she opened her fingers and the knife clattered onto the floor. Speares backhanded her, sending her flying.

At the same time, he stepped back from Yakima's table and raked one of his big Remingtons from its holster. A grin pulled up the corners of his mouth, revealing his big yellow horse teeth. His mustache was flecked with beer foam, and a lock of silver hair hung down over his forehead.

The smile did not reach Speares's brown eyes. "Breed, you're gonna wish like hell—"

Yakima bounded up out of his chair, lifting his table like a shield and throwing it into Speares. The sheriff cursed as the Remington popped, the bullet blasting a hole through the table six inches to the right of Yakima's thrusting arm.

Yakima put his head down and laid his forearms flat against the underside of the table, pushing Speares straight back against the wall. Speares gritted his teeth and yowled.

The Remy belched once more, and a bullet slammed through the table, raking across Yakima's left side with an icy burn.

As Yakima flinched, Speares lowered his own head, and the table rammed against Yakima, shoving him back the way he'd come. He fell onto another table and rolled sideways across an ashtray, scattering beer and shot glasses, coins, and playing cards. Men scuttled away like mice from a pitchfork, bellowing.

As Yakima hit the floor on his right shoulder, he looked up.

Speares stood over him, backing away from the two tables and bringing his Remy to bear. "As I was sayin'—"

Kapop!

The bullet carved a stinging line across Yakima's left cheek as he threw himself sideways. Hearing the *snick-click* of the hammer being cocked once more, he kept rolling.

The Remy barked two more times, both bullets crashing into the stone floor as Yakima rolled to his left. The Remy barked again, the bullet plowing into the leg of a table as Yakima rolled under it. The next bullet slammed through the tabletop.

As Yakima rolled out the table's far side, he grabbed a chair. Speares was thumbing back the Remy's hammer and lowering the barrel once more.

Yakima slung the chair. The edge of the seat clipped the sheriff's forehead, then shattered against the adobe wall.

Speares dropped the revolver and stumbled back and sideways, grabbing his bloody head. Yakima bolted off his haunches. Speares got his feet beneath him, squared his shoulders, and swung his right fist at Yakima's face. Yakima ducked, and the fist sliced the air with a dull whistle.

He came up and buried first his left fist and then his right into Speares's belly.

The sheriff grunted as he stumbled back. When Speares stopped and lifted his head, raging like a bull buffalo with a Comanche arrow in its lungs, Yakima leapt straight up in the air. Two feet off the ground, he wheeled in a full circle and drove the heel of his left boot up and out.

Speares had turned his head, so Yakima's heel smashed into the center of the man's nose. There was a dull smack and a crunch as the nose exploded like a ripe tomato, blood splattering in all directions. The nose itself lay sideways against the sheriff's bloody face.

"Unnnhhhh!" Speares's own boots left the floor, and he wheeled as though caught in a cyclone. On his way down, his head hit a chair, and then he was on his belly, arms and legs spread, flopping and groaning.

Yakima stumbled forward. A thunderous blast shattered the sudden, dense silence, and he wheeled right. Anjanette's grandfather, Old Antoine, stood ten feet away—a dark, wizened little man in a soiled apron and with long gray hair held back by a red bandanna.

He held a double-barreled shotgun straight out from his side. Smoke ribboned out of the right-side bore. Adobe chunks and wood slivers sluiced out of the fist-sized hole in the ceiling above his head.

The man turned his molasses-black eyes on Yakima, glanced at the groaning Speares, then indicated the door with his shotgun. "Out wit da *bot* of youss!"

Yakima turned. Anjanette sat on her butt against the wall, knees drawn up, breathing hard. Her hair was in her face. Yakima went over and helped her up. "You okay?"

She slid her fearful gaze to Speares and nodded.

"Out!" her grandfather shouted once more.

Yakima tossed a couple of tables and a chair out of his way, then stopped to pick up his hat, Winchester, and saddlebags. He didn't want to leave Anjanette here with

Speares, but since Old Antoine obviously knew how to handle the shotgun, and seemed eager to use it, he headed toward the door through the hushed crowd forming a broad circle around the wrecked tables and chairs and the nearly unconscious sheriff.

"Don't have to tell me twice." He stooped to pluck a cigar from the floor, and stuck it in his mouth. Continuing toward the wind-jostled batwings, he glanced at Speares. "I think the sheriff's gonna need some help, though."

He pushed between two gawking freighters and out the batwings. At the edge of the porch, he glanced down to inspect his side. His shirt was red and sticky. The bullet graze burned like a fresh brand.

"Shit," he groused around the cigar in his teeth.

He hiked the saddlebags higher on his shoulder, turned to glance over the batwings, then stepped off the porch and angled across the night-cloaked street. He strode down a trash-strewn alley, then around several goat pens and chicken coops, and made his way through the sage and creosote to the cottonwood-lined bank of Saber Creek.

Dropping down the six-foot bank, he pushed through the willows to where the creek lay, not much more than a trickle this time of the year. The silvery water shone in the starlight, speckled with cottonwood leaves and pine needles.

Yakima dropped to his knees and removed his neckerchief. He soaked the faded red cloth in the stream, then opened his tunic and shoved the neckerchief inside. He winced as the cold water seared him. As he continued dabbing the wound with fresh water, cleaning it, he decided there was no real damage. The bullet had carved a neat furrow between two lower ribs and continued out behind him.

When he'd stopped the bleeding, he continued pressing the wet cloth against the wound, then carried his rifle, bedroll, and saddlebags over to a mesquite tree, rolled out the two heavy trade blankets, and sagged down against the tree's trunk.

"Yakima Henry, you're a damn fool," he grunted. "When are you gonna stop chasin' saloon girls?"

He stretched out his legs, crossed his boots, dug a lucifer from a tunic pocket, and snapped it to life on his thumbnail. He doffed his hat, rested his head against the mesquite trunk, and sat staring out at the star-shrouded night, listening to the stream's quiet chuckle and slowly puffing the cigar.

He wasn't sure how much time had passed when a stone rattled down the bank to his right. In half a second his Colt was in his fist, its hammer cocked.

Anjanette's sexy, raspy voice: "Yakima?"

He groaned and depressed the hammer. "Shit."

Chapter 5

Yakima lowered the Colt to his thigh as he said, "Come on in if you're alone."

There was the rattle of more dirt and gravel down the creek bank. He heard soft footfalls, then turned to see Anjanette's silhouette take shape against the starry sky. She wore a wide-brimmed hat and a black cape, and she was carrying a couple of folded blankets under her arm.

She stopped a few feet away and stared down at him. "Figured you'd be down here since you weren't in the livery barn. Thanks for helping me out back there."

Yakima grunted.

"I shouldn't have gotten you involved," the girl said. "I should have just backshot the son of a bitch with Old Antoine's shotgun."

Yakima twirled the Colt and slipped it into its holster. "What the hell's a woman like you doing with Speares?"

"I'm not *with* Speares. He just *wants* me to be. Follows me around like a hind-tit calf. Told me if I didn't start acting a little more *friendly*, he'd slit my throat."

"Charming bastard, huh? He won't come after you

with that broken nose of his. If he does, shoot him. The town won't hang a girl that looks like you."

"I'd prefer to cut his throat."

"I reckon you damn near did." Yakima glanced at the small knotted scar on her chin. "Where'd you learn to fight with a knife?"

Anjanette quirked a knowing half smile. "I was raised in the desert around wild men. You oughta see Old Antoine wield a pigsticker." She knelt down, set the folded blankets beside Yakima. "You'll need these tonight. It's gonna get cold." She fell silent as she looked him over. "Are you hurt?"

"Nothin' serious."

She nodded toward his bloody left side. "Let me take a look."

"It's all right. I cleaned it out. The cold water numbed it."

She leaned toward him and began pulling his tunic up from his waist. "Let me take a *look*."

He sighed and pulled the damp tunic up his chest, exposing the gash, over which a thick curve of blood had jelled. She leaned forward to have a better look, ran a finger along the furrow. He could feel her warm breath on his belly. Her hair slid off her shoulder to brush across his chest.

Yakima's blood warmed. Her pull was elemental and strong. "You're right," she said huskily. "Doesn't look too ba—"

She looked up as he slid her hair back from her face with the back of his hand. He rested the hand against the side of her head. His chest rose and fell as he stared down at her. She placed her own hand on his belly and lifted her head toward his.

He pulled her toward him and closed his mouth over her lips, which parted for him as she turned her head slightly, returning the kiss, closing her hands over his shoulders, digging her fingertips into his flesh.

She pushed her body against him, wrapping her arms around his neck and pressing her breasts against his chest. Passion engulfed him, his loins throbbing, his buckskins drawing taut across his thighs. He pushed her back and reached down to peel the cape up and over her head.

As he tossed the cape aside, her hair fell back in a tangled mass around her head and shoulders. Her chest heaved as she quickly unbuttoned her blouse, flung it aside, then lifted the lace-edged chemise over her head, exposing her full breasts—two shadowed mounds in the near-darkness.

Yakima leaned forward, shucked out of his tunic, and lowered his head to her breasts, nuzzling each until the nipples rose and the girl was groaning and sighing and running her hands brusquely through his hair.

After a time, she scuttled down between his legs, pushed him back against the tree, and began unbuttoning his buckskin breeches, nuzzling his member as it pushed out against the pants. Yakima rested his head against the mesquite and closed his eyes as she opened his pants and jerked them halfway down his thighs.

As she closed her mouth over him, he ground his elbows into the ground and sighed.

*   *   *

Later, after they had made love three times, Anjanette leaned forward, wrapped her arms around his neck—her legs were already around his waist—and kissed him hard. She pulled away and smiled as she gazed into his eyes and smoothed his hair back from his flat, chiseled cheeks. "Gotta break a leg, lover."

"So soon?"

He ran his hands down the insides of her thighs, and she jerked with a shiver. "I'd love to stay all night, but if Old Antoine wakes and finds me gone, he'll come looking for me." She kissed him again. "With his shotgun."

She rose and dressed quickly, shivering in the chill night, teeth clattering, breath puffing like cotton. When she'd stomped into her men's boots, she leaned down, kissed him again, and, without saying anything more, strode off in the night, her boots clattering on the rocks. He heard her labored breath as she climbed the bank, and then she was gone.

Silence enveloped him. The only sounds were the creek's gurgling and some night creature, probably an armadillo, milling in the brush on the opposite bank.

Yakima wrapped up in the quilts, which were still warm from their lovemaking, turned onto his side, and closed his eyes. It seemed only minutes before he opened them again and saw a milky wash above the eastern horizon. He heard cactus wrens and desert larks chirping and flitting about the brush. The creek to his left glittered like quicksilver.

When he threw the quilts back, the morning's metallic chill smacked him like an open hand. He rose and strode naked to the stream, where he leaned down for a long drink, then, hissing and grunting, slapped water across his body. Gooseflesh rose over every inch of him, but by the time he'd finished the bath and was heading back to his bedroll to dry himself with the quilts, he was as awake as he'd ever been.

He got dressed, stomped into his boots, donned his hat, and rolled his blankets. The sky was only slightly lighter when he propped his saddlebags and bedroll on one shoulder, climbed the creek bank, and, holding the Yellowboy in his right hand, traced a meandering course through the chaparral, back toward the town.

The liveryman, Suggs, was up and shaving in his lean-to living area off the main barn, so Yakima paid the man what he owed him for lodging his horses, then saddled Wolf and the paint and led them over to the mercantile up the street from Charlier's Tavern, which was still dark, the doors closed. The mercantile owner, Ralph Dixon, was sweeping off his front loading dock, his eyes not quite open yet, his gray hair showing the comb tracks through the pomade.

"Christalmighty, can you give a man a chance to drink a cup of coffee first?" he complained when Yakima tied both Wolf and the paint to the hitchrack and mounted the loading dock, where a bur-laden cur slept by a barrel of penny nails.

Yakima plucked his mercantile list from his tunic pocket, glanced at it, then gave it to Dixon. "I'm gonna have a quick breakfast. Be back in twenty minutes."

"You expect me to fill this in *twenty minutes*?" Dixon said, adjusting his steel-rimmed spectacles as he scowled down at the notepaper, clamping his broom under his right arm.

Yakima grinned and canted his head eastward. "You're burnin' daylight, Mr. Dixon." He moved down the loading dock's steps to the boardwalk below. He shucked his Winchester from the saddle boot, then ran his hand down Wolf's sleek, blazed face and scratched the paint's right ear. "I'll be back in twenty minutes. You two don't pick any fights."

Wolf snorted, eager to be on the trail again.

Yakima headed back down the street, toward the café run by a Mexican woman named Ma Chavez. Smoke wafted from the squat adobe hovel's stout chimney, smelling of burning mesquite, frijoles, and roasting lamb. As he passed the Wells Fargo bank across from the tavern, he saw a light inside. Someone wasn't keeping banker's hours. No doubt getting ready for the gold shipment the marshal had mentioned.

"Hey, breed!" someone called softly from above.

Yakima glanced up at the bank's shake roof. One of the men he'd seen yesterday in the sheriff's office squatted there, holding a double-barreled shotgun across his thighs. His battered Stetson shaded his face, but a line of white appeared when he stretched his lips back from his teeth.

"Heard you busted Speares's snout for him." The man chuckled, the deputy sheriff's star on his worn blue shirt jostling slightly. "The sheriff is one sore hombre, up all night cussin' and drinkin' whiskey to dull the pain. His nose is big as a damn beer schooner."

"Yeah?" Yakima said. "Maybe he'll keep it closer to home from now on."

The deputy chuckled again, shaking his head. "He's gonna make you pay. He's gonna make you pay *big*."

"I reckon he'll try," Yakima said, stepping off the boardwalk and crossing the side street toward the café on the opposite corner.

Inside the dimly lit, earthen-floored café, he was taking a sip from his steaming tea mug and waiting for his food, when through the window beside him he spied movement on the opposite side of the street—a tall, broad-shouldered, blond-headed man in a funnel-brimmed Stetson, worn denims, and a red wool shirt under a deerskin vest to which a sheriff's star was pinned.

Speares was moving slowly this morning, almost lightly, as if every step pained him. He wore a big white bandage on his nose, fixed there with a broad white strip around his head, just beneath his hat. The light wasn't at the right angle for Yakima to make out much of the lawman's face, but he could tell the nose was swollen to nearly twice its normal size and was a shade darker than the lingering night shadows.

Speares passed the café and paused before the harness shop on the opposite corner, near Charlier's, and clamped his Winchester under his left arm as he reached up with both hands to gingerly adjust the bandage.

Yakima muttered, "That must hurt like holy hell," then blew ripples on his tea as he sipped it.

When Ma brought the hot skillet of eggs, green chiles, a pancake-sized slab of roast lamb, and several steaming tortillas, Yakima rolled up his shirtsleeves and dug in. He was half finished with the plate when his nearly empty tea mug began rattling softly on the table before him.

Growing in the distance, there came the rumble of wagon wheels, screech of leather thoroughbraces and trace chains, and thud of horse hooves. A six-horse hitch, judging by the sound. A deep-throated bellow rose from up the street, in the direction of the bank. *"Whooooo-ahhhhhhhh!"*

The gold shipment.

Yakima gave the stage only passing thought. It reminded him of the deputy marshal. He hoped he hadn't tied the rope too tight around the lawman's wrists and ankles. If he had, the man had most likely been discovered by Apaches drawn to the burning cabin and was dying slowly over a honey-basted mound of fire ants.

Hearing businesslike voices and commotion outside, Yakima finished his last bite of lamb. His mug began shaking again. It shook so hard it slid around in the little ring of condensation left on the table. Yakima's knife and fork rattled against his plate. He felt the earthen floor quivering beneath his boots.

Outside, thunder rumbled. A horse whinnied. For a second, Yakima thought a rainstorm was approaching. Then he looked out the window, craning his neck and peering east down the street.

He froze.

A gang of riders appeared, riding hell-bent for leather toward the café—a wild-looking bunch in dusty trail clothes, wielding rifles or revolvers as they flew as if driven by a wildfire, their wide-eyed horses laying their ears flat against their heads. The three lead riders—two wearing sombreros and short charro jackets, the third in a bearskin coat and bowler hat—began triggering their pistols or rifles, the one in the bear coat howling like a rampaging Indian.

More thunder sounded nearer the bank, and Yakima turned to see another group of howling desperadoes approaching the bank from the side street between Charlier's Tavern and the harness shop. Yakima couldn't see the bank or the stagecoach from this angle, but there was no doubt that both sets of riders were making a beeline for the gold shipment.

As both groups converged at the intersection west of the café, checking their mounts down to skidding, hoof-grinding halts, a barrage of gunshots rose suddenly. Pistols and rifles belched smoke and fire, the reports echoing around the canyon of adobe, wood, and sandstone facades.

Men howled and yelled. Horses whinnied and screamed.

Bullets spanged and barked into wood or thudded into dirt.

A double-barreled shotgun spoke above the cacophony—first one booming report, then another—making the window near Yakima rattle like a wind chime.

Seconds after the first group had passed the café, Yakima grabbed his Yellowboy and jacked a shell into the chamber as he threw open the door. He'd taken a step onto the dilapidated stoop when a stray bullet plunked into the doorframe to his left, puffing dust and throwing splinters with a shrill *ka-piinggg!*

He flinched as he dropped to a knee, raising his rifle to port arms and looking toward the bank, where the desperadoes—a good fifteen or twenty men—were laying down a serious fusillade against the bank and the stagecoach from atop their milling horses.

This was no holdup, Yakima saw as one shotgun guard—probably a contract man hired by Wells Fargo—was blown off his feet and into the coach behind him. It was a massacre.

Another guard lay beneath the open coach door, one leg resting atop the iron-banded, padlocked strongbox, his rifle lying in the dust to his left. The stage's driver stood in the box, returning fire with his two revolvers, triggering one pistol, lowering it, then raising and firing the other until two of the desperadoes drilled him at the same time—one bullet slamming into his chest while the other smacked his right cheek. The driver screamed and triggered another shot as the bullets flung him straight backward.

At the same time, a woman in a green traveling dress poked her feather-hatted head out the stagecoach door, screaming, her mouth forming a dark O against the porcelain white of her face. A bullet slammed into her shoulder and threw her back into the coach while three more bullets drilled through the coach's thin wooden wall in front of her, clipping her screams.

Yakima drew a bead on the desperado who'd shot the woman—a brown-bearded gent wearing a fringed buckskin tunic over which brass-filled bandoliers were crossed, and sitting astride a hammerheaded piebald. The man was pulling back on the pie's reins with one hand, howling like a warlock, and triggering a Winchester carbine with the other, when Yakima's slug tore through the crown of his snuff-brown hat.

The man's head jerked sideways and the hat flew off his head, revealing the bloody, bullet-smashed crown of his skull. As he dropped his carbine and the reins at the same time and sagged down the other side of the pie, several other desperadoes jerked startled, exasperated looks toward Yakima.

Yakima blew one out of his saddle while another rested the barrel of his Henry on his forearm and triggered a slug into the porch support post near Yakima's head. Yakima racked another round and drilled the shooter through his right forearm.

The man screamed and dropped his rifle. Reaching for it, he released his reins, and his bucking dun flung him off its back and into the dust-churned street below, where another dancing mount kicked him in the head and tossed him end over end.

There was so much gun smoke in the street—from the desperadoes' guns as well as from Speares, the shotgun guards, and the sheriff's deputies—that Yakima could see little but vague outlines of horseback riders dancing about the stagecoach.

He didn't give a good goddamn about Speares's men or the gold or the coach. He was worried about his horses. Wolf and the paint were tied before the mercantile on the other side of Charlier's. They were no more than forty yards from the fighting, well within range of stray gunfire and ricochets.

Quickly, Yakima thumbed fresh shells into the Winchester's loading gate and then, flinching at a ricochet that plunked into the stock trough before the café, bolted into the street, angling toward Charlier's. When he was halfway between the café and the harness shop, two bullets drilled the street before him. Another tore through the slack of his right buckskin cuff.

Yakima dove behind a stock trough and whipped his rifle over the trough's lip, aiming in the direction of the three bullets but seeing little except men milling inside the smoke cloud with here and there a fresh puff and a stab of gunfire adding to the growing, thickening web.

On impulse he fired at a horseback rider, hoping the rider was a desperado and not a stage guard—it was no longer possible to tell who was who in the chaos of men, horses, and gunfire—and cast a look up the street beyond Charlier's.

His glance went back to the tavern. A black-haired girl was hunkered down behind the well coping in the street before the tavern, a water bucket in one hand. She held the other arm above her head as if to shield herself from the gunfire.

Anjanette.

She had gotten trapped at the well when the desperadoes thundered into town.

Beyond, Wolf and the paint stood where he'd left them, at the base of the mercantile's loading dock. Both horses bucked against their reins knotted around the hitchrack. A man stood at the hitchrack, and suddenly the black bolted away from the mercantile.

The man followed Wolf into the street, then grabbed the saddle horn with one hand as he held the reins in the other and, hopping on one foot to keep pace with the skitter-stepping stallion, shoved his boot toe into the stirrup and swung into the saddle.

Wolf buck-kicked defiantly, reluctant to carry anyone but Yakima. The desperado held fast to the apple and slammed his pistol butt across the top of Wolf's head.

"Bastard!" Yakima growled as he lunged forward.

At the same time, obscured by gun smoke, a rider cut around the stone well coping, stretched out from his saddle, and grabbed Anjanette around the waist. The girl gave a clipped cry as the man, his laughter booming beneath the gun pops, pulled her across his horse's withers.

Anjanette shouted, "Let me go, you son of a bitch!"

Yakima snapped the Winchester to his shoulder, then let it sag in his hands. He might hit Anjanette.

She flailed with her arms on one side of the horse while kicking her legs against the opposite stirrup fenders. Holding her down with his right hand, triggering pistol shots with his left, the man spurred his screaming dun straight down the street toward Yakima.

Yakima let his Winchester hang low in his right hand and set himself to lunge for the girl. When the dun was twenty yards away, the laughing rider extended his revolver straight out from his shoulder, aiming at Yakima's head.

As the bullet plunked into an adobe wall, the horse's left shoulder slammed into Yakima's side. He grunted as the air burst from his lungs, and pinwheeled toward the other side of the street, piling up against a stock trough.

"Help!" Anjanette screamed above thundering hooves

and gunfire, as the dun galloped on through the wafting smoke and sifting dust.

Yakima pushed up on his elbows, saw Wolf lurching toward him, the rider crouched low in the saddle, lips stretched back from his teeth.

Drawing air into his battered chest, Yakima rose to his knees and reached for his Winchester, keeping his eyes on Wolf. "That's my horse, you son of a bitch!"

The sentence hadn't died on his lips before a man shouted, "Move 'em out, boys!"

As the stage began careening eastward along the street, adding more dust to the gauze fogging the air, Yakima whipped his head to the right. Wolf was within twenty yards and closing, shaking his head and bucking defiantly as the desperado ground his spurs into the black's flanks.

Yakima stood and brought the Winchester to bear on the man in the saddle—a slender, hatless hombre in a frock coat and with a long, black mustache hanging down both sides of his mouth. He crouched forward, clamping his left arm to his bloody side.

Yakima snapped off a shot. Lead skidded along the side of his head, just above his ear, snapping his own shot high. At the same time, a pistol popped to his right, and Wolf and the desperado bolted on past Yakima and down the street behind the fleeing stage.

Ignoring another slug that whistled over his head, Yakima ran into the street. Thirty yards ahead, Wolf lurched to one side, buck-kicked, and craned his neck to peer back toward Yakima.

The mustang's black eyes were wide with fear and fury.

Again, the rider slammed his pistol atop Wolf's head and rammed his heels into the black's sides, cursing wildly. As Wolf stretched into a gallop, Yakima spat a curse through taut lips and drew a bead on the rider's back.

The rifle boomed. At the same time, Wolf jerked to the left, and the slug flew wide, shattering a window up the street.

The rider continued gouging the black with his spurs. Wolf loosed a shrill whinny, and the horse and rider tore around a bend and out of sight.

Yakima wheeled frantically, looking around for a horse. A riderless dun stood against the side of Ma Chavez's café, cowering under the brush arbor, ears pricked, trembling. Yakima ran toward it.

A rifle exploded to his right, blowing up dust at his boots.

"Hold it, breed!"

Yakima whipped his head around. Sheriff Speares knelt in the street before the bank, racking a fresh shell into his Winchester's breech while aiming the barrel at Yakima. "You ain't goin' *nowhere*!"

Chapter 6

Yakima stared at Speares through a red veil of anger. "Put that rifle down, fool. They took Anjanette." He turned his eyes toward the hills where the gang had disappeared. With each passing second, the desperadoes were putting more ground between him and Anjanette and Wolf.

Speares curled his upper lip and stared at Yakima through the swollen mask of his face and the thick gauze over his nose, which was nearly as large as a child's clenched fist. Around him, a good ten men lay in bloody heaps, gun smoke wafting in the air. It was impossible to tell which were the Wells Fargo guards and Speares's deputies and which were the desperadoes.

Near the tavern, a horse sat back on its haunches, like a dog, struggling to rise while blood gushed from several wounds. Another horse lay dead.

"Don't play me fer no fool," Speares growled. "I know you're one o' *them*. I seen you take out Fisk."

Speares canted his head toward the man lying draped across the stock trough fronting the bank. It was one of the deputies Yakima had seen in Speares's office the day before. Blood washed down the side of the trough beneath the deputy's chest, the tin star drooping on his shirt.

Yakima slid his eyes back to Speares. "If I shot him, it was because he was shooting at *me*."

Speares snapped his rifle to his shoulder, squinting down the barrel. His voice broke as he shouted shrilly, "Shut the hell up and drop that rifle! Stretch out on the ground, belly down. Now!"

Yakima stared back at the man, his chest rising and falling sharply. He wanted to take a chance, dodge right, and snap his rifle up, but Speares had him dead to rights. And Yakima would be no good to either the girl or the horse if he was dead.

He crouched, set the Yellowboy in the street, then, holding his hands shoulder-high, palms out, turned, dropped to his knees, then leaned forward and planted his chest and belly in the dust.

"Hands to the back of your head!" Speares shouted.

As Yakima did as he was told, another voice said in a horrified, bewildered tone, "What . . . what a horror. They took the stage . . . and the strongbox. . . ."

Speares said, "Shut up, Franklin" and moved toward Yakima. Out of the corner of his left eye, Yakima watched the sheriff crouch beside him, lift the Colt from his holster, then stand and wedge the revolver in his cartridge belt.

The sheriff had just opened his mouth to speak when one of the bodies near the harness shop moved. The desperado—a beefy man with long red hair and a beard—spat a curse from clenched teeth as he rose up on his arms, as though he were about to attempt some exercises. Blood and viscera stringed down from his bulging belly.

Speares swung his rifle around, taking three steps back from Yakima—out of Yakima's kicking range—and fired the Winchester. The bullet carved a black hole through the redhead's cheek, throwing the man sideways onto his back, where he expired with a loud fart and a deep sigh.

Speares swung back toward Yakima, loudly ejecting the smoking shell and seating fresh. "If you don't want the same, get up and start movin' toward the jailhouse."

"Christ," the man called Franklin said bewilderedly, as Yakima gained his feet. Yakima didn't have to look to know he was the dapper little man who'd been in the tavern last night with Speares. The banker. "So many . . . dead."

"I told you to shut up, Franklin. Less'n you wanna be one of 'em." Speares poked his rifle barrel into Yakima's back, prodding him forward.

As Yakima began moving toward the jailhouse, at the east end of the street, he stared ahead at the chaparral-covered hills beyond the town. The sun had not yet risen, but there was enough gray light that he could see his black stallion, not much more than a slim shadow from this distance of three hundred yards, crest a low hill stippled with sage and saguaros and disappear down the other side.

His stomach contracted anxiously, and he glanced over his left shoulder at Speares. The man was too far away to attempt a kick. Even with Yakima's finely honed abilities, he would only buy himself a bullet. The banker followed at a distance, looking around at the carnage, lower jaw hanging, his gray muttonchops glowing in the early morning light.

Yakima would bide his time, find another way out from under the sheriff's thumb. . . .

As Yakima approached the jailhouse, the banker strode up quickly behind Speares, his shoes grinding dirt and gravel, his voice shrill. He held his black bowler in one hand, revealing the pink crown of his head. "They got the gold, Speares. Every damn coin! What the hell are you going to do about this?"

Speares stopped and wheeled toward the banker, keeping the Winchester aimed at Yakima, who stopped before the jailhouse's closed door and turned halfway around.

"I'm gonna throw this damn half-breed in the slammer, and then I'm gonna gather a posse," Speares said tightly. "There ain't much more I *can* do, now, is there? Less'n you want me to sprout wings and *fly* after 'em."

He glanced across the street. The liveryman, Suggs, poked his head out the livery barn's doors, a wary expression on his face, his hair still mussed from sleep. Shouting, jerking his head back toward Yakima standing before the closed jailhouse door, Speares ordered Suggs to round up every man in town who could shoot halfway straight.

"Have them meet me, mounted and with a couple days' trail provisions, in front of my office in one hour."

The liveryman looked to his left. A man stood before

Stendahl's Tonsorial Parlor in a faded red robe, night
sock, and slippers, the parlor's bullet-pocked door standing partially open behind him. He shuttled his eyes between Speares and Suggs, then jerked as though he'd
been slapped and shuffled back into the barbershop,
slamming the door behind him.

Yakima snorted softly.

Speares's eyes bored into his, and he raised the rifle
toward Yakima's head. "Get on in—"

Hoof thuds rose up the street, from the direction of the
bank, and both Yakima and Speares cut their eyes in that
direction. A man astride a blaze-faced dun rode between
the bank and the tavern, turning the horse around the
dead men sprawled in the street and gazing down at each
one, as if counting them. He held his jittery horse's reins
tight in his gloved right fist. When he looked up and
gigged the horse down the street toward the jailhouse,
Yakima saw the saddle-leather skin of the man's face between pewter sideburns and the copper star winking on
his buckskin coat.

Inwardly, Yakima cursed. The marshal. Yakima's luck
was draining fast.

The man reined up before Speares and shifted his
gaze between the sheriff and Yakima. The right side of
his face was swollen and purple, with a two-inch gash
where Yakima had kicked him, over which blood had
jelled. The marshal jerked a thumb over his shoulder, in-
dicating the men lying dead in the street. "How long
ago?"

"Not fifteen minutes," said Speares, staring at the man
curiously.

The man looked at Yakima again, recognition narrowing his flat eyes, then switched his gaze back to Speares. "Name's Patchen." He shifted his weight. His sweat-lathered dun hung its head with fatigue. "Deputy U.S. marshal out of Prescott."

"Well, you're about fifteen minutes late," Speares said smartly.

"You gettin' a posse together?"

Sneering, Speares canted his head toward Yakima. "Soon as I lock up this son of a bitch. The breed here's the only one o' the gang that didn't buy a bullet or light a shuck."

"I'll be ridin' with you soon as I get a fresh mount and trail supplies." Patchen favored Yakima with another flat stare. "Watch his feet. Bastard kicks like a damn mule."

Patchen reined the dun toward the livery barn. Speares turned toward Yakima, wagging the rifle barrel. "Inside."

Yakima glanced east again, where the gang had disappeared into the chaparral, and shot his angry gaze back to Speares, his jaw hard. "Every second you waste on me, they're gaining ground."

Speares's chest rose sharply, his face reddening, nose swelling even larger. "Inside!"

Yakima threw the door open and walked into the nearly dark office. From the door, Speares said, "Take the key off the desk and open the cell door. The one on the right. Make one wrong move, and I'll drill a hole through your spine. I'd just as soon watch you dangle from a hang rope, but droppin' the hammer on you wouldn't break my heart."

"You're a damn fool, Speares," Yakima growled as, having snatched the key ring from the desk, he poked a key in the door of the far right cell.

He opened the door and turned to Speares once more, clenching his right fist at his side. The sheriff stretched his lips back from his horse teeth in a mocking grin and squinted one purple-rimmed eye down his Winchester's barrel. Yakima snorted and stepped into the jail cell.

Speares stepped forward and threw the door closed with an echoing clang. He turned the key in the lock, and the bolt clicked home. Speares withdrew the key, lowered the rifle, and shoved his face up close to the bars, sneering.

"I'll accompany Miss Anjanette to your hangin'. You'll wanna take care not to soil your trousers."

Yakima threw his right fist forward. Speares pulled his swollen nose back from the door an eye wink before Yakima's fist slammed against the bars, rattling the cage's entire front wall.

Speares's eyes snapped wide. Then he smiled as Yakima rubbed his sore knuckles in his left palm. He'd torn the skin across the middle knuckle, but he kept his eyes on the sheriff, who slowly backed away from the cell, laughing.

When Speares left the jailhouse, Yakima sucked a deep, edgy breath, wrapped his hands around the bars of the cell door, and shook the door on its hinges. It rattled loudly, dust sifting from the low stone ceiling, but held firm.

Yakima turned and saw a window in the outside

wall—a small rectangle with four iron bars. He wrapped his hands around two of the bars, and held his breath as he pulled back and down, the veins standing out in his neck and forehead.

Finally, when he could hold his breath no longer, he dropped back to the floor, his chest heaving, and cursed. No give in the window, either.

He turned back to the cell door, slumped down on the cot, and lowered his head to his hands. He kept hearing Anjanette's angry cry and Wolf's defiant whinny as he sat there on the edge of the cot, at once berating himself for not slipping free of Speares and trying to figure a way out of the cell and onto the trail of the girl and the horse.

He had no faith in Speares's abilities. Even if the sheriff found a way to rescue the girl, he'd leave the horse. Wolf meant nothing to him.

Yakima pulled his hair and stared at the earthen floor between his boots. Silly, probably, to worry about his horse when so many men had been killed and a girl's life was at stake. But the only things Yakima had—all that he valued—were his Yellowboy Winchester, a gift from an old friend, and the black mustang he'd traded an old Ute for when Wolf was just a colt.

As light in the cell grew, so did the sounds outside. Occasionally Yakima would look up to see a ranch wagon pass or a couple of men carrying a bloody body eastward, probably to the dead man's home. From time to time Speares's voice rose, shouting orders, and horseback riders began appearing out the jailhouse window—green, edgy-looking townsmen armed with Spencer or

Springfield rifles. Most looked as much at home in a saddle as they would in a kid's tree house, and they looked like they wanted to be here as badly as ten-year-old boys wanted to be in church.

Nearly an hour after he'd locked up Yakima, Speares threw the office door open and strode inside. He was carrying Yakima's Yellowboy repeater in his right hand. The U.S. marshal, Patchen, followed him into the office.

Patchen was smoking a long black cigar, holding his own Henry over his right shoulder, the high crown of his snuff-brown Stetson nearly scraping the ceiling, his stovepipe boots clomping along the floor. Out the open door behind him, the posse men waited atop their fidgety mounts, grumbling among themselves.

Yakima rose and wrapped his hands around the cell bars as he stared at Speares. "That's my repeater, Sheriff."

Speares opened a desk drawer, glanced at Yakima. "Damn fine gun. Too fine for a breed. Besides, you ain't gonna be needin' it where you're goin'."

He glanced at Patchen, and both men laughed.

Speares set several boxes of .44 shells on the desk. "Help yourself, Marshal." He chuckled as he began thumbing cartridges from a box into his cartridge belt. My shells are your shells—long as the marshal's office reimburses me, that is."

Patchen stepped toward the desk, nodding his head at Yakima. "Who you got guarding him?"

"Me." A bulky figure in a blue shirt and calfskin vest slumped through the jailhouse's open door, holding his double-barreled shotgun, broken open, under his right arm. The liveryman, Suggs. "Fifty cents a day, right, Sheriff? Till you get back?"

"That's right," Speares said, feeding shells into the Yellowboy's breech. "Till I get back. Which shouldn't be long—if'n we can cut off that gang before they get to the border and lose themselves in the Sierra Madre." He reached into the same drawer from which he'd produced the cartridges, and set a corked bottle on the desk. "Drink for the road, Marshal?"

"Don't mind if I do."

Speares grabbed a tin cup off the stove in the middle of the room, scrubbed it out with a gloved finger, set it on the desk, and splashed whiskey into it. He held the bottle up to Patchen. "Luck."

Speares tipped the bottle back, and the bubble slid toward the bottom as the sheriff took several heavy swallows. Patchen watched him, one pewter brow arched.

When Speares lowered the bottle, sighed, and corked it, the marshal said, "I hope you plan on staying clear, Sheriff. This gang—the Thunder Riders, they're called along the border—is nothing to trifle with."

"I don't aim to trifle with 'em, Marshal. I aim to kill 'em." Speares chuckled and ran his sleeve across his whiskey-moist lips and mustache. "But without a little medicine to dull the pain in my beak—thanks to that son of a bitch right there!—I wouldn't make it to the edge of town on horseback."

Patchen raised the cup. "Touché. It does look a mite on the sore side." He threw the whiskey back, set the empty cup on the desk. He stuck his cigar between his teeth, shouldered his Henry, and made for the door.

Speares told the liveryman, Suggs, to stay in the jail-house with the prisoner as much as possible and to keep away from the cell except to pass a food plate once a day through the slot in the bars. "And whatever you do, don't open that door. I don't care if the damn town's on fire! Understand?"

"I understand," Suggs said, thumbing wads into the shotgun's tubes as Speares headed for the door. "Don't forget—you promised a half-dollar a day."

Speares cursed and left. He stepped out from under the brush arbor into the sunlight, heading for his zebra dun tied to the hitchrack. One of the posse men milling under the arbor—a tall bearded man in a cloth cap and checked shirt—lifted his rifle onto his shoulder and swung around toward his own horse.

As he did, the end of his rifle clipped the sheriff's nose.

Speares gasped as he pulled his head to one side and clapped his left hand over the swollen appendage. *"Uhhhnnnn!"* He froze there, chin down, holding his hand over his nose. From the window, Yakima could see his shoulders trembling slightly.

A few of the others muttered, but Yakima couldn't hear what they were saying.

Speares lowered his hand and turned his head sharply left. His voice owned a pinched, nasal twang. "Goddamn it, Hank, watch where you swing that rifle!"

"Sorry, Sheriff."

"Sorry, hell." Speares made a sour face as he sucked a breath through his lips. "Anyone comes within six feet of my damn nose, they're gonna be prying their rifles out of their assholes—understand?"

When the posse men had grumbled their affirmative, Speares mounted up. He and Patchen swung out away from the jailhouse, and the others—about a dozen men by Yakima's rough count—followed them east of the jailhouse and out of sight, the drumbeat of the horses' hooves dwindling behind them.

Suggs snapped his shotgun closed, sauntered over to the door, and looked out. He left the door open. Except for the one small window to the left of it, and a couple small ones in the cells, the door provided the only light—a trapezoid of molten copper laid like paint across the earthen floor just inside the threshold.

Suggs sat down in the squeaky swivel chair at the desk and held his shotgun across his chest, caressing the forestock.

"Well, breed," he said through a self-important sigh. "Fine mess you got yourself in, now, ain't it?"

Chapter 7

The leader of the Thunder Riders, Jack Considine, crested a low rise and, giving the horse its head while holding Anjanette down across the mount's withers with his left hand, glanced over his shoulder. The stage was a good half mile behind him, as were most of the other desperadoes—keeping pace with the gold, afraid to let it out of their sight.

Those boys didn't have a single trusting bone in their bodies.

Considine grinned under his silver-trimmed Stetson as he turned his head forward. At the same time, the girl twisted toward him, one hand on his saddle horn, her face taut with anger. She swung her arm up, whipping the back of her hand toward Considine's face.

The desperado leader laughed as he grabbed her wrist.

"Let me off, you son of a bitch!" the girl screamed.

"Want down?" Considine slid out of the saddle, grabbed her by the back of her skirt and one arm, and pulled her brusquely off the mare.

The girl's feet hit the ground, and she yelped as her

momentum drove her stumbling backward into a mesquite thicket. She tripped over a clump of Mormon tea and fell on her butt, red-brown dust blowing up around her, her wide black eyes glistening with fury beneath her calico bandanna.

She picked up a rock and threw it hard. It bounced off Considine's right shoulder and landed in the dirt at his boots.

He stood frozen for a moment, taken aback, his cobalt blue eyes darkening slightly in spite of the early sunshine bleeding out from behind a high eastern peak. His brown mustache hung down both sides of his mouth, rimed with trail dust and blood from a bullet burn across his lower right cheek.

He glanced at the rock and strode over to the girl, his eyes glazed with lust.

Anjanette slid backward on her butt. "Get away from me, you son of a bitch!"

"Take your clothes off."

"No!" She scrambled to her feet and ran into the mesquite, weaving around the shrubs until she came to a stone escarpment blocking her path. She turned, pressed her back against the rock. "Please, leave me alone!"

Considine strolled toward her, grinning. She looked around wildly, but the mesquite pushed up close to the scarp, wedging her in. Considine stopped in front of her and slid his pearl-gripped revolver from its holster with one hand while unbuckling the cartridge belt with the other.

As the belt and empty holster dropped to the ground

at his boots, he aimed the revolver at the girl's chest.
"Take your shirt off."

Anjanette glanced at the gun and pushed her back
against the uneven rock wall behind her, digging her fingers into the crevices. "No!"

Considine clicked the hammer back and held the revolver six inches from the girl's heaving chest. Menace
edged his voice. "Take it off."

Anjanette looked at the gun again and curled her lip.
She threw her head back, tossing her hair back from her
face. "You're a bastard."

Considine laughed. "How did you know?" He flicked
his gun barrel against the third button on the girl's green
plaid shirt. A small silver cross dangled down her cleavage.

"Take it off, or I will." Considine grinned coldly. "And
if *I* take it off, it won't be fit to wear again."

Slowly, she lifted her hand to her blouse, began undo-
ing the buttons, her breasts rising and falling sharply,
making the shirt rise and fall as well. Her eyes were
dark, her jaw hard. When the last button was freed, the
blouse hung slack, revealing half of each full, round
breast, the cross dangling between them winking in the
growing morning sunlight.

"No under frillies," Considine observed. "It's almost
as if you were expecting someone. . . ."

He slid the gun barrel down her cleavage, tracing the
inside line of the right breast, then suddenly flicking the
blouse back away from it, revealing the entire pink-
tipped orb, full as a cantaloupe and the color of var-
nished oak.

The girl stared at him, her brown eyes hard, her lips slightly parted to reveal the edges of her two front teeth. "Filthy pig."

Considine chuckled. "Sooner or later, you're going to run out of insults." His expression suddenly hardened and he flicked the other flap of the shirt back from the other breast. "Take it *off*!"

She jumped with a start, then raised her hand to her shoulders, peeled the shirt down her arms, let it fall back between her boots and the base of the scarp. Considine swallowed and ran the revolver barrel across each nipple in turn. Each turned hard, pebbling out from the areola.

He took the gun in his left hand, massaged the amazing orbs with his right, pinching the nipples. Anjanette's face went slack and her chest rose and fell more heavily. As Considine rubbed her breasts, her head fell forward, hair cascading down her shoulders.

"If you're going to rape me, you bastard, get on with it," she breathed.

Considine dropped the gun, leaned forward to unbutton the girl's skirt, which dropped to her boots, revealing her finely muscled legs. He ran his hands across her buttocks, then released her to unbutton his black denim trousers and peel them and his long underwear down to his knees.

The girl groaned as he shoved his pelvis toward hers and slid his hands under each thigh, at once lifting and shoving her back against the scarp.

His hat tumbled off his shoulder and dropped to the ground. He gave a savage grunt as he entered her. She cursed and sagged forward, wrapping her arms around his neck, her legs around his waist.

Considine ground up and into her, and she rose and fell against the escarpment as though riding a green mustang over broken terrain. Her hair bounced over Considine's shoulders and down his back.

Considine gave a final grunt, sighed deeply. His knees bent, and they dropped slowly together, raking air in and out of their lungs, down the rock wall to the ground.

Anjanette buried her face in his shoulder, and Considine leaned his head against the scarp behind her. Gradually, their breathing slowed.

"I'm sorry, Chiquita," Considine said, clearing his throat and smoothing her hair back from her face with both hands. "I shouldn't have thrown you over my horse, given you such a hard ride. I only wanted it to look convincing."

Anjanette's black eyes softened slightly. "You nearly killed me, making me ride that way. You're too rough sometimes, Jack."

"I forgot to bring you a horse. I'm sorry." He kissed her gently. "Forgive me?"

She lifted her chin defiantly. "I also thought you were coming *yesterday* morning."

"My man from the bank sent me a cable yesterday in Javelina, said the company delayed it a day to throw off possible"—he smiled, broadening his mustache and showing a chipped front tooth—"holdup artists." He lifted her chin with his gloved right hand. "Did you miss me, baby?"

Anjanette hiked a shoulder and quirked a corner of her mouth. "I got along."

Considine stared back at her, his eyes pensive. Finally, he stretched his lips in a broad smile and caressed her cheek with the palm of his hand. "I can tell you missed me. You're not nearly as tough as you make out. There isn't a woman alive—not even the desert-rat granddaughter of Old Antoine—who has yet been able to resist my charms."

The thunder of hooves and wagon wheels rose behind Considine. He turned to look back through the chaparral, where a dozen riders loped toward them. Behind them came the stage, bouncing through the greasewood and cactus, weaving around shrubs and boulders while Wolf MacDonald whipped the reins over the team's backs and bellowed long-practiced curses.

Considine turned back to Anjanette, dropping his head to nuzzle her breasts, licking her nipples. He'd met her four months ago, when he and the rest of the gang except for Mad Dog McKenna had split up after robbing an army payroll caravan near Pima Tanks. Considine and McKenna had meant to spend only one night at Charlier's Hotel and Tavern, then light out for New Mexico.

But that was before Considine laid eyes on Old Antoine's granddaughter. Anjanette had sashayed around the saloon that night, grinning and smiling and cavorting like one of the boys, her colored bandanna holding her Indian-black hair back from her finely sculpted face, her breasts pushing like ripe melons from behind her white cotton blouse, skirts swishing about her legs.

When she set down a beer and a tequila shot before

Considine, sitting slumped back in his chair, he could tell from her eyes—cool but with little sparks of copper—that her attraction to him was as keen and immediate as his for her. Her breasts swelled and her light brown cheeks flushed. Her passion was like heat radiating from a stoked boiler.

They spent the entire week frolicking in Anjanette's bedroom every night after Old Antoine took his customary bottle to bed and drank himself to sleep. One night, unable to wait until Anjanette had finished sweeping the saloon, they made love atop the long mahogany bar, her blouse ripped open, skirt thrown up across her belly, his denims bunched around his ankles.

At the end of the week, Considine had promised Anjanette he would spring her from the confinement and boredom of Saber Creek and her grandfather's tavern and show her a world of adventure she'd only dreamed about. A month ago, when he'd learned of the Wells Fargo gold shipment from an hombre working in the Saber Creek bank, he'd figured he'd found a way to do just that.

They decided to make her exodus from town look like a kidnapping, to make a posse afraid of getting a hostage killed, and to keep her face off wanted dodgers. She, unlike the other Thunder Riders, wasn't a seasoned owl-hoot, after all.

Now Considine lifted his head and kissed the girl's lips. "We best go meet the pack."

As he and Anjanette walked back through the mesquite thicket, holding hands, Anjanette said, "Speares will be gathering a posse, you know."

"Sure. But it's suicide to ride after us. More than one lawman has found that out the hard way." Considine glanced at her, giving his rakish smile. "Besides, Chiquita, isn't that what you're for? To slow him down? Your sheriff wouldn't want us to kill our lovely hostage—the loveliest girl in Saber Creek, if not all of Arizona."

He kissed her cheek and snaked an arm around her waist as they moved out of the mesquites. Before them, the other gang members were dismounting their dusty, sweaty horses, casting knowing grins and smirks toward Considine and Anjanette.

The stage driver, Wolf MacDonald, drew back on the team's reins, bellowing.

"I almost killed him last night," Anjanette said tightly. "He pushed me too far."

Considine looked at her again quickly, and grinned. "I don't doubt it! Is that how he got that—?" He gestured to indicate the wrapping over Speares's broken nose.

Anjanette shook her head, staring at the stage stopping twenty yards away, the horses lurching back in their collars, digging their hooves into the dirt. "A friend stepped in."

"Hey, pard, I think we oughta ditch the stage here!" A tall man in faded Union cavalry trousers, wolf coat, and stovepipe hat rode up on a cream barb. He was round-faced, unshaven, with long, straight black hair and silver hoop rings dangling from his ears. On his right cheek a dog's face had been tattooed. The other cheek and eye had been horribly disfigured by Apaches when Ernst "Mad Dog" McKenna was only five years old, and his

Scottish parents were ranching in the White Mountains. "No point in haulin' it any farther. Country breaks up only a few clicks farther south. Let's strap the lockbox to a couple horses and light a shuck due south."

Considine strode between several horses, squinting against the dust, and approached the stage. MacDonald set the brake and began climbing down from the driver's box.

"Anybody still alive in there?" Considine asked, nodding at the bullet-riddled carriage housing.

MacDonald chuckled and wiped a stream of dusty chaw from the right corner of his mouth. "Shit, if all the bullets flying in town didn't kill 'em, the ride I just gave 'em *did*!"

As MacDonald leapt to the ground with a grunt, Considine drew his pearl-gripped Peacemaker and opened the coach door. A woman in a green traveling dress rolled halfway out, head and arms dangling toward the ground, glassy eyes staring up at Considine as if with a puzzling question. Blood dribbled from her lips and from the holes in her right temple and shoulder.

Considine shuttled his gaze from the woman to the coach's dark innards, where two men and an old woman in a black dress with white lace trim lay sprawled every which way. The desperado leader winced and shook his head as he holstered the Colt.

"Well, that makes it easy."

He reached in, pulled the woman in the green dress out, then reached in again, found the handle on the strongbox, and yanked it out from beneath the gray-haired lady, grunting with the effort.

"Dog, help me here!"

Mad Dog McKenna swept his bear coat back from the big bowie sheathed over his belly and grabbed a handle of the strongbox. Together, he and Considine lifted the box, which must have weighed over a hundred pounds, to the ground beside the dead woman in the green dress.

"Must be payday soon out to Fort Chiricahua," Considine said with a laugh.

"Ah, shit," Considine said, "what do those soldiers need with money, anyways? There's nothin' to *buy* up in them bald hills."

MacDonald stepped forward, rubbing his big hands together. "Come on, Jack, open her up, will ya? I wanna see all them coins!"

Considine drew his Colt, stepped back, and triggered the gun. He had to fire once more before the heavy iron lock broke and hung slack against the stout wooden box. Holstering the revolver, he knelt down, removed the lock from the chains, and opened the lid.

Several lumpy burlap pouches, tied with rawhide, snuggled in the box like baby pigs at their mother's belly. Each one was marked WELLS FARGO, LORDSBURG, N.M.T.

MacDonald whistled. "Can I open one?"

"Not till we get to the tavern." Considine looked around. "Prewitt, Cooper, Sanchez—separate these pouches, rig them to a couple of the stage horses."

As Prewitt and Cooper stepped forward, Cooper said, "Sanchez didn't make it out of Saber Creek, Jack."

Considine cursed and cast his gaze around the well-armed men—mostly Yanquis but a few greasers, a black man, a half-breed Sioux, and a former Apache cavalry scout humorously known to the desperado gang as Kills Gold-Hairs because of his predilection for towheaded whores. There was also a round-bodied Mexican woman named Toots, sister of one of the Mexicans, who could shoot better than some of the men, and who hunted, trapped, cooked, washed dishes, and tended wounds.

Considine brought his eyes to Mad Dog. "How many we lose?"

"Four," said Ben Towers, the only black man in the group—a former slave and hide-hunter whom Considine and McKenna had met in Yuma Pen's infamous snake pit. Towers had gone on a bender and killed several men in his hide-hunting outfit, and found that he enjoyed killing men more than buffalo, and robbing banks more than stretching hides for a living.

"But Eddie—he's not in good shape," said Toots, standing among the men who'd gathered in a semicircle around the strongbox. She was a Duke's mixture of Pima, Mexican, and Irish. She turned her barrel-shaped body to indicate the man sitting on a tall, blaze-faced black stallion about forty yards away.

The man was crouched forward in the saddle, hatless, curly auburn hair blowing in the breeze. The horse's head was up as the animal looked around, twitching its ears and snorting angrily.

Considine cursed again and pushed through the crowd toward the man, Eddie Tomlain, a young outlaw from Kansas. Knowing Considine's gun reputation, Tomlain had called him out in the main street of Tularosa one drunken Saturday night. Considine had known a good, albeit green and gassy, cold-steel artist when he saw one, so he'd shot the kid's gun out of his hand, beat him to a bloody pulp, and invited him into the Thunder Riders.

"Ah, shit, Eddie." Considine reached up to pull the kid's crossed arms away from his lower right side. "What the hell those bastards do to you?"

Tomlain raked out through gritted teeth, "I'll be all right, Jack. Bullet went through my side. I'll be all right . . . once I get to O'Toole's."

"Well, you sure got you a nice horse there, Eddie." Considine stepped back to inspect the horse. Wolf lowered his head and gave Considine an angry stare, expanding and contracting his nostrils. "Where'd you find him?"

Tomlain forced a smile, and blood gushed from one corner of his mouth. "He was tied in front of the mercantile. Sure is a fine one, ain't he?"

As he reached out to pat the black's sleek neck, the horse lunged suddenly, lifting its front hooves a good six feet in the air and loosing a shrill whinny. Considine bolted back with a start as Tomlain gave a cry and tumbled off the saddle, somersaulting and hitting the ground with a heavy thud and an anguished grunt. Considine grabbed the black's reins, planted his heels in the turf, and held tight as the horse whipped around, buck-kicking, then rising off its front hooves once more.

The horse nearly pulled Considine off his feet, but the desperado leader held the reins taut and didn't let the horse turn. With this stallion's strength and fury, if he got turned around, he'd be halfway back to town in five minutes.

"Help me, Latigo!" Considine shouted as the horse began to pitch once more.

The biggest, most muscular man in the group—Latigo Hayes—rushed over and grabbed the reins in front of Considine. When the men got the horse reined down, Latigo held the reins up close to the bit, then led the horse a few yards away and tied it tightly to a stout cottonwood.

"Fine horse," said Latigo in his slight German accent, running a hand along the quivering beast's arched neck. "Boy, is he pissed!"

Considine had already turned back to Tomlain. Several of the others stood around him as well, while the rest of the group watered their horses or separated the bags of gold coins for packing on a couple of stage mounts.

Breathing hard, Tomlain looked up at Considine. "I reckon I'm gonna need a hand up," he said with a chuckle. "D-damn hoss. I'm gonna knock some sense into his head . . . show him who's boss."

Considine glanced at the others gathered around the wounded desperado, then smoothed his mustache and pinched his denims up his thighs, and squatted down. "You took a bad one, Eddie." He removed his hat and worried the brim with his fingers. "I hate to remind you of the rules at a time like this, but . . . well, you know we can't let wounded riders slow down the rest of the group. And we couldn't leave you here. One, it wouldn't be fair to you. Apaches or bobcats might find you. Two, if a lawman found you, he might make you tell him where we're headed."

Tomlain's eyes turned dark in the sunlight as his chest

rose and fell, blood gushing out from the hole in his side, sopping his shirt and vest. "You son of a—"

His right hand reached for the Smith & Wesson holstered low on his right thigh in a black rig he'd had tooled and stitched in Durango on their last trip to Mexico. Considine's own hand closed around the gun's grips before Tomlain's could reach it, however, and he slid the .45 from the holster.

He held the oiled weapon up close to his face, looking it over. "Sorry, Eddie. Anyone you want me to notify?"

"Come on, Jack. I can ride. Put me back on my horse."

Considine sighed, stood, and regarded the other five men facing him. Anjanette stood off to his left. The other woman, Toots, stood near Anjanette, rummaging around in her saddlebags as she glanced over her right shoulder at Considine.

"I did the last one, so I ain't gonna do Tomlain. I don't wanna get the reputation of bein' an *executioner*." He glanced at a short, sharp-featured man in a bowler hat decorated with bear claws, with a string of wolf teeth around his long, thin neck. "Luther, I know you and Eddie were tight, so I won't ask you."

Considine raked his gaze across the other four men, his eyes expectant, waiting.

"Hold on." It was Toots, standing beside her horse and facing the group, with a hand-rolled cigarette drooping from her lips. She held a lucifer in her left hand. A smile shaped itself slowly on her round, fleshy face, the pug nose peeling from sunburn.

She scraped the lucifer to life on the cartridge belt wrapped around her thick waist, on the outside of her wool poncho and deerskin leggings, and cupped her hands to the cigarette, puffing smoke. Drawing deep on the quirley and tossing down the spent match, she walked over and took the Smith & Wesson out of Considine's hand. Staring at the desperado leader, she held the gun out toward Anjanette.

"If she wants to be in this group, let her show how much sand she's got under those purty tits."

Chapter 8

Following the tracks of the dozen galloping riders and the stagecoach fishtailing through the chaparral, deputy U.S. marshal Vince Patchen galloped his steeldust over a low butte crest and down the other side. He followed the tracks and the trail of torn sage and cactus toward a mesquite thicket standing in a shallow bowl and checked the steeldust down twenty yards from the abandoned stage.

The six-hitch team was gone, their harness scattered about the scrub, the wagon tongue drooping.

Dismounting, Patchen shucked his rifle, levered a round, and approached the stage warily, swinging his head from left to right. He didn't want to get himself bushwhacked as his old ranger friend, Wilson Pyle, and Pyle's young partner had done.

Patchen squeezed the Henry in his gloved hands and licked his lips. Poor sons of bitches had been shot down like dogs.

When he'd scrutinized the area thoroughly, concluding the gang had moved on, Patchen walked back to the

stage and knelt down beside a woman lying near the
coach's open door, in a blood-splattered green traveling
outfit. The woman's sandy blond hair had fallen from its
bun to hang in disarray about her pretty face.

Patchen didn't bother lowering his head to listen for
a breath. The open eyes were death-glazed.

Horse hooves thudded and tack squawked behind
him. He straightened, looked over his shoulder at the
twelve-man posse galloping toward him, with Speares
in the lead, then poked his head through the stage door.
Inside the coach, three more bodies lay, bloody and broken, in a single pool of slowly congealing blood on the
floor between the seats. Flies droned. The blood smell
hung heavy in the close quarters.

"I figured they'd dump the stage sooner or later."
Speares drew up beside Patchen's steeldust. Blood spotted the thick gauze wrap over his nose. Adjusting the
bandage with one hand, he said, "They'll be picking up
the pace now, headin' for the border, no doubt."

"That means we're gonna have to pick up the pace,"
Patchen said, his jaw hard as he raked his gaze over the
posse pulling up to either side and behind Speares. The
catch party was made up mostly of shop owners and
their sons, with one Mexican vaquero and three Anglo
market hunters whom Speares had lassoed in one of
Saber Creek's saloons.

"I can't ride any faster than this," said the bank owner,
Franklin, wincing as, with one hand on the cantle, he
shifted in his saddle. "You men better go on ahead. I'll
only slow you down. I'll go back and alert the army out
at Fort Chiricahua, have them send a patrol—"

He stopped as Speares raised his Remington to his head and thumbed back the hammer. "Isn't that *your* money we're chasin', Franklin?"

As the banker turned toward the sheriff, his lower jaw dropped, his face flushing with outrage. "Really, Speares!"

Speares squinted one eye. "Ain't you the one responsible for all that Wells Fargo gold? You tell me if I'm wrong."

The others, except Patchen, snickered as Speares held his gun barrel against the banker's left temple. Franklin's mouth opened and closed several times before he finally loosed a few words. "Well . . . yes, of course I'm responsible. But—"

"But nothin'," Speares said through gritted teeth. "I'm shorthanded the way it is, since all my deputies were gunned down tryin' to protect your gold. Now, I realize you ain't no gun hand, but, by God, I need every warm body I got, if for nothin' more than keepin' an eye out for an ambush. In other words, you ain't goin' nowhere but south with me and this posse, and you ain't comin' back till either *you're* dead or we've killed every last one of that bunch of border snipes that invaded *my town*."

Franklin shifted his eyes nervously, swallowed. "You don't think someone should notify the army?"

"Take too long. Besides, those blue-bellies got their hands full with them bronco Apaches." Speares pushed the revolver's barrel more firmly against the banker's head, causing Franklin to stretch his lips back from his gold-capped teeth. "Have we come to an understanding now, Mr. Franklin?"

The banker slid his gaze to Patchen, standing before the posse, grinning and holding his Henry over his shoulder. Finding no help there, Franklin returned his gaze to Speares. "I guess I have, Sheriff—"

A voice from behind cut him off. "What I wanna know is what's in it for *us*?"

Patchen glanced at the man riding directly behind Speares—one of the market hunters in a broad-brimmed hat, chaps, and a long tan duster. He was probably twenty-five and, like his two compatriots, carried himself like a man who knew how to use his well-tended sidearms.

"I mean," the man said, sliding his flinty gaze to the sheriff, "I think there should be a reward."

"Yeah," said the man sitting on an Appaloosa to his right. "Me and Jim and Nudge was just ridin' through when that gold was hit. We got no ties to this town. We hunt for a livin', and by God if we're gonna hunt that gang of cutthroats and your loot, we want a *re*ward!"

Speares gigged his horse forward, turned it around to face the three market hunters. "They took a girl. That ain't enough for ya?"

The one on the far right glanced at the other two, then turned back to Speares. "Hell, her old man ain't even ridin' after her. Last I saw, he was curled up drunk behind his bar."

Speares glared at the man, but checked his anger. Aside from the marshal, these three were the best of the posse. He couldn't afford to lose them.

He looked at Franklin, then canted his head to indicate the townsmen flanking the market hunters. "Mr. Franklin here guarantees you each two hundred and fifty dollars—if the gold *and* the girl are recovered." Speares looked at the banker, flushing beneath the brim of his black bowler. "Ain't that right, Franklin?"

Speares didn't wait for a response. "Move out!"

"Sheriff," Patchen called.

As the others spurred their horses south, Speares turned back to Patchen, standing before the stage. The deputy marshal looked at the woman in the green dress. "What about your dead?"

Speares just stared at him as if he had no idea what the man was talking about.

"You're not going to bury them?"

"The best way to honor the dead," Speares said, holding his skitter-stepping mount's reins taut in his right fist, "is to shoot the shit outta those that killed 'em!"

The sheriff turned his horse and put the steel to its flanks.

Yakima whiled away the afternoon and early evening in the Saber Creek jailhouse by counting the stones in the ceiling, then in the floor, and by trying not to think about how far Wolf and the girl were getting away from him.

By nine o'clock it was fully dark, and the street traffic had died down. Yakima, lying on his bunk, ankles crossed, stared through the cell bars at the shotgun in the hands of the liveryman, Suggs, who slept tipped back in the sheriff's swivel chair.

The shotgun lay across Suggs's broad thighs. Fifteen feet away. But with the bars between the gun and Yakima, it might as well have been in the next territory.

Yakima's heart did a slow, hot roll.

He had to get out of here tonight. By sunrise tomorrow, the gang, Wolf, and Anjanette would be deep into Mexico—probably too far away to track. Speares and his men would most likely be dead, their bloody carcasses strewn about some isolated arroyo.

The door latch clicked.

Yakima shuttled his gaze to the front wall as the door opened. A pretty redheaded woman in a low-cut red and black dress and a lacy black shawl poked her head through the opening, her plucked eyebrows arched. She'd gone heavy on the eyeliner and war paint, and the mole off the right corner of her mouth stood out from the rouge.

Suggs had jerked with a start when the door hinges had squawked. His shotgun slid off his thigh and hit the stone floor with a clatter. As he bent forward with a nervous grunt to retrieve it, the redhead laughed.

"It's me—Polly."

Suggs looked up at her, and the lines in his face planed out.

"Kinda slow tonight," the redhead said, closing the door and stepping into the room. "I knew you were alone over here, with orders not to leave, so I thought you might be lonely." Her eyes grew soft, and she sucked a breath to lift her opulent breasts. "Want a poke? Half price for the man guardin' that killer in there."

Suggs picked up the shotgun and sat back in the chair. "I don't think so, Polly. If Speares got back and caught me . . ."

Polly stepped forward, hooking her thumbs into her bodice and pulling it down to her waist, the large, pale breasts jolting free. "That your last word on the subject, Charlie?" She stopped before Suggs's chair, smiling. Suggs stared at her breasts like a little boy staring at a jar of colored rock candy on a mercantile counter.

He set the shotgun down against the desk and reached forward, palms out. "My, those're some jugs!"

Polly stepped back with a laugh. "Let's see the lucre, Charlie!"

Suggs scowled, glanced at the door, then the window, then turned back to the girl. "I reckon Speares won't be back tonight."

He glanced at Yakima, who peered out from beneath the hat tipped low over his eyes, lifting his chest slowly and regularly, feigning sleep. Suggs stood and poked a hand in his pocket, flipped a couple of coins on the desk. "Hell, since he's gone after them damn Thunder Riders, Speares prob'ly won't *ever* be back. No point in deprivin' myself of a half-priced poke!"

"Now you're talkin'!" Unpinning her hair from the back of her head, Polly skipped toward the open door of the jail's only other cell, to the right of the one Yakima was in. She glanced at Yakima, wheeled toward Suggs. "What if he wakes up?"

Suggs chuffed. "So? The breed ain't long fer this world."

Yakima continued raising and lowering his chest

slowly as Suggs followed the girl into the cell, awkwardly dancing a little jig and humming a few bars of "Old Arizona." Yakima could see part of what they were doing out of the corner of his right eye, without turning his head.

When Suggs had pulled his pants down to his knees, nuzzling the girl and giving her ass a couple of sporting slaps, they crawled onto the cot on the other side of the barred wall. Suggs raised the whore's dress above her waist, positioned himself between her spread legs, and began thrusting.

Yakima let them get going hot and heavy, grunting and sighing and giving the cot's leather springs a good workout, before he poked his hat back off his forehead. He dropped his boots to the floor, eased across the cell, and stuck his left arm through the bars. He wrapped the arm around Suggs's neck and slammed the man's head against the cell wall so hard that both cages shook.

The redhead and Suggs screamed at the same time. The redhead stared up in horror as Yakima slammed Suggs's head once more against the bars and held him there, closing his arm taut around the liveryman's neck. Suggs groaned and choked, his face swelling and turning red as the redhead rose up on her elbows, yelling, "Stop! No!"

Yakima turned his gaze on her. "Get the keys from the desk or I'll kill him!"

She tried wedging her fingers between Yakima's arm and Suggs's neck. "Let him go! You're *killing* him!"

Yakima tightened his grip. "I *will* kill him if you don't fetch those keys pronto! I'll tear his head clean off his shoulders!"

Suggs gasped, eyes bulging, and threw his left arm out, gesturing toward the desk.

Sobbing, the redhead scrambled out from beneath the liveryman, rose from the cot, and ran into the main office. She grabbed the key ring off the desk and started back toward the cell in which Suggs was slumped on the cot, head grinding into the bars.

Yakima turned to stare at her over his right shoulder. "Unlock my cell door!"

She slipped on the stone floor, nearly falling, as she turned suddenly and lunged toward Yakima's cell. She hadn't pulled her dress up, and her big breasts bounced and her red hair hung across her shoulders as she fumbled the key into the lock. It took her several tries to finally get the key turned, and then the bolt gave with a satisfying clank.

As the door swung slightly outward on its rusty hinges, Yakima released Suggs, turned around, and pushed it wide.

He'd taken one broad step toward the desk, over which his cartridge belt and holstered .44 were coiled on a hat peg, when the outside door sprang open. A thin, long-haired man in a wool tunic and a broad-brimmed felt sombrero stumbled in, then stopped suddenly, eyes bright, as two others came up beside him—including the Mexican, Spanish Lluna, whom Yakima had fought on his last visit to town, in the

Saguaro Inn. All wielded rifles, revolvers hanging off their hips or under their arms.

"Well, well—looks like we got here just in time, gents!" The thin man cocked his rifle and aimed from the hip at Yakima's belly. "The breed was about to take a stroll!"

Chapter 9

Yakima froze, glanced at the shotgun leaning against the sheriff's desk.

"Forget it, breed," said the third man, flanking the thin gent, raising his own Winchester and narrowing his flinty eyes. "You'll never make it."

"Hey, don't go and spoil our necktie party, heathen," said Spanish—a bulky Mexican wearing a green greatcoat, red bandanna, and low-crowned sombrero. A streak of white, like lightning, marked his shaggy black beard.

They were ten feet away, but Yakima could smell the liquor on their breath.

The thin gent's glassy hazel eyes slid to the whore standing near Yakima, who quickly pulled her bodice over her breasts. Suggs was on his hands and knees on the cell floor, shaking his head as if to clear it as blood dripped from the gash in his right temple.

"Hey, Suggs," said the thin man, laughing while keeping his rifle trained on Yakima. "Speares might not have felt the need to specify, but I believe he wanted you to guard the breed, not turn the jail into a whorehouse."

Lluna and the third hombre laughed.

"That's real funny, Boyd," Suggs said, rising stiffly while dabbing his cut temple. "Put the son of a bitch back in his cell, will you? There'll be a couple nights' free stablin' for all three you boys if'n you don't tell Speares."

"No need," Boyd said, grinning at Yakima. "We're gonna throw a necktie party in the breed's honor—out front of the saloon. A couple of the boys are building a bonfire, and Old Antoine is tapping a fresh keg."

Suggs grabbed his underwear and held them over his crotch. "Speares ain't gonna like it."

"Sheet," said the big Mexican. "Speares ain't comin' back. They make him look bad. Take his girl. He'll fight, but them Thunder Riders will fill him so full of holes he won't be able to hold one *leetle* sip of wheeskey." With that last, the Mexican held up his right hand, spreading his index finger and thumb about an inch apart and squinting at it.

His middle finger had been chopped off at the first knuckle, leaving a swollen purple stump of gnarled flesh. Yakima hadn't meant to cut off the man's finger; he'd meant to bury the man's own stiletto in his gut. The Mexican had been faster than he looked, however, and he'd sidestepped while throwing an errant hand toward Yakima's wrist.

Not long after the finger had dropped to the floor and been kicked under a table, Speares and three deputies had run into the saloon, armed with Winchesters and a double-barreled shotgun.

The thin gent said, "You an' Polly can stay here and

hump. Now, get the hell outta the way, Polly—less'n you wanna give the breed one last rut before he hangs."

"Shut up, Boyd!" Polly dropped her arms and stalked into the cell where Suggs was quickly dressing.

Boyd chuckled as he moved forward and right, keeping his rifle trained on Yakima. At the same time, he removed two lengths of braided rawhide from the back of his belt, tossed them at Yakima's feet.

"Tie one around your wrists, the other around your ankles. We done seen how you can *kick*."

"And Spanish here done seen what he can do with a pigsticker," said the man by the door, a weasel-faced little hombre with no front teeth and a pinto vest.

"Shut up, Squires," Spanish said, sliding his lower jaw from side to side, like a cow chewing its cud. "'Less you want me to cut off *your* finger and feed it to you raw."

The Mexican moved slowly toward Yakima, holding his rifle up high across his chest.

"Back off," Boyd ordered. "Let him put the ties on."

Yakima relaxed his shoulder and straightened his spine. "This doesn't seem very sporting, boys. At least Spanish and I made a fair fight of it."

"There's no fight, breed," Boyd said. "We wanna watch you dance without your boots touchin' the ground." He frowned at the Mexican, whose bushy black brows beetled, black eyes bright with simmering rage.

"I said back off till he's got the damn ties on, Spanish!"

"He can put the ties on *after* I've broken his *jaw*!" The Mexican thrust the rear stock of his rifle forward, checked the motion, and slashed the barrel toward Yakima's face. Yakima had leapt back to avoid the rifle stock. Seeing that the move was just a feint, he still managed to angle his head so that the barrel clipped only his left cheek.

"Spanish!" Boyd shouted.

The shout hadn't died on Boyd's lips before Yakima had lunged forward and buried his right knee in the Mexican's groin. As the Mexican screamed, Yakima twisted, throwing the big man in front of him as Boyd's rifle exploded.

There was a dull *whump* as the bullet tore into Spanish's lower back. Yakima wrapped both hands around the Mexican's rifle and aimed it toward Boyd. Before he could get his own finger through the trigger guard, Spanish tripped the trigger himself.

"*Owwwww!*" Boyd cried, collapsing over his bullet-torn belly, knees bending as he dropped his rifle.

The third hombre shouted, "Son of a *bitch!*" as he triggered his own Spencer repeater. The slug sizzled through the air over Yakima's right shoulder and sparked off a cell bar behind him. Yakima jerked the Winchester from Spanish's grip and, turning toward the door, racked a fresh shell.

The third hombre screamed like a marauding Indian as he cocked his own repeater and, squaring his shoulders and spreading his feet, extended the Spencer from his waist. He screamed again, toothless mouth wide, and stared down at the Spencer's jammed action.

Yakima squeezed the trigger of Spanish's Winchester. Impossibly, the hammer clicked, empty.

At the same time, the toothless man and Yakima tossed aside their rifles. As the toothless hombre reached for the butt-forward S&W on his left hip, Yakima crossed the room in two long strides, grabbing the man's gun hand with one of his own while smashing the other fist across the man's jaw.

The jawbone broke with an audible crack, and the hombre yowled. At the same time, Yakima took the man's gun arm in both his hands and jerked forward and down, lifting the man off his feet to turn a forward somersault and hit the floor on his ass, facing the desk.

Yakima leaned toward him, wrapped his right arm around the man's neck, and jerked.

Crack!

The man fell sideways to the rock floor without a peep.

Yakima froze, staring toward the cell in which the redhead was cowering behind the half-dressed Suggs, peeking around the burly man's shoulder, her eyes wide and glistening with horror. Outside, men were yelling, their voices growing louder.

Yakima sprang forward. The redhead yelped and pulled her head back behind Suggs, who dropped the shirt he'd been holding and raised his hands, palms out. "Please, don't . . ."

As Yakima slung their cell door closed, Suggs and the redhead stumbled back toward the outside wall. The door latched with the loud crack of a rifle report.

Yakima scooped his hat off the floor, then dashed into his cell for his sheepskin vest. Shrugging into the vest, he grabbed his six-shooter and holster off the peg over the sheriff's desk and quickly wrapped it around his waist as the voices outside and the thud and ring of spurred boots grew louder.

He plucked the dead Mexican's Winchester off the floor, found a box of .44 shells in a desk drawer, and shoved a handful of cartridges into his vest pockets. Running to the door, he glanced outside, thumbing cartridges through the Winchester's loading gate.

Several men—it was too dark to see how many exactly—were moving toward the jailhouse, within fifty feet and closing. Lamplight winked off gun iron and steel spurs.

When Yakima had shoved six shells into the Winchester's breech, he bolted outside and into the street. He stopped about ten feet out from the hitchrack, planted the Winchester's butt against his right hip, and levered five shells into the ground in front of the approaching men.

He must have misjudged one shot and drilled it through a boot toe, because a high-pitched howl rose amid the shouts and curses, one man dropping and grabbing his knee as the others ran for cover on the near side of the street.

As the men continued shouting and the man with the wounded foot continued howling, Yakima ran straight out from the jailhouse and down a side street, clinging to the shadows on the right side of the street while thumbing more shells into his Winchester's magazine.

Above the shouting, howling, and milling behind him, Suggs yelled as though from the bottom of a well, "Don't let the redskin git away, boys, or Speares'll have my *hide*!"

Another man screamed, "Son of a bitch shot my *toe* off!"

Yakima stopped before six horses tied in front of a whorehouse. A girl's laughter and the squawk of bed-springs rose from behind the red-curtained windows. Yakima quickly ran his glance over the horses, then, picking out a blue roan with straight legs and a broad chest and a sorrel that appeared second-best of the lot, he unwrapped the reins from the hitchrack, backed the horses into the street, and leapt onto the roan.

In less than a minute, he was on the outskirts of Saber Creek, galloping east through the chaparral, leading the sorrel along behind.

When he'd pushed the horses hard for a good mile, he checked them down to a trot. No point in risking a broken leg. He was a good twelve or thirteen hours behind the Thunder Riders, but he had to be patient. He'd tracked in the dark before—his eyes were keen and there was more light than one might figure—but he'd have to take his time, riding one horse, then the other, and keeping a close eye on the sign.

He was trotting through a creosote-stippled flat about three or four miles from town when the thud of hooves—three or four sets—rose behind him. He reined the horses down and turned his head, listening. Voices rose in the silent night, and bridle chains jangled.

Shit. Men from town were following him.

He turned the horses off the trail and into a nest of rocks and saguaros. Tying the horses a good thirty yards away from the trail, he ran back to the rock nest and hunkered low, peering above the V formed by two boulders.

He waited, hearing the hoof falls and the occasional ring of an iron shoe. Fifty yards back along the trail, three jostling silhouettes took shape in the darkness, starlight flashing off bridle bits and rifle barrels held across saddlebows.

Yakima straightened and raised the Winchester to his shoulder. He loosed five quick shots, one after the other, blowing up dust a few feet in front of the horses. The horses whinnied and the men shouted.

When the echo of the last shot had died, the silhouettes were gone. The thuds of galloping horses dwindled in the hushed night.

With a satisfied chuff, Yakima turned and walked back toward his own mounts while thumbing fresh shells into the Winchester's loading gate. He mounted the sorrel, deciding to give the roan a rest, and angled back out to the trail pocked with the shoe prints of a dozen galloping horses and the two ragged furrows of the stagecoach.

He found the stage a half hour later, a black smudge in the darkness before a mesquite patch. Brush wolves were growling and yammering around the carriage, snapping brush, and Yakima didn't stay to see what they were fighting over.

He kicked the sorrel ahead, wrinkling his nose at the smell of blood and viscera wafting toward him from the stage, and continued following the gang's sign through the rocky desert. Two hours after finding the stage, he switched horses, loosening the sorrel's saddle cinch and slipping the bridle bit, and continued astride the roan, with the sorrel's reins dallied around the saddle horn.

He rode hard all night, losing the trail only twice and having to backtrack to pick it up again. At dawn, he watered the horses at a runout spring, then sat on the ground with his back against a boulder. Fatigue was heavy in his bones. His eyelids drooped, and he was out.

In a dream, he was standing in the yard of his cabin, digging a root cellar, when Wolf trotted toward him from the corral, head down, a playful cast to his molasses-colored eyes. The mustang nuzzled his neck, the bristled lips tickling.

Yakima lifted his head sharply, heart beating fast. The roan jerked its head back with a startled snort, turned, and trotted to the end of its tied reins.

Yakima picked up his rifle, stood, and peered eastward. Rose touched the horizon, dimming the stars and ribbing the high, long clouds with red, purple, and gold.

He mounted the sorrel, dallied the roan's reins around the horn, and headed south.

Chapter 10

That evening, just as the sun set, the posse's tracks angled off the desperadoes' trail into a notch in the rolling, scrub-covered hills. Probably to bed down for the night. Yakima pulled on past.

He had two good horses; he could keep riding for another couple of hours before the mounts would need rest. The desperadoes would probably hole up soon as well, which meant Yakima would continue gaining on them. He might even catch up to them by morning.

What he'd do when he did catch up to them, he wasn't sure. He couldn't take down the entire gang alone. He would have to wait for dark, steal into their camp, rescue the girl and Wolf, and then get the hell away without getting drilled.

A tricky maneuver at best.

Two hours later, he made camp in a dry arroyo, staked out the horses in the sparse grass growing among the cottonwoods. There was no water, but he'd filled his canteens at the last rock tank.

When he'd let each mount drink from his hat, he unsaddled both of them, rubbed them down with grass, scrubbing off the sweat foam and dust, then built a small fire and made coffee with the supplies he'd found in the saddlebags. There was little food—only a few strips of jerky and some biscuits—but that with some wild roots he'd dug up near the cottonwoods would be enough to sustain him until he caught up to the gang.

He slept fitfully for three hours, huddled up in his blankets as the temperature fell to near freezing. Waking and shivering, he built up the little fire again. He heated the remaining coffee and had another cup with his last biscuit before kicking sand on the fire, shrugging into his sheepskin vest, and saddling the horses.

His breath fogged under the stars. Hoarfrost glazed the rocks, brush, and cottonwood limbs. The thuds of his horses' hooves seemed loud as gunshots in the cool, quiet air, under the shimmering stars, as he rode up out of the arroyo and back onto the trail of the Thunder Riders.

It remained cool even after the sun rose. Cresting a steep saddle, Yakima shivered as the chill wind blew up from the valley below, over the ruins of a ragged gathering of crumbling pueblos and rotting brush pens spread across a slope stippled with cedars and ironwood clumps.

A blocklike adobe church with an empty bell tower stood amid the pueblito's ruins, its wooden cross lying on the ground before the stout gray doors, which opened and closed gently in the breeze. On the slope behind the church, amid elms and oaks, lay a cemetery spotted with leaning wooden crosses and cracked adobe shrines.

Yakima scrutinized the village for a time but saw no

movement. He gigged the horses down the deeply rutted wagon trail, aiming for the stone well coping in the middle of the main street, riding slowly and raking his gaze across the fire-blackened adobe hovels, pens, and corrals on both sides of the trail.

It appeared that no one lived here anymore, but Yakima saw the remains of a couple who had—no more than skeletons clad in threadbare white slacks and tunics, Yaqui arrows protruding from their remains. Apparently, the attack, which had occurred a good five or six years ago, judging by the decay and the brush that had grown up around the buildings, had been swift and efficient, leaving no one from the village to bury their dead.

Yakima stopped the horses near the well. A skeleton lay about twenty feet away, at a corner of the church and beside an overturned hay cart. The dead man's empty eye sockets stared at Yakima, a thin, faded red bandanna whipping around the neck to which only a few strips of dried brown skin remained. Yakima wrapped the reins around the roan's saddle horn and turned to the well.

Though the village appeared abandoned, someone apparently tended the water source, as the wooden bucket sitting upside down on the low stone wall had been patched several times and a new hemp rope attached to the handle.

Yakima dropped the bucket into the well and pulled it back up, water sloshing over the sides. He filled his two canteens, then set the bucket in front of the horses. He hadn't yet released the handle when a bullet tore into the ground beside him, the rifle's crack cleaving the breeze-swept silence, the horses whinnying and jerking back with a start.

Yakima slapped his .44 and wheeled toward the church.

At the same time, a familiar voice shouted, "Hold it, breed!"

Sheriff Speares stood just inside the church's open door. Speares no longer wore the bandage on his face, and his swollen, crooked nose resembled a purple-yellow gourd. He aimed Yakima's own Yellowboy repeater straight out from his left hip. Movement to the right of the church attracted Yakima's eye, and he turned to see the deputy U.S. marshal, Patchen, moving up along the church's cracked adobe wall, snugging the stock of his Henry rifle against his shoulder.

"Less'n you wanna buy a bullet from your own rifle," Speares said, "you best pull that six-shooter nice and slow, drop it on the ground."

Yakima cast his gaze from Speares to the marshal and back again. He'd been concentrating so hard on the desperadoes, he hadn't kept an eye on his back trail. The posse had caught up to him.

He kept his hand on his pistol grips. He didn't want to kill them, but he wouldn't let them take him again.

"Drop it!" Patchen shouted, as though reading Yakima's mind.

The man's echo hadn't stopped before Yakima at once jerked his stag-butted .44 from its holster and dove behind the well coping. Speares and the marshal fired their repeaters, both slugs slamming into the well coping and spraying chipped rock.

The horses nickered and pranced and shied away from the well. Speares fired again, and the roan screamed hideously behind Yakima, who snaked his Colt around the coping and fired three quick rounds, two drilling the church wall near the marshal, the other chewing into the door to the right of Speares and sending the sheriff lunging inside the church's heavy shadows.

Yakima rose and wheeled toward the horses.

The roan was down, legs quivering, blood gushing from the hole in the side of its head, just beneath the ear. Yakima swerved wide of the thrashing horse and ran to the sorrel, which was sunfishing toward the other side of the street. The horse was planting its rear hooves, ready to gallop, when two more shots sizzled over Yakima's head.

Sprinting up to the left of the sorrel, Yakima grabbed the saddle horn. The sorrel lunged forward, and Yakima had to fight to maintain his grip on the apple as he hop-skipped on his right foot before kicking his left boot into the stirrup.

As the horse galloped between two ruined adobes, Speares shouted behind him, "Bring the horses!"

Two more rifle shots sounded, one slug drilling a rotting rain barrel just off the sorrel's right hip, the other grinding into the faded pink adobe wall on Yakima's left.

The horse traversed the gap in four long strides, then Yakima neck-reined it left, avoiding an old privy pit, and they shot west, paralleling the village's main street.

Behind him, Yakima heard men shouting and horse hooves thumping, Speares's voice booming above the others.

Yakima crouched over the sorrel's stretched neck as they galloped off across the brush-tufted slope. When they were clear of the village and an old placer digging, Yakima glanced over his left shoulder. The posse was gathered in front of the church, a tall man in a tan duster holding the reins of Speares's horse as the sheriff swung into the saddle. Already mounted, Patchen was pulling away from the group, elbows flapping like wings as the steeldust lunged toward Yakima.

Yakima hipped forward. Ahead, a notch in the northern ridge opened. He reined the galloping sorrel into it, hoping it wasn't a box canyon, and the sorrel tore up red gravel along the bottom of an ancient riverbed.

A couple of old stone shacks sagged along the low banks, and the horse's drumming hooves startled a small herd of Sonoran deer, which bounded up the left slope, disappearing among the rocks and piñons.

The sorrel followed the riverbed's slow curve westward. Yakima cursed, hauling back on the reins when the bed of the ancient river disappeared under a towering wall of wagon- and cabin-sized boulders. Tufts of brown and faded green grama grass pushed up between the rocks, and a couple of stunt pines twisted, leaning as though under a heavy wind.

Yakima jerked a look behind. Speares's posse was out of sight around the bend, but the clattering of shod hooves on rock grew steadily louder.

Turning toward the ridge, Yakima picked out a narrow game trail angling up the side to the left, meandering around boulders.

He rocked forward, grinding his heels into the sorrel's flanks. "Go, horse!"

The horse hit the slope on the run and dug its rear hooves into the sand and gravel along the trail, flinging its front feet out for purchase. Yakima crouched low and gripped the horn with both hands, batting his heels against the mount's ribs.

A shrill laugh rose from below, amid the grinding of hooves and squawk and rattle of tack. "Boys, we got us a duck on a millpond! Aim and fire at will!"

Yakima jerked a glance down the slope. The posse, led by Speares and Patchen, was storming toward the base of the ridge. Speares flung himself out of the saddle and shucked the Yellowboy from the boot. Yakima was a long way from the ridge crest, and well within range of the posse's rifles.

The horse was moving so slowly, it made a good target. Without the horse, Yakima was doomed.

He slid his left foot from the stirrup and dropped down the horse's side. He was about to ram his rifle butt against the horse's hip, hazing it up the ridge—he would catch up to it later, after he'd discouraged the posse—but a bullet fired from below did his work for him.

The sorrel leapt with a start and lunged up the trail, lifting dust and loosing gravel in its wake. At the same time, Yakima rammed a fresh shell in his carbine's breech and ducked behind a boulder.

Shots cracked from down the slope, one bullet slamming into the boulder, another ricocheting off a flat rock to Yakima's left. He doffed his hat and edged a look toward the riverbed. The posse had dismounted, one man leading their horses back down the canyon while the others spread out among the rocks.

Speares leapt a boulder, heading for another. As several rifles puffed at the ridge base, Yakima drilled a round into the boulder Speares had just ducked behind, then another at a man wedging himself between a cedar and an arrow-shaped rock on the right side of the gravelly gorge.

He pulled the rifle back behind his own cover and glanced up the trail weaving away to his right. The sorrel was a good sixty yards away, and not far from the ridge crest, but it had slowed to a walk, looking back down the ridge behind it.

Yakima drilled a round into the rocks near its rear hooves. The horse buck-kicked, whinnied, and galloped up the ridge, heading for the crest and, he hoped, down the other side to safety.

Bullets tore into the rock and gravel around him. He returned several shots, then looked around, choosing a path up the ridge. He returned several more shots, bounded out from behind his cover, and ran several yards up the ridge before ducking behind a petrified tree root, a slug blowing sand across his boots.

Someone yelled from below, the words unclear beneath the sporadic gunfire and ricocheting lead. He peered around the petrified root.

Speares was zigzagging up the slope on Yakima's left, holding the Yellowboy straight up and down before him. Patchen was lunging up the slope on his right, his tan face framed by his silver sideburns, sunlight winking off his rifle barrel. The other posse members remained at the ridge's base, covering the lawmen, slugs whining around Yakima's head or grinding into the root before him.

Yakima pressed his cheek against the root, brushing sand from his right eye.

When he began hearing the clatter of running feet, he fired three rounds downslope, then bounded up toward the ridge. He zigzagged for thirty yards and, as a bullet nipped the heel of his right boot, dove into a hollow amid several wagon-sized boulders.

He rose to his knees, snaked his rifle barrel around the right side of the rock. Patchen was running toward him, breathing hard, holding his rifle across his chest. When he saw Yakima bearing his aim down on him, his eyes snapped wide.

Yakima's rifle exploded. The marshal gave a yelp as the bullet tore into his left thigh. Mustachioed lips stretched back from his white teeth, he pushed off his right foot and dove into a rock nest shrouded in prickly pear and Mormon tea.

The rifle fire from downslope had ceased, as the other posse members couldn't see over the curve of the slope.

Hearing boots and spurs coming up the slope on his left, Yakima ejected the smoking shell from the carbine and sidestepped into a narrow gap between several large boulders. He continued through the gap, turned right around the back of one of the boulders, turned right again and worked up the side, circling back toward the front, intending to slip up behind Speares.

When he was nearly back to where he'd started, he saw the sheriff step into the large gap between the boulders, aiming the Yellowboy from his shoulder.

Yakima snugged his rifle against the back of the sheriff's sunburned neck.

Speares froze.

"I'll take my rifle, Sheriff."

Holding the rifle he'd appropriated from the jailhouse in his left hand, he held his right hand out where Speares could see it.

Speares's back twitched, his head turning slightly to the right.

"Don't be stupid," Yakima warned.

"You'll kill me anyway."

"Maybe." Yakima snapped his fingers. "The rifle."

Speares remained frozen for a few seconds, and then his shoulders slumped slightly. He held out the Winchester Yellowboy, and Yakima wrapped his hand around the rear stock. The smooth, familiar walnut and remembered weight of the brass receiver felt good in his palm.

He prodded Speares's back with both rifle barrels. "Belly down. Nice and slow."

Speares growled, "What're you gonna do?"

"Belly down!"

Speares dropped to his knees, glanced over his left shoulder, his eyes dark with dread, then kicked his legs out and fell to his belly. Again he turned his head to peer over his shoulder. His shaggy blond hair flopped over his forehead.

Yakima crouched to remove Speares's revolver from his holster. He tossed the Remington in the rocks, then aimed the Yellowboy at the back of the sheriff's neck. "If you can't take *me* down, how do you expect to take the *gang* down?" He angled the Yellowboy at a mole behind Speares's right ear. "Face the dirt."

Speares winced, set his chin on the ground. "Please . . . don't." His heart thudded and all the blood in his body seemed to rush to his battered nose. He hated the pleading tone in his own voice. "Goddamn it, I'm unarmed. Don't shoot me."

He squeezed his eyes closed, pressing his chin and knees to the ground, every muscle taut, waiting for the bullet.

A voice sounded along the slope before him. "Where the hell is he?"

Speares lifted his head sharply. Patchen lay twenty feet away, aiming his Henry rifle out from behind a rock and a stunted cedar, squinting down the barrel. His red face was pinched with pain and fury.

Speares turned to look over his left shoulder. Only sun-bathed rocks and brush behind him.

The breed was gone.

Chapter 11

Thirty miles south of Yakima and the posse, the Thunder Riders rode in a long line, two abreast, up a winding mesa trail sheathed in creosote, sage, and ocotillo, with large boulders pushing up around the lone oak or elm. Jack Considine sat astride Wolf, while Anjanette rode a claybank gelding off Considine's right stirrup.

She wore a fringed leather vest over a blue plaid shirt, and the small silver crucifix nestled in her cleavage winked occasionally in the crisp winter sunlight. Her man's Stetson was secured to her head by a horsehair thong swinging free beneath her chin, her rich hair flowing across her shoulders.

She'd appropriated the clothes from the saddlebags of the young outlaw she'd been forced to shoot. She had blood on her hands, but she'd been forced to kill before, when she and Old Antoine had been prospecting in bandito-infested mountains. The pleas of the young gunslick were little more than whispers.

She was glad to be away from the choked confines of Saber Creek, the tavern, and her owly, alcoholic grandfather. She felt a sense of freedom riding into the misty blue distances of southern Sonora toward an outlaw hideout known to the Americans as Junction Rock with the infamous, heart-wrenchingly handsome Jack Considine and his notorious Thunder Riders.

From there, Jack had promised, they would make their way to the coast and set sail for Cuba—just him and Anjanette—where Considine had often dreamed of buying his own sugar plantation.

As they rode, the men of the gang smoked and talked in desultory tones, one man chuckling at a joke. Another was cleaning the rifle resting across his saddlebow. The only other female in the gang, Toots, rode with one leg hooked around her saddle horn. She was trimming the nails of her pudgy, curled toes with a pocketknife.

The group crested the mesa and their horses continued through the scrub, passing a small adobe shrine along the trail and scaring up an armadillo. The mesa spread before them—a table surrounded by layers of distant blue mountains and high purple clouds between which golden sunlight angled.

A couple of hundred yards beyond, what looked like a modest-sized hacienda sat in the middle of the mesa, sheathed in green high-desert scrub and surrounded by ruined stone buildings and brush corrals. Smoke gushed from the stone chimney on the near end of the house.

Considine turned to Anjanette. "You will have a soft bed tonight, Chiquita. O'Toole keeps the best roadhouse in Sonora."

She smiled, her tapered cheeks dimpling. "*We* will have a soft bed tonight, my love." She leaned toward him, wrapped her left hand around his neck, and was about to kiss his cheek when the black mustang, sensing the rider's distraction, suddenly put his head down and kicked his back legs out, snorting like a mule, trying to unseat his rider.

"Goddamn beast!" Considine shouted as the horse leapt suddenly, sunfishing.

Wolf's hooves hit the ground. He half turned and, throwing his head forward, bucked savagely again.

Considine had wrapped one hand around the saddle horn, but he hadn't been prepared for the viciousness of the horse's pitch. His butt rose high out of the saddle, and his boots shot out of the stirrups. Flying over the horse's lunging left shoulder, he turned a somersault before hitting the gravelly ground left of the trail on his back.

"Jack!" Anjanette dropped out of her saddle.

"*Woo-hooooah,* boy!" shouted Considine's partner, Mad Dog McKenna, gigging his own mount up and reaching for the pitching black's reins.

Wolf jerked his head away, and the reins slipped out of Mad Dog's reach. McKenna cursed. Wolf bounded off his back hooves and galloped forward and right of the trail, tracing a broad circle to head back the way they'd come.

"*Git after him, boys!*" McKenna shouted.

As a half dozen of the other riders booted their mounts after the fleeing black, trying to cut him off, Anjanette dropped to one knee beside Considine. The desperado winced and lifted his head from the ground, his thick auburn hair in his eyes, mustache caked with sand.

"You okay?" Anjanette asked, one hand on his shoulder. "Maybe you better lie there a minute."

Considine shook his head as if to clear it, then sat up, lowering his head and massaging the back of his neck. "Somebody catch that damn beast!"

Mad Dog McKenna chuckled. "Hey, Jack, you want me to ride that black from now on? Maybe he's too much horse for you, amigo."

Considine told his scarred, earring-wearing partner to do something physically impossible to himself.

Toots checked her own mount down closest to Considine and dropped out of her saddle with a grace odd for a woman her size. "Or maybe me, huh, Jack?" She smiled as she knelt on the other side of the desperado leader from Anjanette, snuggling close and massaging the inside of his thigh with her hand. "I can always ride a stud!"

She laughed, locking stares with Anjanette.

Turning to Considine, who was still rubbing his neck as if to work some knots out, Toots softened her voice. "You okay, good-lookin'?"

Considine was grumbling and cursing as he pushed away from both women and stiffly gained his feet. "I'll be just fine when I get my hands on that goddamn horse!"

Toots picked up Considine's hat, dusted it off, and held it out to him. Considine turned toward the large dust cloud down the trail a good fifty yards, where three desperadoes had their riatas looped around the stallion's neck and were trying to lead him back.

When the men finally got him turned, with English

Cooper slapping his quirt against the black's ass, they put their mounts into gallops, heading toward Considine. Wolf galloped reluctantly, head up and snorting, eyes flashing small lightning bolts of fury.

Considine donned the hat and stepped forward, shucking his pearl-gripped Remy from his holster. "Only thing for a horse like that's a bullet."

Anjanette caught up to him, put her hand on the gun, pressing it down. "Don't shoot the horse, Jack."

Considine eyed her suspiciously. "Why not?"

Anjanette hesitated. "Think of the money you'll make on him at Junction Rock."

Considine snorted as the three riders reined up before him, swinging sideways while holding their lariats taut. The black stopped a good twenty yards away, hanging its head, its black eyes sharp with fury.

"The girl's got a point, Jack." Mad Dog McKenna came up beside Anjanette, hitching his threadbare cavalry breeches higher on his hips, the silver hoop rings dangling from his sun-black ears. "That horse'll bring five, six hundred dollars at Junction Rock. Now, I know we got the gold, but you know how long we all can hold on to a poke." Considine's partner chuckled and dropped his eyes to Anjanette's prominent bosom. "Never know when you're gonna have to exchange the horse for a woman."

"A *real* woman," said Toots, grinning up at Considine.

"He's got a woman," Anjanette snarled. "But you can never have too much money—isn't that right, my love?"

Considine walked up to the black, grabbed the dangling reins. "I'm not gonna kill him. My anger's done passed." Suddenly, he raised his pistol and swung it down hard against the horse's fine black snout, raking the front sight along the side of his nose.

As the horse jerked his head up, then lowered it, Considine raked the gun barrel across the other side of Wolf's snout, carving a thin line from which bright red blood oozed.

"Remember *that* next time you decide to throw me, you hammerheaded, snake-eyed son of a *bitch*!"

Holding tight to the reins, just beneath the bridle and glaring into the horse's dark eyes, Considine holstered the revolver. Wolf's nostrils opened and closed. He chuffed and snorted angrily against the ropes, twitching his ears and rippling his withers.

"Now, then," Considine said, easing around the horse and reaching for the horn. "We gonna be pards?"

As Considine swung into the saddle, Anjanette stepped forward, raising a gentle hand to the long cut along the horse's snout.

"Leave him," Considine ordered. He glanced at the others. "Let's go. I need a drink."

When the column was again moving toward the large adobe casa growing above the chaparral before them, Considine turned to Anjanette, showing his perfect white teeth in a grin. "He's behavin' right fine now." He patted the black's right shoulder. "I reckon we're friends!"

Anjanette didn't turn toward him but continued riding stiffly beside him, facing straight ahead.

He frowned. "You know who owns this hammerhead?"

Anjanette glanced at Wolf, looked away, then pooched out her lips to hide her pensive expression. "I never saw him before."

As they rounded a bend, the thatch-roofed adobe barn and log corrals slid back to the left, revealing an ancient windmill with a large stone tank. Water streamed into the tank with a steady metallic murmur. Around the tank stood ten or so rurales, in their customary dove gray uniforms, Springfield rifles hanging down their backs—a dusty, unshaven lot with pinched eyes and evil sneers.

They held the reins of their horses, most of which were drawing water from the tank, though a couple lifted their heads toward the approaching desperadoes, swishing their tails nervously. A cream Arab with a silver-mounted saddle jerked its head up from the trough and whinnied.

The rurales turned their heads slowly to watch the gang heading toward the roadhouse. One of them spoke quietly to the man standing beside him—a rangy Mex carrying his Colt revolvers in a double rig across his chest.

Considine grinned and threw a hand up. "Howdy, boys!"

The rurales didn't say anything. Several of the desperadoes behind Considine chuckled. The lone black man in the group, Ben Towers, grumbled, "The only truck I got with Mexico is all the greasers."

"Especially those in uniform," added Mad Dog McKenna, riding directly behind Considine.

"And them with their hands out," said Latigo Hayes, loosening his Buntline Special in its oiled holster and swinging his sawed-off shotgun around to hang down his chest.

As the desperado leader put his horse up to the hitchrack, a face appeared just over the top of the road-house's batwing doors. It was a square, pale face with short gray whiskers. The light blue eyes caught the afternoon light and flickered humorously.

The man chuckled, pushed through the batwings, and said in a heavy Irish accent, "Well, I be damned. Chacon was right—you boys *were* headed this way, sure enough!"

"Mick," Considine said by way of greeting, then turned his head to glance at the rurales around the windmill. "We got a welcoming party, I see."

"How in the hell Chacon knows you're coming, I'll never know!" Mick said, planting his small, freckled hands on his hips as he stood before the doors, running his gaze up and down the group flanking Considine, Anjanette, and Mad Dog McKenna.

The roadhouse proprietor wore a buckskin tunic and a bloodstained apron around his considerable paunch. A .36-caliber revolver was wedged behind the apron. His eyes settled on Anjanette for a time, the corners of his small mouth rising slightly as he said, "I see you gotta new woman."

"Anjanette, meet Mick O'Toole. Came to fight the French and stayed to run a whorehouse. Mick . . . Anjanette."

Mick nodded, his eyes brazen.

"The pleasure's mine," Anjanette murmured, the

man's gaze making her aware of her breasts pushing out from behind the flannel shirt and fringed leather vest.

"My old friend inside?" Considine asked Mick.

Mick tore his gaze from Anjanette's breasts. "Sure."

Considine and Mad Dog shared a meaningful glance. "Boys," Considine said, lifting his voice so the others could hear, "why don't you water the horses?"

He glanced at Anjanette. She was studying him, her fine black brows furrowed.

"You can stay out here where it's safe," Considine told her, swinging down from his saddle. "But the adventure's inside."

Mick chuckled, adjusted the pistol in his pants, turned through the batwings, and disappeared into the roadhouse.

Anjanette threw her hair back from her shoulders, swung down from her saddle, and tossed her reins over the hitchrack. "Well, then, I reckon I'm going inside."

"I kinda figured you would." Considine grabbed her shoulders and kissed her.

"Break it up, lovebirds," Mad Dog said, mounting the porch steps. "We got business."

Considine chuckled and turned through the saloon doors behind his partner. Anjanette followed Considine, squinting against the hazy light and the wafting blue woodsmoke rife with the smell of roasting pig and harsh Mexican tobacco.

Considine and Mad Dog stopped a few feet inside the door, and Anjanette squeezed in between them. The three shuttled their gazes around the large stone-floored room and the makeshift bar on the right.

Mick had taken his place behind the bar, grinning, fists on the bar's rough-sawn planks. Several wizened peasants in serapes and frayed sombreros were playing dice on the floor in a corner, a scrawny, spotted cur gnawing a knucklebone nearby.

A couple of fat whores in sack dresses and heavy rouge were hunched over stone mugs and playing cards at a table close to the bar. One had a cigar snugged in a corner of her mouth. They glanced at the newcomers with interest, but when their gazes fell across Anjanette, hope leached from their eyes and they returned to their drinks and poker.

Considine's eyes were on the table at the far end of the room, near the narrow stone steps rising toward the roadhouse's second floor. Two men in rurale uniforms, jackets unbuttoned, sat at the table, plates and bowls before them.

The man on the left—short, round-faced, and curly-haired—sat back in his chair, ankles crossed, thumbs hooked inside the bandoliers crossed on his chest. Seeds and dust matted his tight black curls.

He was grinning at the other man, Captain Chacon, a grossly fat mestizo with long silver-streaked hair hanging down both sides of his broad, fat face, and silver-streaked mustaches hanging down both corners of his mouth.

A young girl, no more than eighteen, straddled the captain's right knee, facing the table. She had full lips and wide-set light brown eyes, with a faint mole on the nub of her right cheek.

She was topless, and the captain was flicking the

brown nipple of her right nubbin breast with his index finger, laughing and glancing back and forth between the girl and the curly-haired man, Lieutenant Miguel Pascal Ferraro, as if the jostling nipple were the funniest thing he'd seen in a long time. The girl stared down at the table, bored.

Considine turned to look past Anjanette at Mad Dog, then sauntered forward. Heading toward the captain's table, he called to Mick for a bottle.

Chacon and Ferraro jerked their heads up and around at Considine's voice. Chacon spread a grin. He was missing both his eyeteeth, and it gave his fat, savage face a strange, rabbitlike look.

"Ah, Senor Considine and Senor McKenna!" the captain said, removing his hand from the girl's breast but keeping his arm wrapped around her shoulders. "It is an honor and a privilege to see you both again!"

Considine sighed. "I'd like to say the feeling's mutual, but I never tell lies in Mexico. Too many Catholics."

"Ain't it funny," McKenna said, "how you always seem to know when we cross the border."

While Ferraro remained staring cow-eyed at the three newcomers, as if the English were too fast for him, Chacon threw his head back on his shoulders and laughed from his belly, shaking the girl sitting on his knee so that her long, dark brown hair fluttered on her shoulders.

When the captain's laugh had settled to a slow boil, he said, "It would indeed be a strange coincidence if it were not for the fact that I watch the border so *closely* and have three Yaqui amongst my border guards. They, as they themselves boast, can smell a gringo from as far away as the last full moon!"

Again, he threw his head back and laughed.

Ferraro glanced at his superior, skeptically amused, and his thick upper lip curled slightly.

"Yaqui, huh?" Considine said, hooking his thumbs behind his cartridge belt. "Well, I'll be damned. That's almost like cheatin'!"

"Reckon you gotta watch them snake-eaters pretty close, don't ya?" said Mad Dog. "I mean, I've heard they'd as soon cut a rurale's throat as look at him."

The captain's laughter stopped abruptly, and he absently brushed his fingers across the whore's nipple, making it twitch. "My men respect me, Senor McKenna. Even the Indios." His gaze strayed to Anjanette, and turned smoky. "I see you have, uh, found a new companion, Senor." Again his left hand lightly caressed the young *puta*'s tender breast. "An especially fine one, if you don't mind my saying so, Senorita."

He cupped the whore's breast with his hand, rubbing it, while staring lewdly into Anjanette's eyes.

Anjanette returned his stare coldly, saying nothing. Considine laughed and wrapped a proprietary arm around her neck, drawing her toward him and kissing her cheek. "Captain Chacon . . . Lieutenant Ferraro . . . let me introduce the lovely Anjanette."

The lieutenant's drunken gaze flickered up and down Anjanette's curvy body, a deep flush rising in his broad, dark cheeks. The captain closed his hand around the young whore's breast and gave a courtly nod. "They are getting more lovely every trip, Senor Considine. My compliments. If only I could find one as lovely as she in this godforsaken country."

He shifted his gaze to the desperado leader, slitting one eye. "What will you take for her?"

Anjanette's back tensed. She opened her mouth to speak, but Considine gripped her more tightly and laughed, "She's not for sale, Captain. Not this trip, anyway!" He laughed again, nuzzled Anjanette's stiff neck, and muttered in her ear as he glanced toward the bar. "Mick's lookin' lonely over there, Chiquita."

Meeting the captain's lusty, glassy gaze with a hard one of her own, Anjanette turned slowly. "Reckon I better buy him a drink." She hooked her thumbs in the waistband of her long wool skirt, and strolled over toward the bar.

When Anjanette had gone, Considine glanced at Mad Dog, then kicked a chair out and sat down. During the introductions, Mick had brought two stone mugs and a bottle of the pulque that he brewed himself and mixed with tequila—a heady, gut-wrenching combo.

"Well," said Considine, leaning forward on the table and popping the cork from the bottle. "I reckon you're lookin' for what you're usually lookin' for."

"Our border pass," said Mad Dog, removing his hat and sweeping a hand through his long, greasy hair, jingling the hoops hanging from his ears. "Me and Jack been wantin' to talk to you about that, Captain."

Chacon exchanged glances with Ferraro. The girl sat on the captain's knee, seemingly oblivious of her exposed breasts, staring into space.

Considine said, "We work hard for our living—me

and Mad Dog. Stealin' gold from stagecoaches and banks and trains—shit, that takes a lot out of a man. And me and Mad Dog ain't gettin' any younger." He glanced at his partner. "Ain't that right, Mad Dog?"

"We sure as hell ain't, Jack."

"We're gonna have to slow down a little here pretty soon. The fifty-six thousand we took out of Saber Creek won't last more than a few months. Not the way we like to drink, gamble, and fuck." Considine chuckled. "So we've readjusted your fee, Captain."

As Considine reached into his shirt, Chacon and Ferraro tensed in their chairs.

Considine froze, smiled. "At ease, boys."

Slowly, he lifted out a rawhide pouch. He jerked his hand, breaking the leather lanyard hanging around his neck, and tossed the pouch onto the table with a dull thud.

"Take it or leave it," McKenna growled.

Lips pursed, nostrils expanding and contracting angrily, Chacon plucked the pouch off the table and hefted it, frowning. Ferraro stared at the pouch as he held one hand beneath the table, his fingers no doubt wrapped around a revolver.

Finally, with a dubious glance at Considine, Chacon turned the pouch upside down.

Sand and penny-sized stones sifted onto the table, the stones clattering against the planks. Something larger dropped along with the stones, and when the dust had cleared, the two rurales leaned forward, staring down at the black, dust-floured tarantula crawling around atop the debris.

The whore jerked back against the captain's chest, her eyes regarding the furry black spider with revulsion. With a soft cry, she scrambled off the captain's knee and backed slowly away from the table, staring in horror at the tarantula moving its hairy legs about the sand and rocks.

"Muerta!" she rasped, her pleated skirt buffeting about her bare brown legs.

Cutting a glance at her, Mad Dog snorted. Considine slid his gaze to his partner, then back to Chacon, and chuckled.

Chacon's eyes brightened and his lips stretched back from his rabbit teeth. He chuckled then too, head bobbing, eyes shuttling between the desperadoes and the lieutenant, who appeared baffled. As the desperadoes and the captain cut loose with booming, belly-deep guffaws, the lieutenant grinned. Soon he joined them, laughing and pounding the table with his open left palm.

Behind the bar, Mick's eyes were dark as he stared at the four laughing men.

Anjanette picked up a shot glass from the bar, raised it slowly to her lips, her hands shaking slightly, and tossed the drink back. When she set the empty glass on the bar, the men stopped laughing all at once, as though her setting the glass down had been a signal.

Silence.

The fire snapped, echoing in the adobe-lined room. Outside, a horse nickered. Sensing trouble, the fat whores, the dice players, and the dog scuttled outside.

The whore backed up against the bar, between Mick

and Anjanette. Slowly, staring toward the four men at the table, she lifted her hands to her ears.

Chacon's laughter had faded without a trace. His eyes hard, his lips set in a grim line, he shuttled another glance between Considine and Mad Dog. Then he leaned back in his chair and snapped his right hand to his side.

At the same time, the two desperadoes fired beneath the table—Considine at Chacon, Mad Dog at Ferraro. Chacon screamed and dropped both hands straight down toward his crotch as Ferraro bolted up, hands crossed beneath his belly. Throwing his chair back, he twisted around and fell. The lieutenant rolled to his side, raising his knees toward his chest, yowling, blood oozing down the insides of his thighs.

On the floor to his left, Chacon screamed as a great cacophony of gunfire sounded outside, like a sudden army battle or an Indian attack. His misery-pinched eyes rose to Considine's, and his jaw hardened as his right arm jerked again toward his holster.

Casually, as the gunfire continued outside, men and horses screaming, Considine slid his chair back, extended his revolver straight across the table at Chacon, and drilled a neat round hole through the middle of the captain's forehead.

To his left, Ferraro bellowed and fumbled his Colt Navy from its holster. He bellowed again, lay back, and extended the revolver toward Considine.

To Considine's right, a gun boomed, and the lieutenant's head jerked back. He fired a round into the ceiling, dropped the gun, and grabbed his bloody throat with both hands, gasping, choking, his eyes bulging from their sockets.

After several seconds, his body relaxed, his hands sagged to the floor, and his eyes glazed with death.

Considine glanced at Mad Dog, who still held his silver-plated Smith & Wesson out before him, smoke curling from the barrel. He arched an eyebrow at Considine.

"What?" Considine said. "I never covered your ass before?"

Behind him, someone whistled. Considine and Mad Dog turned to see Cal Prewitt—a strap-thin former cow waddy in a high-crowned Stetson and patchy beard—hanging like a devious schoolboy between the half-open batwings. He had an arm draped over each door, knees bent, boots about a foot off the floor. His eyes were round with excitement.

"Hey, Jack! Mad Dog!" Prewitt swung back and forth between the batwings. "What you want us to do with the carcasses?"

Considine holstered his revolver and fastened the keeper thong over the hammer. "Drag 'em off so ol' Mick doesn't have to live with the stench. Lead the horses off and let 'em go. And, for Pete's sake, get off those doors, less'n you wanna pay for 'em!"

"They stink as bad alive as they do dead," said the roadhouse owner, staring down at the two dead rurale leaders. He turned to Considine, rubbing his hands on his apron. "But I appreciate the gesture, Jack."

Considine walked over to Anjanette, standing back against the bar, her eyes on the dead men, one hand holding a recently refilled shot glass before her lips. Considine took the drink out of her hand, threw it back, set the glass on the counter, and wrapped his left arm around the girl's shoulders.

As he grabbed the bottle off the table and began leading Anjanette toward the stairs at the back of the room, he said, "Are you having an adventure yet, Chiquita?"

Chapter 12

By the time Yakima had climbed the ridge above the posse, leaving Speares to soil his trousers among the boulders, it was late afternoon. He caught up to the sorrel grazing along the opposite slope and traced a winding course through the darkening canyons, hooking up with the desperadoes' trail a few miles southwest of the burned-out village.

He rode for a couple of hours and camped that night under an overhanging lip of layered limestone. He built a small fire and a makeshift spit, upon which he roasted the two large jackrabbits he'd killed with a Jesus stick. The fire was well concealed by boulders lining the bivouac. Waiting for the meat to cook, he hunkered on his haunches, his Yellowboy standing between his knees, and stared down the slope and across the valley cloaked in velvety darkness at a pinprick of flickering orange light growing brighter as the darkness thickened.

The posse's fire.

They were a persistent bunch—he'd give them that.

Yakima sat staring across the star-capped desert,

hearing the fire crackle and the rabbit skins sizzle and split. Absently, he fingered the rifle's smooth barrel.

An idea occurred to him. He'd been wondering how he was going to rescue Anjanette and Wolf from so large a group. Why not let the posse try to take them down first? While the desperadoes were distracted by Speares and Patchen, Yakima would steal up behind them, grab Anjanette and the horse, and hightail it back toward the border.

The tactic made as much sense as anything else he'd come up with.

When the rabbits were done, he ate one hungrily, tearing off large chunks with his hands and licking the grease from his fingers, washing the meat down with hot black coffee. He wrapped the other rabbit in burlap, stuffed it into his saddlebags for tomorrow, then enjoyed one more cup of coffee before kicking dirt on the fire and rolling up in his blankets.

The distant keen of a cougar lulled him to sleep.

He woke at first light to a fine layer of frost on his blankets and on the hat brim pulled low over his eyes, his breath puffing in the gray dawn air. Flinging his blankets aside, he rose, grabbed a spyglass from his saddlebags, and leapt atop a flat boulder at the edge of his campsite.

Squatting, he trained the glass down the slope, toward the cactus-studded valley below. Two hundred yards away, a tiny pink flame guttered amid the scrub. Shadows flickered around the fire, and in the misty gray light, Yakima saw the horses tied to a picket line between two cabin-sized boulders.

Since the posse was taking time for breakfast, Yakima would, too.

He went back to his fire ring, built a low blaze with crushed sage branches, and made coffee, which he sipped while he nibbled on the bones of the cooked rabbit. He kept a close eye on the posse. Ten minutes after they'd moved out, heading southwest along the trail of the dozen hoofprints scoring the desert floor, he doused his fire, packed up, saddled the sorrel, and followed.

He trailed the posse from five hundred yards throughout the morning, slowing when they slowed, stopping when they stopped. Near noon, trouble. When pulling the sorrel away from a small spring bubbling around mossy rocks, a loud, ironlike clatter rose from below.

Dread scalding his gut, Yakima glanced down. The horse's left front shoe dangled from its hoof. Slipping out of the saddle, Yakima crouched to inspect the shoe. Only one nail remained, and the shoe itself was cracked. What was worse, after examining the hoof, he found that the frog was swollen and tender. The horse couldn't be ridden until the hoof was wrapped for at least six hours with a cool mud pack and then reshod.

Yakima removed the shoe, tossed it into the brush, and glanced ahead, his jaws set with frustration. Shit.

The only thing he could do was lead the horse along the posse's trail and hope he came upon a village or estancia where he could trade the horse for a fresh one. Barring a trade, he hoped for a portable forge and blacksmith's tools where he could pack the hoof and shape a new shoe. He would lose valuable time, maybe lose the gang's trail, but there was little choice.

He wished he had his moccasins to make the walk easier, but the soft-soled shoes were in his saddlebags atop Wolf. By the time he reached a settlement, his own feet would no doubt need as much attention as the sorrel's.

As he led the horse along the desperadoes' trail, over-lapped by that of the posse, minutes stretched to hours. The stockman's boots drew taut around his swelling feet, and he could feel the skin on the balls of both feet tearing, then oozing inside his socks, grieving him with every step.

After a couple of hours he sat down on a rock, re-moved his boots and socks, and cut away the loose skin on his feet with the Arkansas toothpick he always car-ried in a makeshift ankle sheath. He had nothing to pad the boots with, even if he *could* have squeezed in any-thing besides his socks and his swollen feet, so he donned the socks, slid his feet back into the boots, and continued walking, fixing his attention on the flora and fauna—the creosote shrubs and mesquite snags and oc-casional white-throated swift darting about the chaparral—to keep his mind off the ache.

He crossed a valley, then a low saddle, before tra-versing a maze of ancient arroyos so choked with brush and boulders that it became difficult to stay on the rid-ers' trail. From a distance, he saw two cougars, a lynx, at least fifty turkey buzzards feeding on a rotting bear carcass, and a half dozen wolves snorting around an old deer kill.

Luckily, no Indians.

At about six o'clock that evening, he followed a

winding trail up the side of a broad tabletop mesa, then continued following it to the edge of an open area in which a large rectangular adobe sat to the right of several crumbling barns and corrals.

An old rancho, by the look of the place. The twang of a guitar and celebratory voices rising from inside the house, in addition to the half dozen Arabian horses tethered to the hitchrack out front, bespoke a roadhouse. Smoke puffed in deep gray clouds from the chimney on Yakima's side of the house, rife with the smell of roasting pork.

A slender brown-haired girl stood at the stock tank at the other end of the yard, dipping a wooden bucket into the water. She wore a flour-sack skirt and, despite the evening's chill, a low-cut blouse, one strap hanging down an arm barely bigger around than a shotgun barrel.

Barefoot, lugging the sloshing water bucket in both hands before her, she shuffled back toward the roadhouse. She didn't turn her head toward Yakima. She kicked up dirt as she went, long hair blowing in the wind.

Yakima gave a gentle tug on the sorrel's reins and started toward the roadhouse.

"Hold it right there," a man's Irish-accented voice growled to his left. "One more step and I'll blow you all the way to the rock gods!"

Yakima turned to see a short, pudgy man with close-cropped gray hair and a gray-bristled beard move out from the open door of the adobe-and-log barn on his left, aiming an old Springfield trapdoor rifle straight out from his shoulder.

"I don't allow 'Paches. . . ." The pudgy man let his voice trail off as he sidestepped slowly up to Yakima, keeping his cheek snugged against the Springfield's stock, as if facing a mountain lion in its own den. He grunted uncertainly. "You ain't 'Pache, are ye? Too damn tall. What the hell are ye, then?"

Yakima glanced at the sorrel flanking him on his left. "I'm looking for a trade. He's got a bum hoof, but it'll heal with tending."

The Irishman lowered the rifle from his cheek but held the barrel steady on Yakima's chest, slitting one eye skeptically. "You with that posse that tore through here a few hours ago?"

"Do I look like one of them?" Yakima didn't wait for an answer. "I need that horse. . . ."

"I don't have no horse, just a big mule I use for skidding wood up from the draws. He don't carry riders, and he ain't for trade. But I got a forge and bellows in yonder you can shoe him with." The Irishman canted his head toward the barn on Yakima's left. "But I gotta make a livin'. . . ."

"You have some burlap I can wrap his hoof with?"

"Sure do. And you can even sleep with him in yonder."

"Mighty pale of ya. How much?"

The Irishman lowered his rifle and grinned. "For three dollars—or you can split me a cord of ash and cottonwood over yonder, keep my fire goin' tonight. I'm entertainin' Don Garcia-Viejo's *segundo* and his greaser riders, and I'm slow-roastin' a sow hog. Like to make a good impression on the local gentry, don't ya know!"

Yakima glanced at the two-foot logs scattered among the sage near the barn, then turned back to the Irishman. "I'll split your wood. But you better throw in a warm bed and grub."

"Hell, I'll even throw in a fat whore. That wood-splittin' grieves my rheumatism!"

"Save your whore for El Segundo, but I'll hold you to the rest."

They shook.

After the man who'd said his name was Mick O'Toole had returned to the roadhouse, Yakima set to work firing up the blacksmith forge in the barn. While the forge heated, he applied a compress of cool mud and whiskey to the sorrel's hoof, wrapping it tightly, then set to work on a shoe. When he'd hammered one to the shape of the hoof, he left it on the anvil, ready to be applied first thing in the morning, after he'd removed the compress.

The horse needed a good two- or even three-day rest, but overnight would have to do. Yakima had to get after Speares's bunch and the Thunder Riders. Hopefully, he would find someone willing to trade mounts with him farther along the trail.

Finished with the horse, which he stabled in the barn's shadows with measured amounts of oats, hay, and water, he took his boots off and applied some of the mud and whiskey to the bottoms of his own feet, sucking air through his teeth at the alcohol sting. He wrapped both feet lightly, then set to work splitting the firewood north of the barn.

He was weary from the long walk and the work in the barn, but hefting the mallet and smashing the blade down through the logs, working up a rhythm, loosened his back and arms and focused his mind, distracting him from wondering how Anjanette and Wolf were faring among the outlaws. He'd half expected to find the girl dead in the desert, and hoped he could get to her before the gang tired of her and cast her off like trash.

The desert air turned crisp, drying the sweat on his back. An especially large wolf pack yammered in the hills north of the mesa, and Yakima vaguely wondered what had stirred them into such a frenzy.

When he had a half cord of wood split, he gathered an armload and started toward the roadhouse shining like a rough, well-lighted jewel in the starry darkness. A fiddle had replaced the guitar, making more squawking noise than music, and several more horses stood before the hitchrack, swishing their tails or drawing water from the stock trough before them.

Yakima mounted the porch steps, pushed through the batwings, and looked around through the smoky shadows in which three or four groups of Mexican men clumped, some playing cards while a few merely sipped from stone mugs and sat back in their chairs with dreamy, drunk expressions, enjoying the fiddle music of the skinny vaquero in ragged trail garb.

A couple of fat whores were at the table where five well-dressed vaqueros sat, smoking and drinking. One of the whores sat between two tall Mexicans, laughing and twirling a pudgy finger around in her shot glass while one of the men leaned toward her, whispering in her ear.

The other whore was bent forward over the table while another Mexican—the best-dressed one of the lot, with a white streak slashing through his thick black hair—spanked her with his black-gloved hand. Yakima knew enough Spanish to know the man was chastising her for being fat—"Why in the hell don't you stop eating, woman?"

She laughed, going along with the chiding but wincing a little with each slap.

The Irishman, Mick, watched the table from behind the bar, wearing a strained smile as he ladled pulque into mugs.

Yakima dropped his load of wood near the fireplace, in which two shanks of hog sizzled and sputtered.

"Bring in another load, and I'll fill you a plate," Mick told him as he hustled the two stone mugs of pulque out from behind the bar, heading for the table with the well-attired vaqueros and the fat whores. He shook his head, muttering, "What I don't put up with to stay on the don's good side . . ."

Yakima glanced at the Mexicans' table again, then went back outside, where he split a few more logs, then headed back to the cabin with another armload. Near the corner of the dark barn, he stopped suddenly as a girl's scream rose from inside the roadhouse. There was a sharp slap, and a man shouted in Spanish, "Bitch, you'll do as I order!"

Yakima continued forward as the Irishman's voice

sounded in placating tones from the other side of the batwings. The fiddle had fallen silent, and all Yakima could hear from the roadhouse was the first man's angry voice booming above Mick's.

A horse snorted as Yakima passed the hitchrack and mounted the porch steps, the patter of running bare feet growing louder. He was a foot from the doors when he heard a girl's sobs, saw a small, slender, long-haired silhouette growing out of the shadows before him. It was the girl he'd seen earlier at the water tank, her eyes now silver with tears.

The enraged voice rose again behind her. "Get back here, *puta*!"

Yakima lunged to the right as the girl flew through the batwings, hair streaming out behind her. She ran across the porch and leapt off the steps and into the yard, heading for the barn.

Yakima turned back toward the door. The tall man with the white streak in his hair was striding toward the batwings, boots pounding the flagstones.

Yakima leapt back to the right, a log falling from the pile in his arms.

A wink later, the Mexican burst through the batwings like a bull from a chute. "I warn—"

Instinctively, Yakima kicked his left leg out in front of the doors. The Mexican's left boot hooked under Yakima's ankle, and the man gave an indignant cry as he flew across the porch, fell down the steps, and rolled into the yard.

Groaning and cursing, the man pushed off his chest

and lifted his head toward Yakima, still standing to the right of the batwings with the split wood in his arms.

The man spat, ran a sleeve across his mouth. His voice rose shrilly, shouting in Spanish something like, "That better have been an accident, friend, or you have made a fatal mistake!"

Chapter 13

Yakima hadn't wanted any trouble here. He'd only wanted to tend his horse and light out free and clear the next morning, to get back on the trail of Anjanette and his mustang.

The delay itself was galling, knowing that the Thunder Riders were pulling farther and farther ahead. But the added complication he now found himself in was about as welcome as a blow from an Apache war hatchet.

He hadn't *meant* to get involved in the girl's trouble. His boot had leapt out in front of the batwings as though of its own accord.

Now he stood in the shadows of the roadhouse porch, facing the well-dressed Mexican with the white streak in his hair—the vaquero *segundo* whom the Irishman had mentioned earlier, Yakima assumed. The man was climbing heavily to his feet before the porch, looking around wildly and snarling. His head swung toward Yakima, and he froze.

He chuffed with indignance. "Did you *trip* me, Senor?"

Yakima pushed back against the roadhouse wall as though trying to merge with the adobe. "Sorry, friend. My foot slipped."

The man chuffed again, louder this time. "Your foot *slipped*? I don't think so, Senor!"

Yakima sighed. Shit. Holding the wood in his arms, he stepped out from the wall. He kept his voice reasonable. "I meant no offense. Just seemed the girl was tired of your company is all." Yakima's eyes shifted slightly. The slender shadow stood by the open barn door, facing the roadhouse.

The Mexican laughed caustically, curling one hand around his revolver. "You are in error, Senor. It is merely a game she plays. And just to show you how big a mistake you have made . . ." He slid his revolver from his holster with self-assured negligence.

Just as the barrel cleared leather, Yakima dropped his arms, his right hand coming up and grabbing a split log from the top of the falling stack. As the wood thundered onto the porch, Yakima swung the log back behind his shoulder and slung it forward with a clipped grunt.

"Ack!" El Segundo screamed as the log slammed into his right wrist with a dull smack and the gun hit the ground with a thud.

Out of the corner of his right eye, Yakima saw a couple of silhouetted faces peering over the batwings. The smoke of strong tobacco laced the air. He sidestepped to the edge of the porch as the *segundo* looked up at him, hissing and growling like an enraged cur guarding a prized bone.

"You will pay dearly for that, you son of a bitch! I assure you!"

A voice rose from the shadows over the batwings. "Trouble, Jefe?"

"Trouble?" said El Segundo. "No trouble, Pablo. Just a gringo half-breed who needs to be taught some *Mejican* manners."

There was the *snick-click* of a gun hammer being pulled back. The batwings parted, and one of the other vaqueros stepped out, the pistol that he held before him reflecting the umber light from inside.

"I think a good lashing with my bullwhip might save him from more trouble later on." El Segundo chuckled, backing away from the porch while squeezing his wrist with his other hand. "Pablo, take his gun."

The first man through the batwings stepped toward Yakima, aiming his revolver from his belly, a short cigarette glowing between his lips. Four more vaqueros, two wearing sombreros, flanked him, all sliding their six-shooters from their holsters and thumbing back the hammers. As the first man moved toward him, Yakima raised his hands up, palms out.

"*Por favor*, El Segundo, no more trouble, huh?" It was the Irishman, peeking out between the batwings. "Ligia is too young for your rough pleasure. Come back inside. You can have Esmeralda on the house tonight. For free, eh?"

"This dirty half-breed tripped me," El Segundo said tightly, keeping his hard eyes on Yakima.

The man with the cigarette slowly extended his right

hand toward Yakima's holstered revolver. The other four vaqueros flanked him, their own guns drawn.

El Segundo spat and scooped his revolver from the dust, brushed it off, and clicked back the hammer. "It cannot be overlooked."

As the man with the cigarette leaned toward Yakima, his mustachioed lips spread away from the quirley in his teeth. Yakima didn't look down, but he felt the man's hand release the keeper thong over his .44's hammer, then begin to ease the revolver up out of the sheath.

Suddenly, Yakima chopped his open right hand straight down against the man's wrist. There was an audible crack of breaking bone. The man grunted and let Yakima's Colt slide back down in its holster.

At the same time, Yakima jerked the man's gun hand wide. The Schofield belched smoke and fire, the bullet plunking into a support post. Holding the man's right wrist, Yakima spun him around, then grabbed his own revolver, ratcheted back the hammer, and snugged the barrel against the vaquero's right ear.

The vaquero was breathing hard, grunting with the pain of his cracked wrist. His cigarette dropped from his lips; it glowed against the porch floor.

Yakima stared out from behind the man's head at the four other vaqueros facing him, crouching, extending their revolvers straight out from their shoulders.

He didn't say anything, just sidestepped slightly, keeping Pablo between him and the five men bearing down on him.

"Pablo, you are a damn fool!" screamed El Segundo.

Pablo groaned and cursed.

"If your amigos don't drop those six-shooters and ride on out of here, Pablo," Yakima said in his cow pen Spanish, "I'm gonna bore a hole between your ears with a .44 slug."

El Segundo and the other four vaqueros held their positions, guns aimed. Yakima pressed his own revolver's barrel harder against Pablo's ear.

One of the vaqueros glanced at El Segundo.

El Segundo stared at Yakima, shifting the gun around before him, trying to get a bead on Yakima's head. His chest rose and fell sharply. The white streak through his hair shone in the darkness.

Yakima rammed his gun barrel hard against Pablo's head.

"El Segundo!" Pablo cried.

El Segundo cursed and lowered his revolver, depressing the hammer.

"Toss 'em down, amigos," he growled disgustedly as he dropped his own gun in the dust. "The don will not be pleased if we ride back to the hacienda with an empty saddle."

Reluctantly, the vaqueros leaned down, set their guns on the porch.

Yakima shoved Pablo out away from him. "Mount up and ride. Don't try circling back. I've got good ears and good eyes."

Pablo and the four vaqueros grabbed their reins off the hitchrack. Silent as scolded children, they backed their horses away from the rack, then swung into their saddles.

"Gringos like you don't last long in Mejico." Keeping

his eyes on Yakima, El Segundo slipped his reins from the hitchrack, swung into the saddle, and reined the horse around. "We will meet again, Senor!"

He ground his spurs against the Arabian's ribs and galloped out of the yard.

The others glared at Yakima, then spurred their own snorting mounts after El Segundo, their bouncing silhouettes soon blending with the desert's inky darkness.

The batwings creaked, and Yakima turned to see the Irishman step out onto the porch, staring after the Mexicans.

"Bastard done killed one of my whores a few months back," the man growled. "They were bound to kill Ligia, too—or mark her so she ain't worth spit."

Yakima glanced at the logs on the porch floor. "There's your wood." He turned, began striding toward the barn. "I'll stay out yonder, in case they circle back."

As he crossed the yard, the girl stepped out from behind the barn door. He stopped ahead and to the left of her. She was little more than a brown smudge in the darkness, her straight dark hair framing her oval-shaped face.

He remembered another young dove he'd saved from hardcases in Colorado, and his heart pinched. Faith. He walked up to Ligia, laid his hand gently against her smooth cheek. "Are you all right, Senorita?"

She nodded, lowering her eyes demurely. *"Sí, Señor."*

She stepped around him and headed for the road-house, where the Irishman was plucking the logs off the porch, still grumbling and looking after the Mexicans.

She mounted the porch steps, pushed through the batwings, and disappeared inside.

Yakima fetched his rifle from the barn and headed back to the woodpile.

When Yakima finished splitting wood a half hour later, he dug a small pit in the chaparral near the barn and built a coffee fire. He would sleep here, under the stars, where he could keep a sharp eye and ear out for the Mexicans. He doubted they'd try to even the score tonight, but if they did, he'd be ready for them.

He sat back against his saddle, his coffee cup on a rock beside him, hands behind his head, staring up at the starry sky. Gravel crunched softly to his left. In an instant, he grabbed his Yellowboy and cocked it, swinging the barrel around.

A slender shadow jerked. "It's Ligia!"

She stood in the greasewood, holding a steaming plate in one hand while extending the other in a beseeching gesture. She wore a thick shawl that fell to her knees and fur-trimmed moccasins. Yakima lowered the rifle, depressing the hammer.

"I brought . . . food," she said in broken English, stepping forward haltingly. "You must be hungry."

Yakima scooted up higher against his saddle and set the rifle on the rock beside him. "Starving."

The girl moved forward and held the plate toward him in both hands, keeping her shy eyes on him expectantly. He saw now that one eye wandered inward slightly. Yakima took the plate. His stomach grumbled and his mouth watered at the thick slab of pork and giant help-ing of pinto beans steaming in the chill night air.

"He cooks good food . . . Senor O'Toole."

"Much obliged," Yakima said, picking up the wooden fork and digging in. "I was about to break into my rab-bit, but this looks a whole heap better than day-old jack."

The girl backed away slowly and stood watching him, hands crossed at her waist. She was lingering. Waiting for the plate, maybe. Yakima nodded at the coffeepot resting on a rock beside the fire's low flames. "Help yourself to coffee, if you like. There's an extra cup in one of those saddle pouches."

As Yakima continued to eat hungrily, the girl glanced at the coffeepot and the saddlebags lying on the other side of the fire. She walked around the fire, knelt down, pulled a cup from the saddlebags, then used the leather swatch to lift the pot from the rock and to pour the steaming brew into the cup.

Cup in hand, she rose, moved toward a rock near Yakima, and sat down, pressing her fur-trimmed moc-casins together and setting the smoking cup on her knee. She sat there silently while Yakima ate. She glanced around the campsite from time to time, turning her head with a start when a rabbit rustled the nearby brush, but kept her gaze mostly on Yakima, studying him as though he were a question she was trying to answer.

When his stomach was beginning to feel satisfied, he kept eating but returned the girl's sidelong gaze. "Name's Yakima. Yakima Henry."

The girl said nothing, her brown eyes reflecting the firelight.

"I heard you're called Ligia," Yakima continued. "Pretty name. One of the prettiest I've stumbled across, matter of fact."

He looked up to see her blushing. A dove that blushes . . . Obviously, she hadn't been a dove very long.

"It was *mi mama*'s name." She turned her head slightly to one side and frowned, causing the one eye to slide even farther toward her nose. "You are Indio?"

"Half. My mother was Cheyenne with some Yakima blood. She liked the ocean. Pa was a white prospector. We traveled around a lot. I spent a little time with my ma's people, after she died, but I didn't really belong there. I been drifting ever since."

He tossed his fork onto the empty plate, set the plate on a rock, and wiped his hands on his buckskin breeches. He was a little surprised to hear himself talking so much, but he didn't often get the chance to talk to anyone but his horse.

"I do whatever work I can—ranch work, railroad work. I've ridden shotgun on gold shipments, driven stage-coach, mucked out livery barns. I worked in a place like the Irishman's once. Last year."

He sighed, remembering the night he'd saved Thornton's favorite dove, Faith, from four men who hadn't paid, who'd intended to kill her to get back at Thornton. Then the long trail afterward, him and Faith and Wolf, heading for the Colorado mountain boomtown of Gold Cache, staying ahead of the kill-crazy bounty hunter, Wit Bardoul.

He'd been staring into the fire, forgetting about saving his night vision, lost in his thoughts. He turned his head to see the girl kneeling beside him, running her hand over the brass receiver of the Winchester Yellowboy. Her fingers traced the etching on the side opposite the receiver, of the wolf fighting a grizzly in deep grass.

"Beautiful . . ."

"An old friend gave that to me."

Yakima stared at the receiver. Funny how a gun intended for a territorial governor had ended up in the hands of a gandy dancer Chinaman—a Shaolin monk who had taught Yakima some Oriental fighting practices—and then in the saddle boot of a drifting half-breed. Ralph, as he was known—his Chinese name was too complicated for Yakima to pronounce—had been a first-rate cardplayer, and he'd won the rifle in a poker game. Not believing in guns, he'd given the Yellowboy to Yakima.

Yakima felt the warmth of the girl's hand on his thigh. He looked at her. She was staring at him, eyes bright in the firelight. "You think I am pretty?"

Yakima stared at her clean, smooth cheeks, lustrous brown eyes, and slightly pursed lips. Her neck was long and fine, with two small, dark brown moles, one above the other. Her straight brown hair swayed across her shoulders in the breeze. "You *are* pretty."

She drew her hands inside her cape, then lifted it over her head and tossed it aside. Lifting her hands to the low neck of her dress top, she began peeling the sleeves down her arms.

Yakima reached up, placed his hands on hers, stopping her.

She frowned. "Mr. O'Toole said it was okay."

Yakima shook his head, slid the dress back up the young girl's arms. She was too young, and he was too tired. "You're right pretty, but I think I'll just lay back and watch the stars till I fall asleep."

He leaned back against his saddle, crossed his hands behind his head. She stared down at him, pooching her lips out and frowning, indignant.

He squirmed a few inches toward the cantle end of the saddle. "You're welcome to join me if you want." She'd be safer out here with Yakima, who could protect her, than inside with the Irishman, who probably couldn't.

She dropped to her hands and knees and lay down beside him. He draped his right arm around her shoulders, drew her close to him, so she could share his warmth, and pulled a blanket across them both.

She snuggled her head against his shoulder, pressed her body close to his.

"Look there," Yakima said, pointing skyward. "Falling star."

Chapter 14

Tired as he was, Yakima slept fitfully, waking to listen every half hour or so for approaching bushwhackers. He was accustomed to such sporadic rest, though, and when he rose at four, wriggling his shoulder gently out from beneath Ligia's head, he felt fresh.

The girl groaned and snuggled deeper under the blankets as he built a fire and started coffee. While the fire built itself up, he went into the barn to check on the horse, relieved to find that the swelling in the frog was nearly gone.

He hammered the shoe into place, then led the horse out to where the fire was snapping, the coffeepot chugging. The girl knelt on the ground, rolling his blankets.

As he led the sorrel up to the fire, Ligia looked at him and sank back on her heels. "Now you are going?"

"After some coffee. It'll be light soon."

"I will cook eggs for you."

Yakima shook his head and knelt beside the fire, removing the pot with the leather scrap. "Just the coffee."

He poured them each a cup, and they sat around the

fire, saying nothing, sipping the coffee. When he'd finished half his cup, he leathered his horse, attaching the bedroll and rifle scabbard, praying silently that the sorrel's hoof would hold up until he could trade for another mount.

The gray of the false dawn shone in the east, dimly defining the distant ridges. A nighthawk cried somewhere above the dark adobe roadhouse hunched on the other side of the yard.

Watching Yakima from a nearby rock, Ligia shivered under her heavy poncho. "You go where?"

Yakima slid the Winchester from the saddle boot, began thumbing shells into the receiver. "I'm not sure yet."

"You are pursuing the desperadoes . . . the Thunder Riders?"

Slipping a shell through the rifle's loading gate with a metallic click, he glanced at her.

"They go to Junction Rock. A very bad place. Many badmen there . . . gringos and Mejicanos. All running from the law."

Yakima walked around the horse and stood before her. "Never heard of it."

"I heard the desperadoes talking."

Yakima frowned. "Was the woman still with them? The pretty gringa?"

"*Sí.*"

"She look all right?"

The girl shrugged. "*Sí.*" She smiled knowingly. "Very beautiful."

Yakima set two fingers beneath her chin and pecked her cheek. "Adios, Ligia."

He turned to the horse, swung into the saddle, and reined the sorrel toward the yard.

Behind him, Ligia's voice rose softly in the predawn silence. "Be careful, Yakima. Many banditos and Indios along the trail. Very *bad*!"

Yakima walked the sorrel along the top of the mesa, then down the southwest side. As he bottomed out on the desert floor, the sun rose above the eastern horizon, light shafts spreading across the sky and the broken, red-bronze terrain like a giant blossoming marigold, sweeping shadows along before it.

He was crossing a cactus-choked wash when he reined up suddenly. In the corner of his eye he'd spotted a sun flash—a faint prick of reflected light, brief as a firefly's spark—a mile or so ahead, just to the right of the trail.

It might be only sun reflected off mica or a cast-off bottle, but he had to check it out or risk getting bushwhacked. He cursed. Another damn delay.

He turned off the trail and followed the twisting, turning watercourse generally west, crouching so his head remained below the lip of the south bank. When he'd ridden a couple of hundred yards, he swung straight south, keeping his eyes on a pillar of boulders rising above the chaparral ahead and left, roughly where he'd seen the sun flash.

He gigged the sorrel along, trotting when he thought he could keep his dust trail low, swinging wide of the rocky pillar, then circling to within two hundred feet of its back side. Snorting softly, he shucked his Winchester from the saddle boot.

Five men perched atop the rocks up and down the pillar, two peering around its one side, three around the other, all holding rifles. They wore short charro or fringed deerskin jackets, black leather chaps decorated with hammered silver disks, and sombreros. El Segundo sat the lowest on the pillar, staring around the right side, his sombrero hanging down his back, the white streak in his hair glowing in the morning sunshine.

His head was canted back, and his jaws were moving, as if he were talking to one of the others.

Yakima gently levered a round into the Yellowboy's breech. He snugged the stock to his shoulder and aimed carefully along the side of El Segundo's head, hoping to clip the man's ear, and fired.

The slug drilled the rock before El Segundo with a shrill *pshting!*

El Segundo flinched and grabbed his ear as he wheeled, stumbling back against the rock and dropping his rifle. As the others jerked around toward the source of the shot, snapping their eyes wide, Yakima cut loose with four more quick shots, the other four men grabbing, respectively, an upper left arm, upper right thigh, upper left thigh, and left calf.

When they were all howling like whipped pups, Yakima drilled a hole through one of the vaqueros' sombreros, then planted the stock of his rifle against his hip and pulled the sorrel's reins taut in his left hand.

"Go on back to the hacienda," he yelled, "or next time you'll get more than a friendly tattoo!"

None of the four attempted to raise his rifle. They all stood or sagged among the rocks, clutching their bloody bullet burns and regarding Yakima with awe and fury.

Yakima considered grabbing one of their horses, no doubt tied nearby. But stealing a horse might put their don on his trail with more men than he could outdistance or shoot, for horse stealing in this country was considered more lowly than murder. Besides, Yakima might have to explain the horse's brand to rurales.

Deciding to wait and make a legitimate trade for the gimpy sorrel farther up the trail, he backed the horse away from the five vaqueros, then turned behind a cluster of Joshua trees and heeled the mount into a lope, angling south, hoping the trail of the Thunder Riders hadn't faded.

Later the same day, Speares led the posse through a narrow valley with low, sage-stippled hills on the left and a towering sandstone scarp streaked with bird shit on the right. They passed through a cottonwood copse, the few remaining yellow leaves rattling in the chill wind, and Speares reined his horse to a halt at the lip of a broad, sandy draw.

As the rest of the weary, unshaven posse drew up behind him and around him, Speares cast his gaze to the draw's opposite bank. A good seventy yards away, it was cloaked in tough brown shrubs and occasional sand-colored boulders.

Patchen's horse shook its head as the marshal peered across the draw. "Good place for an ambush."

"There've been plenty of good places for an ambush, and we ain't been ambushed yet." Speares rose up in his saddle to rake his gaze along both sides of the opposite bank, for fifty yards in each direction.

"Don't mean there won't be a first time," said one of the three dust-clad market hunters, Nudge Tobias. "I say we scout it first."

"So do I!" the banker, Franklin, exclaimed haughtily. His saddle-chafed thighs were bleeding through his broadcloth trousers, and every chance he got, he made sure everyone knew how unhappy he was, riding way the hell south of the border with a lowly catch party.

Speares looked at Patchen.

"Not a bad idea," the marshal said. "There's no cover down there."

"Pshaw!" Speares said. "That gang ain't worried about no catch party. They don't have enough *respect* for us to waste time layin' an *ambush*."

Harley Knutson, who owned one of the two gun shops in Saber Creek, mopped sweat from his sun- and wind-blistered forehead. "How in the hell you figure we *can* take them down, Speares? That's what I wanna know. I mean, they're the *Thunder Riders*!"

Speares placed a hand on his cantle and hipped around to regard the beefy shop owner with strained tolerance. "We *can* take them down, Harley, because *they don't think we can.* Hell, I don't even think they know we're on their trail."

"Well, in that case, Sheriff," said one of the other market hunters, a walleyed hombre named Jan Behunek, "why don't you cross first? Just to put our minds at ease."

Behunek cut his self-satisfied gaze to his partners, one on each side of him. The other posse members voiced their own agreement, nodding.

Flushing, Speares looked at Patchen. The marshal offered a lopsided smile inside his silver muttonchops and shrugged. "Looks like you've been outvoted, Sheriff." He reached forward and shucked his Henry rifle from the saddle boot, racked a shell in the chamber. "I'll cover you."

Speares glanced at the men behind him disgustedly before turning forward and shucking his rifle. *"Christ!"* He spurred the horse off the bank and into the sandy riverbed. The sand was deep, nearly hock-high in places, so Speares held the mount to a walk as he raked his eyes along the opposite bank and up the rolling, brushy hills beyond.

Nothing but thick brush and rocks. No sound but the breeze funneling down the dry watercourse.

Speares chuckled and glanced over his right shoulder. The posse was spread out, all holding rifles and watching him warily. Patchen sat slouched in his own saddle, holding his Henry across his saddlebow. He had a tight, slightly mocking smile on his face, which was shaded by his low-tipped hat brim.

Superior son of a bitch.

Speares turned forward. The opposite bank grew before him, rocks and shrubs separating, delineating themselves, showing the vacant gaps between.

When he was ten yards from the bank, brush rustled to his right. He jerked back on the horse's reins, his heart thudding, and swung his rifle around.

A skunk, its nose to the ground, meandered out from behind one moss-speckled boulder, heading for another veiled by Spanish bayonet.

Speares lowered the rifle, felt his face warm. He glanced over his shoulder. On the far bank, Patchen's white teeth shone under his mustache. A couple of the others were grinning as well.

Speares spat to one side, then gigged his horse the last few yards to the bank. He put the mount up a narrow game trail curling through the brush. On a hillock overlooking the riverbed, about forty yards up from the bank, he turned the sorrel and planted his rifle on his thigh, barrel aimed skyward.

He didn't say anything, just stared at the posse on the other side, waiting in truculent silence.

Patchen raised an arm and, as the others fell in behind and around him, put his steeldust down the bank and into the deep sand anchored by occasional clumps of chamisa. The marshal swung his head slowly from side to side, shifting the shade across his chest, making his copper star wink in the sunlight, holding his rifle up and ready.

The others, except for the banker, did likewise. Franklin was too exhausted and miserable to worry about an ambush. His blaze-faced dun fell in behind the others, the banker hanging his head as though nearly asleep.

The walleyed market hunter, Behunek, threw his head back and laughed at something one of his partners said, riding beside him. At the same time, he dipped his right hand into his shirt pocket, reaching for a tobacco sack.

Watching the posse move toward him, Speares ran his tongue over his chapped lips. A cigarette would taste good about now.

The thought had no sooner passed through his brain than a rifle boomed on his right. The rifle was so close, the boom so loud and unexpected, that Speares first thought lightning had struck. Holding tight to the dancing claybank's reins, he turned toward the source of the blast.

Blue smoke puffed above a thick brush tuft.

He snapped his gaze toward the dry watercourse. Behunek was flopping backward in his saddle like a rag doll, the man's frightened horse leaping and pitching as though its tail was on fire.

A veritable cannonade exploded out of the brush before and around Speares. The sheriff saw the smoke of a good half dozen rifles rise above the shrubs. His startled mount bucked sharply, whipping him straight up and over its head. His Winchester flew out of his hands and clattered to the ground at the same moment that he landed in a cactus patch with a burning pain along the backs of his thighs.

Groaning, vaguely aware of screaming men and horses from the direction of the draw, Speares turned onto his belly. Heart pounding, he pushed up on his hands and knees, trying to rise. His head was spinning and throbbing, and he scrambled only a few feet ahead on his hands and feet, then plopped onto his side.

Breathing hard, blood racing, he raised himself onto his elbows.

Through the dust of his fleeing horse, he saw a man moving toward him—a tall hombre in a gray wolf coat and with a hideously scarred eye, silver hoops dangling from his ears. The man grinned as he approached Speares, shifting his Spencer repeater to his left hand while drawing a .45 revolver with the other.

The man stopped suddenly. He raised the revolver, aiming straight out from his right shoulder, angling the barrel slightly down, directly at Speares's head.

Speares was about to raise his hands when smoke and flames stabbed from the revolver's bore.

He didn't hear the shot.

Chapter 15

That morning, Yakima made good time on the sorrel, alternately walking and loping. It helped that the terrain was relatively flat, with no high saddles to strain the horse's tender frog.

By a little after noon, however, the country became broken and rocky, and there were several rugged passes he and the horse had to negotiate, then a deep canyon to cross. Coming up out of the canyon, Yakima felt the horse balk slightly, favoring the right front hoof.

Yakima slowed the sorrel to a walk. This was not country in which you wanted to be stranded afoot. He should have taken one of the vaqueros' horses, the don's wrath be damned.

A half hour later, he rode up out of another, smaller canyon and reined the horse to a stop under a tall pine. He'd dismounted to check the hoof when he glanced westward, then did a slow double take.

A pillar of black smoke rose on the other side of a low mesa.

It could indicate a brush fire, or some Mexican

campesino merely burning slash. Or Indians. If there were Apaches or Yaquis in the area, he wanted to know where they were exactly, and how many.

He tied the horse to a pine and loosened the saddle cinch to give the sorrel a breather, then, keeping an eye on the smoke, shucked his Winchester from the boot. He rammed a fresh shell into the breech, off-cocked the hammer, grabbed the spyglass from a saddle pouch, and jogged west through low brush, zigzagging around rocks. He started up the mesa's sloping, brushy wall at an angle, flushing a big jack he wouldn't have minded roasting for supper and a couple of kangaroo rats.

As he climbed the slope, he thought he could make out some faint, celebratory yowls, and he felt the hair prick on the back of his neck.

Near the mesa's crest, he crouched, keeping his head low, and climbed onto the top of the ridge. He crawled through galleta grass and sage until he had a good view of the canyon on the mesa's other side. Stopping, he set the rifle down beside him, snaked the spyglass out from under his shirt, and trained it down the rocky slope before him.

Trailing the smoke column to its source on the canyon floor, he found three big wagons tipped on their sides, spilling freight onto the sage and rocks around them. A couple of mules lay dead in the traces, while several others milled a distance away, trailing their reins. Two of the wagons were on fire, lying so close together that the black smoke rose as one column.

Seven or eight Apaches in deerskin leggings and calico bandannas scurried around the spilled freight of the unburned wagon, kicking the crates and barrels, plunging knives into food sacks. One held a woman's pink dress up against him, dancing and shrieking while two others watched him and howled, one bent forward at the waist and slapping his thigh.

To the left of the Apache with the dress, another Apache was firing arrow after arrow into the bulky body of a dead freighter from three feet away.

Yakima slid the spyglass right, toward the base of another ridge. The Apache horses, outfitted in rope halters and blanket saddles, their sides bright with war paint, stood in a cluster of low boulders. Two Apaches sat near the horses, nearly concealed by a rocky shelf rising behind them. Passing what looked like a bladder flask, they pointed, talked, and laughed, enjoying the theater being played out on the canyon floor before them.

Yakima turned the spyglass to the horses again. A desert-bred Apache horse would cut across this devil's playground like a hot knife through lard. It was asking for death, or worse, but the sorrel was going down, and an Indian pony had nearly twice as much sand and bottom as most white men's horses.

Keeping his head so low that his chin scraped the ground, he crabbed straight back the way he'd come, then jogged down the slope to the sorrel. When he'd removed the horse's saddle and bridle, he swung the saddlebags over his shoulder and turned the horse toward open country.

"You're on your own, pal," Yakima said, slapping the horse's rump. "A vaquero or campesino will pick you up."

The horse ran off, snorting, hooves clipping stones.

Leaving the saddle in the brush—most Apache horses wouldn't tolerate a heavy stock saddle—he jogged north along the base of the mesa.

Crawling on his hands and knees, he crossed the gap between ridges, so the howling, mewling Apaches wouldn't see him, then scrambled up the butte on the other side. At the top, he stopped between two upthrusts of cracked granite. Straight down and about thirty yards out on the canyon floor, amid the boulders, the Apache horses stood swishing their tails and pricking their ears.

The two Apache guards sat on separate rocks and boulders, still passing the bladder flask of tizwin.

The only thing more sinister than raiding bronco Apaches was raiding *drunk* bronco Apaches.

Yakima scanned the slope, figured a way down to the horses, and dropped again to his hands and knees. Holding the Yellowboy in his right hand, he crawled down the butte, slithering along the base of one of the stone scarps. He kept his head down but his eyes raised, watching the marauding Apaches.

The raw alcohol should make the braves easier to take down.

Setting his rifle and saddlebags against a low rock shelf, Yakima reached into his boot and plucked his Arkansas toothpick from its leather sheath. He hefted the six inches of razor-sharp steel, then glanced through the notch in the shelf. The braves were facing the burning mule train, one yawning widely while the other continued to chatter in his guttural tongue.

Holding the blade tip straight up, Yakima cat-footed to the top of the rocky scarp and crouched atop the crest.

He whipped the knife up to his shoulder, snapped it forward. It careened through the air, angling down the slope, flashing in the sunlight until the six-inch blade smacked into the right Apache's back with a thump.

At the same time, Yakima propelled himself off the scarp, diving, hands straight out in front of him. The stabbed Apache stood and yowled as Yakima closed his hands around the other brave's neck and drove him straight forward, slamming him hard against the ground.

The brave wriggled and lurched, but Yakima kept his hands pressed firmly to the young Indian's neck and, holding his knees tightly against the brave's back, gave a sudden, savage jerk. The neck snapped, and Yakima could feel the shattered bones grind beneath his hands.

He turned to the wounded brave, who lay belly down five feet away, kicking feebly, one hand reaching toward the bone handle protruding from the center of his back. Liver-colored blood spurted out around the blade with each beat of the brave's pierced heart.

Suddenly, he lifted his head, his entire body jerking, sighed, and set his chin in the dust.

Yakima reached over and pulled the toothpick from the brave's back, wiped the blood on the Apache's smoke-stained leggings, and peered through the brush toward the mule train. He saw little from this vantage but smoke and occasional brown figures in red bandannas moving around.

Relief washed over him as he stood and turned toward

the snorting, startled horses. He'd taken one step toward a muscular buckskin when a rifle boomed behind him.

A bullet smacked a rock near his right ankle, the hot lead ricocheting wildly.

Yakima whipped around, grabbing his .44 from its holster and thumbing back the hammer. An Apache crouched forty feet away, ejecting a spent shell from his Spencer's breech, legs spread, a savage snarl bunching his square, flat, saddle brown face.

As the Apache leveled the Spencer once more, Yakima whipped his Colt up and fired. The slug bored a hole through the Apache's left shoulder.

The Spencer boomed and blazed, but Yakima's shot had jerked the Apache's slug wide. As the brave screamed and staggered backward, trying to bring his rifle up, Yakima aimed and fired again, drilling a dark hole through the man's calico blouse and punching him straight back and down behind a rock.

His moccasins hung up on the rock, his brown feet showing through the scuffed soles, twitching.

Shouts rose from the direction of the mule train. Yakima's heart thudded as he snapped a look that way, spotting two Indians running toward him, heads bobbing above the brush. He lurched toward the buckskin, grabbed the reins, and then quickly went down the line, cutting all the reins free of the single picket line they were tied to. Then he fired his revolver into the air twice.

As the Indian ponies whinnied and scattered up the side of the canyon, the Indians' shouts grew louder, the harsh tones of the Apache tongue rising. Yakima didn't bother taking another gander toward the canyon. He just turned the horse by its braided rawhide reins and ground his heels into its flanks.

They were up behind the rock shelf in seconds, and Yakima swooped down to grab his saddlebags and rifle from among the rocks. He draped the bags over the horse's rump and pressed his heels once more into its rib cage.

The stout buckskin had been the right choice. It took off in long, lunging strides, moving so fast straight up the slope that Yakima, used to having a saddle horn to hang on to, had to cling to the horse's mane and grind his knees into its hide to keep from tumbling off.

Rifles popped behind him, the slugs tearing into the slope around the buckskin's hooves, hazing the horse into even faster, longer strides, throwing up rocks and gravel behind. One bullet sizzled just past Yakima's right ear and spanged into the turf with a sharp *clack*. Several more drilled the rocks to his left, one missing him only because the horse had swerved to avoid a coiled Mojave green rattler.

Horse and rider bounded over the ridge crest as three more shots tore the ground just off the horse's hooves.

Ten feet down the other side, Yakima straightened his back, hauled on the buckskin's reins, and leapt down. Holding the reins, he ran back up to the ridge crest. Below, three Indians were sprinting toward the base of the slope, within ten feet and closing. Another one, a wiry youngster with greased hair flashing in the sunlight, bounded up the slope, leaping from rock to rock.

Yakima raised his Winchester and fired three quick rounds, not taking time to aim. A bullet clipped the youngster's right knee. The brave dropped with a howl, hugging his kneecap, while the other three dove behind boulders.

Wheeling, Yakima ran back and leapt onto the confused, prancing buckskin. He gigged it down the ridge, hugging its neck and clinging to the mane, feeling the sure feet working beneath him. At the bottom, he ground his heels into the horse's flanks and shot out onto the rolling desert beyond.

The buckskin hesitated a few times, wary of the stranger on its back, who no doubt smelled as bad to its nose as Apaches did to white men's mounts. But Yakima held the reins taut, not letting the horse turn its head, and continued heeling the hard ribs until he was loping fluidly over the hogbacks.

He glanced behind a couple of times but saw no sign of the Apaches. They were obviously a renegade band and, hopefully, more interested in the spoils of the mule train attack than in seeking the stolen horse or vengeance for their dead and wounded.

Yakima rode hard for the rest of the day, back on the overlapping trail of desperadoes and posse. When the falling sun etched dangerous shadows in the lee of rocks and brush clumps, he rested the buckskin in a dry wash.

At good dark, he set out again, closely studying the hoofprints before him. He hoped that by taking advantage of the bright starlight at this altitude, he would be able to catch up to the gang before their sign was obliterated by wind or rain.

Of course, he would have to somehow skirt the posse again, unless they caught up to the Thunder Riders first, in which case they might prove an effective diversion. On the other hand, they could very well get Anjanette and Wolf killed, and give Yakima no chance at all.

He lost the trail only once all night, which cost him an hour, but at nine o'clock the next morning, having catnapped for ten minutes, he was still following the hoofprints, scuff marks, horse apples, and torn shrubs. Around ten, he halted the mustang at the edge of a cottonwood grove and stared over its head toward a draw cut perpendicular to the trail.

From the draw, a great cacophony rose. Over the draw's lip, dark shapes shifted and bounced. There was the sound of large wings flapping, the occasional enraged shriek of fighting buzzards.

Yakima thumbed the Winchester's hammer back and put the buckskin ahead. The horse chuffed and shook its head, nostrils working, a wary cast to its eyes. When it turned suddenly sideways, balking and threatening a buck, Yakima slid off its back and wrapped the reins around a small cottonwood.

Holding the Winchester high across his chest, he strode slowly forward. As the draw gradually opened before him, the putrid smell of death and the rancid fetor of exposed viscera touched his nose. The buzzard squawks and shrieks rose, rattling his eardrums.

He squatted on the lip of the bank, staring into the draw's sandy bed. A dozen or so bodies lay twisted and strewn in the blood-soaked sand beneath the fluttering blanket of bald-headed turkey buzzards. The buzzards churlishly poked and prodded the flesh and exposed entrails, ripping out several inches of bloodred tissue at a time.

The gang had made short work of the posse and about four of the posse's horses. The buzzards were cleaning up.

"Fools," Yakima growled.

He was about to rise and head back toward his horse when what sounded like a man's scream rose amid the clamor of the feeding, fighting birds.

Yakima slid his gaze right, frowning, raking his eyes around the carnage.

A shrill, horrified scream sounded from about halfway across the draw. "Get away, you ugly bastard! *Git!*"

Yakima rose, slid down the bank, and strode toward the source of the shouts. He stepped through blood-soaked sand between two dead horses, the saddle hanging down the side of one, scattering the chirping birds, and stopped.

Three heads sat in the sand before him, spaced about six feet apart.

The head of Sheriff Speares was on the left, facing up the ravine. His swollen face was scrunched up, wincing, the eyes slitted. Beside him, facing him, was the head of the banker. The man's eyes were closed, his lower jaw slack, his face bruised and sun-blistered, blood leaking from several ragged buzzard holes. To the right of the banker and facing away from Yakima was the pewter-haired head of Marshal Patchen.

The marshal's head moved, and a shrill voice rose from it: "Stay away from me, you son of a bitch!"

Yakima looked toward the opposite bank. In the shade

of a boulder, a buzzard stood facing the buried marshal, one ragged wing outstretched as the bird quivered on its long, crooked talons, preparing to wing over for a quick bite.

"Ah, shit," Patchen said tightly, spitting dirt from his lips and laughing maniacally. "He's comin' again!"

Chapter 16

Yakima raised the Winchester and blew the bird's head off with a single round.

As the headless buzzard hopped around in a wide circle, beating its wings in a bizarre death dance, Yakima moved forward and shuttled his gaze between Speares and Patchen, both buried to their chins in the ravine's fine sand. Their faces were pink with sunburn and mottled purple from bruises and cuts where, Yakima assumed, the buzzards had been working on them prematurely. The sheriff's nose was still swollen, but it didn't stand out so much now, as the rest of his face was nearly as badly inflamed.

It was hard to tell how long the banker had been dead, but his face looked like a gouged clay mask streaked with red. His gray hair, crusted with dry blood, slid around in the breeze.

Patchen spoke through gritted teeth. "You better talk to your jailer, Speares. If he's still alive."

Yakima spread his feet and set his Yellowboy on his

shoulder, gloved finger through the trigger guard. He stared skeptically down at the two buried lawmen.

"Should've known better than to leave old Suggs in charge," Speares rasped.

Patchen chuckled darkly, his head twitching.

"Breed," Speares said, wincing at a sudden sharp pain. "I'll put in a few good words with ol' Saint Pete if you drill a pill through my head."

Patchen ran his dry tongue across his lips, smearing a blood drip. "Give me one, too. I'm about worn out, tryin' to get out of here and hold them predators back. That gang of yours are sick sonsabitches."

"Must be half Apache," Speares mused. "Only they were kind enough to leave our eyelids."

Patchen rolled his eyes toward Speares. "Makes it slower that way."

Yakima poked his hat back off his forehead. "How long you been here?"

Patchen glanced up at him, eyelids fluttering. His eyes were bloodshot, the lids pink and sand-caked. "Since yesterday afternoon."

"Long enough for me," Speares said. "If the buzzards don't get us by sundown, wolves and cats will move in tonight." He spat. "Spare a couple bullets, breed. I'd do as much for you."

Yakima sighed and looked around. A scarred Spencer rifle lay nearby, half buried in the sand. He set down his prized Yellowboy, grabbed the old Spencer by the barrel, and began shoveling sand away from Patchen's chin with the stock.

Patchen watched him skeptically, hopefully. So did

Speares. Neither man said anything while Yakima shoveled the sand away from the marshal's chest, shoulders, and back.

When he'd gotten down to the man's belt, Patchen gazed up at Yakima, incredulous. Yakima pulled his Arkansas toothpick from his boot, reached around, and cut the rope tying the marshal's hands behind his back. Patchen continued staring at Yakima as, planting his hands to both sides, he worked Patchen's legs out of the riverbed.

Yakima straightened, breathing hard. He looked at Speares, now staring at him curiously, one eye squeezed shut. He tossed the Spencer down and picked up his hat and Yellowboy.

"You can dig the sheriff out. I got business ahead."

Shouldering the Winchester, he walked back across the ravine, mounted the bank, and strode through the brush to the buckskin. He grabbed the reins, leapt onto the saddle blanket, turned the horse around.

In the ravine, Patchen was using the Spencer to dig out Speares—slow, weary strokes, the sheriff spitting sand from his mouth. The buzzards squawked and quarreled as they consumed the dead bodies around them.

Yakima put the buckskin down the bank and gigged it through the sand, weaving around a dead man and a dead horse. He glanced at Patchen, who'd stopped working to stare at him.

"Go on home!" Yakima yelled. "Stay the hell outta my way!"

He could feel the two lawmen staring at his back as he

took off on the buckskin up the opposite bank and lit out for the brushy hills beyond.

Midafternoon of the same day, Anjanette and the Thunder Riders galloped over several low hogbacks, twisting around the ruins of an ancient adobe village, and checked their horses down the side of a sage-covered bluff. Beyond, towering sandstone peaks jutted, streaked with the copper light of the west-angling sun.

At the ridge's base, beyond a grassy bank and a line of tall deciduous trees, lay a stream sheathed in downy fog.

The entire gang spread out in a long line just below the hill's brow. Sitting her dapple-gray ten feet off Considine's left stirrup, Anjanette could faintly feel the silky caress of the warm air from the stream against her face.

The sun had shone nearly every day of their ride from Saber Creek, but the air, except for a couple of hours at midday, was cold. She imagined shedding her clothes and soaking in the warm water, the fatigue draining from her saddle-sore bottom and thighs.

She was about to remark on the strange warm stream, when the fog thinned on the other side of the trees and she caught a glimpse of what appeared to be more ruins climbing the side of the far ridge—a honeycomb of houses sitting one atop the other, with crumbling walls and caved-in roofs. Several square or rectangular openings gaped out over the fog-shrouded stream, like the empty eye sockets of an emaciated skull.

The fog closed, and the ruins disappeared.

Leaning forward on his saddle horn, Considine

glanced at her. "Canyon of Lost Souls, the Injuns call it. The stream's called River of No Return. A few miles east it just slips into the ground, disappears."

"As many times as we've been here," said Mad Dog McKenna, at Considine's right, "this place still gives me the creeps."

"Gives everybody the creeps," said Latigo Hayes. "That's why it's a great place to cool our heels!"

"You mean *warm* 'em—don't you?" The black outlaw, Ben Towers, gave a groan of pleasure, hugging his shoulders. "That hell-fired water's the next best thing to a woman!"

Mad Dog glanced at Anjanette, then curled his lip at Considine. "Jack here has the real thing."

"So do I!" yelled MacDonald, putting his horse up beside Toots's mount and wrapping one arm around the big woman's stout neck, guffawing.

Toots rammed an elbow into his ribs, nearly throwing him off the side of his horse. The others laughed.

Considine glanced at the gang members gathered on both sides of him. "We'll hole up here for a couple days. Give the horses and ourselves a rest before we make the last pull to Junction Rock!"

"Sounds good to me, Boss!" shouted one of the men as he and the rest of the gang spurred their horses down the hill toward the trees and the thick fog beyond, yelling and yowling. Toots rode up beside Considine, glowered at Anjanette, then turned a dimple-cheeked smile on the outlaw leader. "If you want a *real* woman to soap your bones, Jack, I'll meet you at the river!"

With that, she ground her heels against her paint's

flanks and, cackling, galloped down the slope in the sift-ing dust of the others.

Considine turned to Anjanette. "Don't worry about her. She's just kiddin' around. She already got herself a beau at Junction Rock—a big bearded mestizo who runs a saloon and hunts bear. She's pure-dee stricken by that fool."

"In that case, it'll be nice to get to Junction Rock," Anjanette said. "I'm getting tired of looking over my shoulder at her."

Considine jerked the black stallion's bit to remind him who was boss. The abrupt reining and the nightly hobbling, as well as several sudden lashes from a bull-whip, had helped take the fire out of the stallion's eyes.

The outlaw leader turned to Anjanette, smoothing his thick, drooping mustache with one hand and dimpling his cheeks. "Come on! A long soak in that water is the closest to heaven I ever been this side of the sod." He winked and ran his gaze down to her breasts and back up again. "*Almost,* that is!"

He raked the black's flanks with his spurs, galloping down the slope while angling left of the other riders. Anjanette glanced once more toward the ruins concealed by the fog, suppressing a sudden chill, then threw her head back, shaking her black hair from her eyes, and put her steeldust after the stallion.

She'd ridden a hundred yards when Considine and Wolf disappeared into the cottonwoods and the fog. Anjanette followed, feeling the air grow warmer the closer she rode toward the river. She followed Considine's path through the trees, the fog enveloping her, the warmth pressing against her, the smell of sulfur filling her nostrils.

The steeldust's shod hooves clattered on the rocks, and then she could see the stream sliding along to her right, murmuring slightly. Ahead, the black stood with its reins wrapped around a stout cottonwood, its neck arched indignantly.

Anjanette looked around. "Jack?" She was surprised by how loud her voice sounded inside the gauzy fog, echoing off the rock wall on the other side of the stream.

Considine's voice came back, nearly as loud, slightly breathless. "Here!"

Anjanette gigged the steeldust ahead, saw Considine's blurred shape hopping around at the edge of the stream, kicking out of his jeans. When the denims lay in a pile among the small black rocks and gravel, he bent forward to shuck off his underwear, then splashed naked into the water, his pistol belt coiled around one arm, a cheroot protruding from his lips.

"Come on, girl!" His voice thundered. "Don't be shy. I got somethin' to show you!"

"Wait!" Anjanette called as she leapt out of her saddle. "You're gonna lose me!"

Ooose meeee, ooose meeeee! faded the echo.

Quickly, Anjanette tied her horse to a deadfall tree, then moved through the fog to the stream's edge, doffing her hat and unbuttoning her shirt. She jerked, startled, when shots exploded upstream—three quick reports followed a second later by a fourth.

A man laughed. Another howled, wolflike, the echoes

filling the canyon, seeming to somehow disturb the gently swirling fog.

Somewhere out in the foggy stream, Considine laughed. "Most Mexicans never come down here. Bad medicine an' such. But the boys must've run into someone who didn't wanna share their camping spot!"

He laughed again. There was the sound of splashing water.

When Anjanette had flung aside her skirt and pantaloons, she hefted her full breasts in her hands, soothed by the silky, warm fog touching every inch of her naked body. She stepped out into the lukewarm water, over the smooth, polished rocks of the bottom, hearing echoing laughter, splashing, and hooting from upstream. The water felt like warm milk as it inched up her calves, knees, and thighs.

She peered into the fog ahead, the far rock wall a purple mass before her. "Jack?"

"Come on, baby!" Considine yelled. "Follow my voice. There's a cave. Our own private bathhouse, and the water's hot enough to scald a pig!"

His echoing laughter was suddenly muffled. Anjanette cursed, at once soothed by the humidity and warm water pressing against her legs and spooked.

Ancient Indian ruins. River of No Return. Canyon of Lost Souls.

The fog became the tendrils of a million ghostly beasts; the laughter of the celebrating outlaws seemed to be the cackling of a thousand ancient Indian demons.

She moved to the rock wall, pressed her hands against the sandstone, and worked her way slowly upstream, raking her left hand against the stone. In the rock, she saw chiseled images of horned creatures and human stick figures with arrows sticking out of them and more figures leaping off a cliff into what looked like the toothy jaws of some snarling biblical beast.

The sandstone wall opened suddenly—the ragged entrance of a cave. The floor of the cave was the floor of the river, with a strong current pushing out of the cave and against her ankles. Ducking slightly under the low ceiling, she moved into the cliff face, the crenellated cave walls surrounding her, adorned here and there with more chiseled figures.

The air was moist and close, steam snaking around the protruding rocks, the smell as cloying as that of wafting powder smoke.

She peered into the steamy shadows, her vision penetrating only a few yards or so. "Jack?"

A voice sounded far back in the chamber, but she couldn't make out the words.

Anjanette continued forward, moving slowly along the cave's bending right wall, trailing one hand along the wall in case the bed of the stream suddenly gave way beneath her. She felt a burn of annoyance—why hadn't Jack waited for her?—and the nettling prick of fear as the bizarre wall etchings gaped out at her.

And yet the steam, the water lit by fires in the earth's bowels, and the exotic, mysterious cavern where she found herself naked, the sand almost hot beneath her feet, sent spasms of sensuous pleasure trembling through her, so that she felt the nipple of her left breast rise beneath her palm.

Even Jack's childish game of hide-and-seek was somehow compelling, alluring. Old Antoine's rough saloon, with its fetid spittoons and puddles of spilled whiskey, beer, and vomit, was already a distant memory.

She followed the stream around a long bend, peering ahead, the water gurgling against her thighs, moving ever deeper into steamy darkness. As the floor of the stream dropped slightly, the thick, warm water inching up to her belly, and all ahead was darkness, she let loose a curse and stopped.

"Jack, goddamn it, I've had enough! Where *are* you?"

She jumped with a startled grunt as arms snaked around her suddenly, hands closing around her breasts, squeezing. The body behind her pushed her forward brusquely. She stumbled in the deep water, the hands on her breasts holding her upright.

"Come on, little bitch," Considine barked. "Spread your legs for me!"

Her knees smashed into a large, flat boulder before her, and she gritted her teeth against the pain. "Jack, goddamn it, you're hurting me—"

Considine cursed and bent her forward across the rock, and before she could protest again, he spread her legs with his knees. She felt the sudden, sharp pain of his violent penetration and the burn of her bare flesh grinding against the boulder.

"Damn you!" she cried as Considine bucked against her, one hand on the back of her neck, pinning her head to the rock.

"You know you want it," he grunted. "You *always* want it!"

She gritted her teeth in pain as the outlaw leader bucked, grunting and digging his fingers into her hips. Her chin against the rock, she groaned and cursed.

Mercifully, it didn't take him long. When he finished and stepped back, releasing her, she pushed off the boulder, straightening, her feet sliding on the rocks.

She slapped him. The crack sounded like a pistol shot. *"Bastard!"*

Considine stared back at her. She couldn't see much of his face in the darkness, but the steady silver light in his eyes—at once cold, savage, insane—sent a chill down her spine.

As she fell against the rock, ready to parry a blow, Considine chuckled. His eyes softened. He brought a hand to his face. "I'm sorry, Chiquita." His voice was low, soft, barely audible above the gurgling stream. "I thought we were only playing."

Anjanette swallowed, crossed her arms over her breasts. "I don't want to play like that anymore, Jack."

She pushed past him and started wading back the way she'd come.

"Don't go getting serious on me, now, baby!" Considine yelled behind her, his voice darting around her like a ricocheting gunshot. "I was only *joking!*"

Chapter 17

At eleven o'clock that night, about three miles from the canyon where the Thunder Riders had holed up, Marshal Patchen filled his coffee cup from a speckled tin pot and sank back against his saddle. He glanced over at Sheriff Speares, who sat on a rock about six feet from the low cook fire, hunkered deep in his wool coat and staring out at the darkness while smoking a quirley and sipping from his own steaming coffee cup.

Patchen could tell that the sheriff was mentally licking his wounds. Speares had been made a fool of by the Thunder Riders, then saved by a man he'd thrown in jail. Knowing now that he shouldn't have jailed the breed in the first place—obviously Yakima Henry wasn't one of the gang members—was even more embarrassing.

Patchen absently fingered a raw buzzard peck on his right cheek. Of course, he was as much a fool as Speares, but Patchen had been a fool before, so he didn't take it as hard.

And he would be a fool again.

No man—especially a *lawman*—could expect *not* to

be a fool now and again on this savage frontier. The trick was to learn from your foolishness and to continue living in spite of it.

Patchen crossed his boots and hunkered down inside his mackinaw, resting his coffee cup on his thigh. "Tell me, Speares—why are you still so determined to take down this gang? Your nose is broken, your posse's been wiped out, you've been buried up to your neck in sand, nearly had your eyes pecked out, and you're over a hundred miles south of the border. Can't just be the *gold* you're after. *Or* the girl."

Speares continued staring into the darkness, holding his Winchester across his thighs. The quirley between his lips glowed brightly. He removed it, staring at the coals as he slowly exhaled tobacco smoke through his nose. "I used to ride with that kill-crazy bastard."

Patchen studied him. "Considine?"

"Several years ago, when I was a kid. He fed me to a catch party. For a *joke*. The bastards strung me up, left me hangin', damn near killed me. But I worked myself free. Gave up the owlhoot trail—'ceptin' a couple times—and vowed that if I ever had the chance I'd kill the murdering four-flusher."

Patchen laughed. "Instead, he got the gold you were guarding, shot up your town, and nabbed your girl!"

Speares turned a hard look on Patchen, holding the cigarette between the thumb and index finger of his right hand. "I'm glad you think it's so damn funny." He lifted his chin and squinted his eyes. "What about *you*? You're just as far from your jurisdiction as I am from mine."

The smile faded from the marshal's face as he stared

into his coffee, absently swirling it. He took a sip, set the cup back on his thigh. "I can tell you a better Considine story than that. About a year ago, he hit the town I was living in, shot up a saloon, and kidnapped my daughter. Took her off the street in front of the haberdashery. I tracked him into the mountains above Tucson, found Peg's naked body in the Salt River Canyon. She'd been beaten, carved up—"

Patchen took another sip of the coffee, his eyes hard as he stared out over the rim. "Before he hit Saber Creek, he shot a pair of rangers. Execution style. That's what I'm gonna do to him."

Speares sucked on his quirley as he looked off through the desert willows. "Not if I get to him fir—" He stopped, frowning, slowly reaching up to pluck the quirley from between his lips.

"What is it?" Patchen asked.

Speares threw out an arm as he continued staring through the darkness. "Quick—douse the fire!"

Patchen threw out the last of his coffee and sprang to his feet, kicking dirt on the fire. A second later he was crouched beside Speares, his Henry in his hands, following the sheriff's gaze through the willows and across the rolling, rocky slopes cloaked in starlit darkness.

It was hard to judge distance in this broken country, but about a mile away, a flickering, cone-shaped light shone. As Speares and Patchen stared, another, smaller light grew left of the first. A minute later, still another light appeared, quickly gaining vibrancy until it was as bright as the first two.

The three fires were about ten, fifteen yards apart.

The lawmen glanced at each other.

"What do you think?" Speares said.

"I think we got company," said Patchen.

"Strange time to be settin' up camp."

Patchen rubbed his sunburned chin. "Ain't it, though?"

"Think we oughta check it out?"

"It smells like a trap."

"If it's the gang, we might be able to pop a couple and get Anjanette out before they do to her what they did to your girl."

"If they haven't already," Patchen said.

"Once she's safe, we could go back in for Considine and the gold."

"On the other hand, we might be wandering into an Indian camp. Or banditos."

Speares smirked, impatient. "Well, now, how in the hell are we gonna know if we don't check it out?"

"I reckon you have a point." Patchen walked back to the doused fire, where smoke rose from the dusty ashes, and began gathering his gear. "We best break camp in case we need to split ass outta here."

When both men had rolled their blankets and saddled up, Patchen swung onto his horse's back. "Let's take it slow. Apache slow. They could be waiting for us between here and the fires."

"You know, Patchen," Speares said snidely, toeing his stirrup while holding his saddle horn, "you ain't the only experienced lawman out here."

Patchen turned his horse and gigged it around rocks and through the willows, heading toward the fires and grumbling. "Maybe not. But at least I *learn* from my experiences."

"I heard that," Speares said, gigging his own mount up beside Patchen's. "You're talkin' about that ambush, ain't ya? Well, goddamn it, I done told you I was sorry about that. Those sonsabitches are slick as damn snakes in a privy pit!"

"Don't be sorry," Speares said, swinging his head from left to right as he walked the horse down a rocky hill, starlight limning the sage, creosote, and occasional pine. "Just keep your mouth shut and your eyes open."

Speares muttered something too softly for Patchen to make out, reining his horse a few yards right of the marshal and raking his gaze across the brush and the low, rolling hills revealed by starlight.

Moving slowly, often stopping and listening, the lawmen worked their way to within a hundred yards of the fires. They dismounted, tied their horses to a couple of low pines in a crease between hogbacks, removed their spurs from their boots, and continued on foot, about twenty yards apart and holding their rifles up high across their chests. They stepped quietly, keeping a low boulder snag between them and the fires, stopping every few yards to look around and listen.

As they moved, they heard only the slight swish of the breeze in the brush, occasional owls and coyotes, and the pops and snaps of the fires on the other side of the rocks. Sparks rose above the rocks, winking out among low cottonwood branches.

Speares moved around left of the rubble while Patchen slipped to the right. The marshal hunkered down behind a boulder, squeezing his rifle in his hands, and peered toward the flickering firelight about thirty yards ahead.

The three fires burned in shallow pits. The wood had burned down some, falling with soft thumps and thuds, but the flames still reached several feet into the air.

Around them, no one. There was no tack or gear of any kind. No extra wood for keeping the fires burning. It was as if someone had merely set the fires and left.

Electricity fired through Patchen's veins. His first instinct had been correct. The fires were a trap.

He'd begun to retreat when the snap of a branch rose on the other side of the false encampment. He stopped, held his position, peering around the rocks.

In the brush beyond the firelight, a shadow moved. Flames winked off steel.

A spur chinged softly.

From somewhere above and left of the marshal, a rifle boomed, shattering the heavy silence. A man grunted, and there was the thud of a body falling in brush.

"It's a trap!" a voice shouted, pinched with fury.

Boots thumped and brush crackled as two figures materialized from the shadows on the other side of the fire, both aiming rifles. Patchen pulled his head back behind the rock as two slugs blasted the side of it, spraying sand and rock shards.

Patchen snaked his rifle around the rock and was about to draw a bead on the shooter, when the rifle above and left boomed again. The man on the other side of the fire screamed and flew straight back into the darkness, throwing his Winchester.

A rifle lever rasped, and there were two more quick shots. A man cursed shrilly to Patchen's left. There was a loud thump, followed by a crunch.

A wail rose, filled with such misery that Patchen's belly flip-flopped.

Patchen peered around the rocks and to the left and saw a man crawling out of the far fire, his back and arms aflame. Still screaming, he pinwheeled, flapping his arms as though trying to fly, and sprinted off into the darkness—a human torch lighting up the surrounding brush and trees.

About twenty yards away, he collapsed against a boulder, clung there for a time, legs moving as though he were trying to climb the rock, and gave another yell. It sounded like a horse's anguished whinny. Finally, the man slumped to the ground and lay there, flames leaping around him.

Patchen spied movement on the far left side of the rocks. Speares came slowly out from cover, crouching over his rifle as he peered into the darkness around the fire.

A shadow jounced in the tree ahead and to the left of Speares. Patchen tensed, brought his rifle up. At the same time, Speares swung his own rifle around, angling it up at the tree.

A familiar voice: "Hold on."

Firelight flashed off a brass rifle casing. A man dropped from a stout branch to the fork of the cotton-wood and from there to the ground, landing flat-footed, bending his knees. Long black hair fell across his shoulders, and his sweat-stained buckskin shirt stretched taut across his chest.

"Damn," Yakima said, shuttling his gaze from the burning man to a spurred boot lying at the edge of the firelight to the dead man behind the fire nearest Patchen. "They only sent three. I was hopin' for a few more."

As Patchen moved forward, lowering his rifle, Speares cursed. "You used us for bait, you son of a bitch!"

Yakima shook his head, peering cautiously into the darkness. "I just set a couple fires."

"You're a crazy son of a bitch, Henry." Patchen's gut burned. He was getting to be as big a fool as Speares, and he wasn't learning a damn thing from his foolishness. "How'd you know they wouldn't all come?"

Yakima shrugged. "I wouldn't send my whole gang to check out three campfires. Especially if I had gold to keep track of." Yakima racked a fresh shell into his Winchester's breech and off-cocked the hammer. He regarded the two lawmen with vague distaste. "If you two are gonna hang around, you might as well make yourselves useful. I've got a *hidden* camp up yonder in the hills. Fetch your horses."

He turned, started away.

Speares laughed caustically. "You gotta lot o' damn nerve!"

Yakima continued walking away. "It's gonna take nerve to take down the Thunder Riders."

"How do *you* propose to do it?" Patchen said, resting his rifle barrel on his shoulder.

Yakima turned, stared at him. "The Apache way." A

faint smile touched the hard, shadowed plains of his face. "The Cheyenne way."

He turned and disappeared in the darkness.

Flanked by the rest of the gang, Considine and McKenna stood before the ancient Indian ruins, at the edge of the steaming River of No Return. They stared toward the three campfires on the dark hillock north of the canyon, watching the sudden fourth blaze die as gradually as the echoes of the gut-wrenching howl that accompanied it.

The men around the gang leaders murmured among themselves.

McKenna turned to Considine. "Sounded like Prewitt."

Considine, who had sent Prewitt, MacDonald, and a northern gunslick named Belknap to investigate the three fires, which had appeared suddenly on the hillock a mile or so away, said nothing as he stared through the snaking steam, thumbs hooked in his pistol belt.

Apprehension trickled a single bead of sweat down the middle of his back.

He kept it out of his voice as he glanced at McKenna. "If the boys don't come back, take a couple of the others out at first light." He turned and walked back toward the gang's own campfires flaming here and there around the ruins, toward his bedroll and Anjanette.

Ben Towers stepped up beside McKenna, who continued staring at the distant fires. "What'd he say, Boss?" Towers asked.

McKenna sighed, glancing at the tall black man. "He

said that if them three don't show by sunup, he wants you to take Hayes, the Apache, and Joolie up to investigate."

With that, Mad Dog clapped Towers on the shoulder and followed Considine's path toward the gang's campfires.

Meanwhile, picketed with the rest of the gang's horses, but with a gunnysack tied over his head and all four feet hobbled with thick strips of braided rawhide, Wolf arched his neck suddenly. Through the burlap, he'd caught a familiar scent on the night breeze.

A recognizable man-smell drifting across the steaming water . . .

The smell was faint and fleeting. Still, the black stallion twitched his ears and snorted, his giant heart quickening.

Chapter 18

Just after sunup the next morning, Yakima, Patchen, and Spears lay belly down atop a low tabletop mesa, staring through rocks and brush toward the hillock where Yakima had set the three fires and killed the three Thunder Riders.

Yakima checked the hillock with his spyglass and saw four other desperadoes now gathered there. Three of them kicked around the brush, while one—a tall black man in a low-crowned brown sombrero and a deerskin jacket—knelt over one of the dead men. The black man held a Spencer rifle in one hand and looked around with the quick, cautious movements of one accustomed to tracking and being tracked.

"Well, they sent one more than last night." Yakima passed the spyglass to Patchen, who raised it to his bruised, sunburned face, adjusting the focus.

"Sent an Apache this time," Patchen said, staring through the glass. "Yasi, known as Kills Gold-Hairs for his preference for gold-headed white girls. He's so

depraved that even his own people won't have anything
to do with him."

"Kills Gold-Hairs?" Speares said with interest. "I
heard there's over a thousand dollars on his head alone."

"Lawmen and army trackers have dusted his trail,"
Patchen said, handing the glass to Speares. "No one's
even come close to him, though several have died
bloody."

"I reckon we're gonna get our chance." Speares lowered the glass and stared with his naked eyes across the
rolling chaparral. "They picked up our tracks, headin'
this way. Just three. The fourth seems to be headin' back
to their camp at the river—to report to Considine and
Mad Dog, no doubt."

Yakima reached over Patchen and grabbed the spyglass from Speares. "Remember the plan. Spread out and
give 'em plenty of sign but not so much they sniff the
trap."

He looped the spyglass's lanyard around his neck and
began crabbing straight back along the mesa. When he
was behind the mesa's brow, he rose and hoofed it back
down the opposite slope.

Their three horses waited at the mesa's base, tied to
scrawny willows. Patchen and Speares followed, grunting at their aches and pains, loosing dust and gravel
down the steep bank behind them, spurs singing softly.

Yakima leapt atop the buckskin and turned toward the
other two men reaching for their saddle horns. "We meet
back here. Don't get lost. It's a big desert."

He heeled the buckskin southwest, cutting through a
sharp draw between mesas. Behind him, Speares turned

to Patchen. "He's got one hell of a mouth for a half-breed."

Patchen swung into the saddle with a great creak of dry leather. "You tell him that, Sheriff."

Chuckling, the marshal turned his own mount north and galloped off around the base of a low piñon-studded mesa.

An hour later, Speares hunkered among boulders spilling down the right shoulder of a rocky scarp sheathed in creosote and gnarled elms. He stared down the other side of the hill, into a tangle of low pines and barrel cactus growing around another split outcrop of black volcanic rock.

Around him, birds and squirrels chattered. There'd been a javelina snorting around behind him somewhere, but it had drifted off not long after Speares had settled into the rocks.

A black widow spider crawled out of a crack in the scarp beneath his rifle, and Speares watched it, a tiny white dot on its tail, crawl up over his rifle barrel, just in front of the receiver, and disappear among pine needles and decaying leaves.

Less than a minute ago, a hoof thud had sounded from the split scarp ahead. Since then, Speares had lain cheeked up to the rifle stock, breathing shallowly through slightly parted lips, staring at the scarp, his heart thudding rhythmically in his chest.

Another thud, and the sheriff increased the tension on the rifle's trigger.

A bobbing horse head appeared—a blaze-faced dun

with a Mexican-style bridle, braided and inset with hammered silver disks. As the dun moved out from the narrow notch in the scarp, the black man in the saddle swung his head around slowly, his back taut but still moving fluidly with the horse's choppy steps.

His face was shaded by the broad brim of his brown sombrero, but Speares saw a short beard, a slender nose, and a wide, pale scar on his neck. The man moved his head back and forth, skittish as a mule deer in bobcat country.

Drawing a bead on the man's short buffalo coat, Speares continued easing back on the trigger until horse and rider slid suddenly behind the hill's brow, heading toward Speares's left.

Speares swore silently, pulled his head and rifle back behind the scarp, and scrambled as quietly as he could to the other side of the rock. He crawled atop the hill's shoulder, left of the projecting rock, and aimed down the slope.

The black man and the dun appeared, rising up out of the hill as though from the earth itself. The rider turned his head away from Speares. The sheriff's heart pounded as he held his breath and settled the rifle's foresight into the notch above the receiver, bearing down on the side of the black man's head.

The man whipped around so suddenly that Speares didn't realize what had happened until his hat had been blown off his head and the rifle report was echoing around the near ridges.

He stared, mouth agape, at the black man's smoking Spencer. The Spencer's stock was snugged to the man's right cheek, and he was twisted slightly in the saddle, aiming the rifle at Speares.

The sheriff's Winchester boomed.

The bullet slammed into the desperado's upper left arm, splitting the coat seam and throwing the man sideways. The horse screamed as the desperado tumbled down the right stirrup with a loud grunt, jerking the horse's reins and twisting the horse's head so sharply that the horse fell hard on its right side, as though its hooves had been cut out from under it.

The man groaned as the air burst from his lungs, and then the dun screamed again, thrashing and shaking its head and scissoring its hooves as it climbed up off the desperado and galloped away, buck-kicking and trailing its reins.

Behind the horse, the desperado writhed about in the dirt and gravel, rolling over several times, groaning, clutching both hands to his arm. His rifle and smashed hat lay several feet away.

Speares ejected the spent shell and rose slowly. The black man lay at the base of the slope, on his back, groaning and wagging his head from side to side. Speares leveled the rifle on him and scrambled down the hill, keeping his eyes on the still, dark form in the brush.

Where the man and horse had fallen, the dust and brush were flattened and blood-flecked. Blood followed the man's trail several yards down the slope, to where he now lay, belly rising and falling sharply, round eyes staring skyward, blood frothing from his nose and lips and down his chin, forming a red bib on his chest.

The desperado's eyes rolled toward Speares, the pupils expanding and contracting slowly.

Staring down, the sheriff grinned. "Sure wish I had time to cut your head off and haul it back to Tucson for the bounty, Towers. With that kinda money, a man wouldn't have to work a *real* job for months."

The man's eyes were flat and glassy, but his right hand moved feebly over the grips of the old-model Colt riding high on his hip. Speares leaned down, grabbed the gun out from under the limp hand, and tossed it down the slope.

The black man's mouth opened and closed several times, blood continuing to spill over his lips, before he was able to rasp, "Finish . . . me. . . ."

Grinning, Speares shook his head. "I'm gonna need all the lead I got for the rest of your gang." He turned, climbed the slope, and stooped to pick up his hat. Frowning, he poked two fingers through the hole in the crown and glared down at the dying desperado.

"Damn your hide! That was my best hat!"

Big, blond-headed Latigo Hayes reined his claybank to an abrupt halt and canted his head, listening to the rifle report. The echo of the first shot hadn't died before another boom echoed across the ridges.

Hayes sat the stout claybank tensely, his heavy jaw hard under its thin coat of curly blond whiskers and dust, wondering who'd gone down—one of his men or one of theirs, whoever "theirs" were. When the second echo had faded, followed by only the chittering of birds and squirrels, the big desperado glanced down at the hoofprints he'd been following.

They'd been leading him into the high, pine-studded hills east of the Canyon of Lost Souls. Lifting his eyes from the fresh tracks, he looked around warily, his thumb on the off-cocked hammer of his rifle. Seeing nothing but heavy brush and occasional pines and cacti, but needled by the feeling that a rifle barrel was aimed squarely on the back of his neck, he touched his spurs to the claybank's ribs.

He followed the tracks into a narrow canyon muddied by a runout spring. Watching the tracks carefully but also keeping an eye skinned on the rocks and brush around him, he followed the tracks out of the canyon and into another, where a small stone shrine nestled between two pines, the faceless figure of the Virgin Mary swathed in tree roots. A spray of wildflowers lay atop the shrine—brown and brittle as the dead leaves and pine needles around them.

The man Hayes had been following had stopped here. His shod hoofprints were set deep in the clay.

Looking around again and turning up the collar of his blanket coat—the air was cool though the sun was bright—Hayes gigged his horse up canyon. He followed the canyon into a wide valley, then into another canyon and through a gorge, taking a circuitous route that led nowhere. The big man's chest tightened, and his hands grew slick inside his gloves.

Tracing yet another, narrow canyon, he drew back on the clay's reins once more and found himself staring down at the same shrine he'd stopped at a half hour ago.

"What the—"

To his left, a horse whinnied. As his own horse answered the whinny, he shot a sharp glance up the ridge and into the pines rising beside him, the sun peeking through the columnar shadows.

Hayes's bowels churned with fear and fury.

He gritted his teeth, looking around wildly. "Where are you, you son of a bitch?"

A calm, deep voice sounded behind him. "Here."

Hayes jerked his horse sideways. Squatting atop the low canyon wall was a man with a high-crowned Stetson, silver muttonchop whiskers and mustache, and a copper star pinned to his buckskin mackinaw. The lawman grinned down the barrel of the Henry rifle aimed at Hayes's chest.

"You ain't Considine, but this is for my Peg just the same!"

Hayes sucked a breath to scream, but he hadn't finished inhaling before smoke and flames stabbed from the Henry's barrel, obscuring the toothy smile of the face at the other end.

Yakima knew the Apache was on his trail, because the Apache pony he himself was riding continued to sniff the breeze and snort, as though it smelled a familiar scent.

Having an Apache on your trail—especially one as infamous as Kills Gold-Hairs—was like having a rogue grizzly on your heels. Yakima couldn't move quietly enough, see or hear clearly enough. And every brush rustle or falling pinecone sent ice through his veins.

He'd been leading the Apache steadily up and over

several relieved ridges for nearly an hour before he found a low saddle with sheltering rocks from which to effect an ambush. He tethered the buckskin on the saddle's backside, well hidden among pines, willows, and rock outcrops, then made his way back to the saddle and hunkered down in a notch on its rocky spine.

Holding his Winchester up high across his chest, he leaned against a rock and stared down the saddle through sage, scattered pines, and occasional berry shrubs.

Minutes passed like hours. Clouds shepherded shadows across the slope and the distant blue ridges darkened as the sun angled west.

Yakima had just begun to wonder if the Indian knew where he was and was going to wait for him to poke his head out of the rocks—nobody could wait like an Apache—when a coyote's howl rose from somewhere downslope and to the right.

It was a wild, manic yammering. It went on for several minutes, lifting the hair along Yakima's spine. Yakima had heard young coyotes, strayed from their pack, kick up such a ruckus. But his gut told him this was no coyote.

Kills Gold-Hairs knew Yakima was here, somewhere among these rocks, and was trying to lure him out, to pink him from cover.

Yakima hunkered down, pressing his right cheek against the stone wall. He edged a look down the slope with his left eye, careful not to angle any shadows on the ground before the notch.

Another long minute passed.

Down the slope, a horseback rider appeared, the

man's long black hair buffeting in the wind. Astride a white-speckled dun, Kills Gold-Hairs moved up the hill toward the saddle, clad in denims and knee-high moccasins, red and black calico shirt with a beaded medallion hanging around his neck, and a floppy-brimmed brown hat.

Two revolvers hung in shoulder holsters. Two knives were snugged up tight against the man's hips, and he carried a Winchester carbine with a leather lanyard across his saddlebow.

The Apache moved easily in his white man's leather saddle, with almost insulting ease, a faint smirk on his face, eyes slitted. He zigzagged the horse through the scattered pines and shrubs, batting its flanks with his moccasined heels.

Suddenly, about fifty yards shy of the saddle, the Indian stopped the horse. He threw his head back on his shoulders, squeezing his eyes closed, opening and closing his mouth until the coyotelike yammering rose up the ridge to Yakima's ears.

The bizarre cry made Yakima's scalp tingle. He eased down his Henry's barrel, snugged his cheek to the stock, and rested a bead on the Apache's calico shirt.

Just as he was taking up the slack in his trigger finger, the Apache threw himself out of the saddle, hitting the ground on his shoulder and rolling. Yakima jerked the Henry's trigger back.

Ka-peewww!

Dust puffed from a bleached log.

The Indian bounded to his feet and ran through the trees and shrubs to Yakima's left. He dove over a low rise as Yakima fired another round. The slug plunked into the short grass a foot off the Apache's left moccasin.

And then the Indian was out of sight behind the brow of the hill, dust from the second strike scattering on the breeze. The riderless horse galloped back the way it had come, screaming and trailing its reins.

Yakima cursed as he ejected the spent shell, seated fresh, and bounded straight out of the notch. Taking the Winchester in one hand, he wheeled and climbed the rocks above the notch, quickly gaining the top of the scarp and squatting, extending the rifle in the direction the Apache had disappeared.

He caught a glimpse of movement, snapped off a shot. Knowing the Apache would try to get around behind him, he bounded down the back side of the scarp and sprinted down the hill. Gaining the crease between hills at the bottom, he turned north, climbed another steep ridge through scattered pines and shrubs, and snugged up to a boulder at the top.

A low rasping sounded on the other side of the boulder.

Slowly, Yakima scaled the rock and edged a look down the other side. Directly beneath him, the Apache clung to the rock in mid-climb, his Winchester hanging by the lanyard down his back. His lips were stretched back from his teeth, and his brown eyes bored into Yakima's.

He was so close that Yakima could see the pores in his sweat-slick skin, the distended cords and veins in his neck, and the missing eyetooth revealed by his stretched lips.

Yakima rose from a crouch, lowered his Winchester's barrel. At the same time, the Indian whipped his hand up toward the top of the rock. Yakima's left boot was jerked out from beneath him, and the ground bounded up suddenly to slam against his back. His finger jerked back on the rifle's trigger, and the sudden boom flatted out across the pine-carpeted ridges below, the slug sailing skyward.

Before Yakima knew what had happened, the Indian was on top of him, slashing down with a stout-bladed bowie. Yakima threw his left hand up, caught the Indian's right wrist, stopping the blade inches from his throat, and bucked straight up with a desperate yowl.

The Indian grunted as he flew, twisting and turning in midair, across the boulder and out of sight.

A resolute thump sounded from somewhere behind and below, and there was the rattle of falling gravel.

Yakima drew a deep breath, wincing at the pain at the back of his head, then lurched to his feet, and glanced down the far side of the rock.

At its crenellated base, the Indian lay impaled, belly up, on a sharp branch sticking straight up from a deadfall pine. The man's arms and legs sagged toward the ground. The eyelids opened and closed several times before freezing half closed. One foot jerked and fell still.

Blood bubbled up around the forked branch protruding from the Apache's torn shirt and belly.

Breathing hard, Yakima sleeved sweat from his forehead. He spat dust and grit from his lips, turned to retrieve his hat and Winchester, then began descending the rock.

The killing had just begun.

Chapter 19

From somewhere beyond the edge of Anjanette's sleep, a light thud sounded.

Considine's arm shot out from under her head. He reached across his own body, grabbed one of the revolvers from his matched holsters, and, thumbing back the hammer, aimed the barrel straight out at the fire guttering in the stone ring near his and Anjanette's blanketed feet.

Sparks rose from a short ash-white log along the edge of which a slender orange flame flickered.

Propped on one arm, Anjanette slid her gaze from the fire to Considine staring wildly at the flames, his index finger drawn taut against the trigger.

"Just the fire," she said, reaching out to push the gun down.

"Shit." Considine depressed the hammer, then slid the revolver into the holster beside him. He fell back against his saddle and drew his blankets to his chin with a yawn.

Anjanette lay back against her own saddle for a time, staring at the luminous sky. It was close to dawn. Behind her, she could hear the gurgle of the river, feel its warmth penetrating the chill night air.

She closed her eyes, drew the blanket up to her chin, but she could tell that sleep wouldn't return. Damn Considine and his nerves. He was always so eager to take a shot at something or someone.

She sighed, threw her blankets back, and rose to her knees.

Considine turned to her sharply, frowning. "Where you goin'?"

"For a swim."

He stared at her, his brows ridged.

"Is that all right?" she asked sarcastically. "Should I have asked permission first?"

"No," the desperado leader said reasonably, resting his head back against the saddle. "That's all right, I reckon." He lowered his hat over his eyes and crossed his arms on his chest. "There's woolly hombres out there. Stay close. Take a pistol."

As Considine's chest began rising and falling rhythmically, Anjanette stood, wrapped a blanket around her shoulders, pulled her boots on, and headed off through the ruins toward the river sliding through the fog at the bottom of the canyon. She stepped around a couple of the sleeping gang members. Knowing that three were posted around the ruins and on the ridge overlooking the canyon, she aimed for a thick stand of cottonwoods lining the river, out of sight from above.

On the shore, screened from the ridge by the stout trees, she kicked out of her boots, shucked out of her skirt, shirt, and underclothes. She shivered, feeling a dank chill in the warm fog. Cupping her breasts in her hands, she stepped into the river.

The water felt like ink rising over her knees and hips as she waded toward a pool in a slight horseshoe a few yards downstream. In the pool, she sank down, enjoying the sensation of the warm liquid closing over her.

For a time she lolled there, thinking about Considine. She regretted getting mixed up with the desperado leader. She saw now that he had two faces. Before throwing in with the gang, she'd been shown only the face of the sweet, roving rogue. He was much coarser, darker, angrier than she'd expected. Anjanette was no hothouse flower, but Considine's predilection for violent lovemaking left her feeling cheap and frightened.

She'd seen what he'd done to Yakima's horse. Any man who would pistol-whip a defenseless animal was no man to keep company with.

But then, if she went back to Saber Creek, Old Antoine would only continue to work her like a rented mule. In five years, she would look like one of those Indian War widows who tended chickens and took in laundry in their brush huts along the creek.

Anjanette cupped the lukewarm water over her breasts, lolling back in the stream.

Yakima.

There was a man who knew how to treat a woman. His touch had been neither too gentle nor too harsh. There was a man who, born and bred in the wild, owned a strange sensitivity. While reveling in his own manliness, Yakima could treat a woman to the sweet sublime. Even now, she could feel his big hands, his lips, the sweep of his long hair on her breasts, his hips thrusting between her thighs, his muscular buttocks flexing beneath her hands.

The problem with the handsome half-breed was that he was as untamed as his horse. Lonely, to be sure. But a loner just the same.

She wondered where he was now. He'd no doubt searched for his horse, because Yakima and the black mustang were like blood brothers. Maybe he'd given up by now, realizing that no one man could tangle with the Thunder Riders. He'd probably bought another horse in Saber Creek and returned to his mountain cabin, alone.

A hand closed over Anjanette's shoulder and she jerked her head around with a start. Behind her in the snaking mist, staring down at her stonily, Toots loomed, silhouetted in the weak dawn light. Naked, the big woman looked like a pale pumpkin with breasts resembling half-filled gut flasks. Her round belly bulged out beneath them. She had pulled her hair back in a bun, a few strands wisping about her plump cheeks and expressionless eyes.

"Jesus," Anjanette said, crossing her arms on her breasts and closing her legs. "You scared the hell out of me!"

Toots held out her hand. Anjanette half expected to see a stiletto in it. Toots slid the grimy sliver of lye soap toward her. "Wash my back."

Anjanette stared at her, the water flowing around her waist and Toots's chubby, dimpled knees.

Toots jerked her hand, frowning impatiently, and said

as though speaking to an idiot, "You wash *my* back, and I wash *yours*."

Anjanette glanced at the soap, then at the woman's eyes, still half expecting a trick of some kind. Seeing no cunning in Toots's expression, Anjanette lowered her arms and climbed to her feet. Toots's gaze slid across Anjanette's breasts, her expression softening.

"If you want your back scrubbed," Anjanette said, taking the soap from the woman's hand, "turn around."

Toots turned. Anjanette crouched to dampen the soap, then rubbed it between her hands until she'd worked up a good lather. She applied the lather to Toots's back, inwardly recoiling at the feel of the woman's soft flesh under her palms, the bowed shoulders, a wedge of flaccid breast peaking out from under her right arm.

"Mmmhhhhhh," Toots groaned, lifting her head. "That feels good."

When Anjanette had finished lathering the woman's back, she held the soap over Toots's right shoulder. "Here."

Toots sank down into the water and plucked the soap out of Anjanette's hand. Again, her eyes strayed across Anjanette's full breasts. "I'll wash you."

"No thanks."

Toots frowned and put some steel in her voice. "I wash *you*."

Anjanette held the woman's gaze. Was Toots, in her own awkward way, trying to bury the hatchet?

Anjanette shrugged, turned around.

"Bend down," Toots ordered.

"Huh?"

"You're taller than me. Bend down a little."

Anjanette bent forward. Toots began running her soap-lathered hands across Anjanette's back. She was a little chagrined at the pleasant sensation of the soft, soapy hands on her skin. Toots stopped scrubbing, touched her finger to a slight bruise just beneath Anjanette's right shoulder blade.

Anjanette sucked a sharp breath through her teeth.

"That hurt?" Toots asked.

Anjanette didn't answer.

Toots continued scrubbing, rubbing both palms up and down and across Anjanette's slender back. There was a faintly mocking tone in Toots's voice. "Jack getting rough?"

"Nothing I can't handle."

"One thing you can expect outta Jack." Toots ran her right hand down under Anjanette's arm, sliding her fingers across the side of Anjanette's round, firm breast. "He'll get rougher."

"I can get pretty rough myself." Anjanette clamped her arm taut against her side.

"Me, though," Toots said, sliding her hand down Anjanette's other side and snaking it forward to cup that breast, palming the nipple. "I can be slow . . . *easy*-like."

Anjanette thrust Toots's hand away and turned, crossing her arms on her chest, an angry flush rising in her cheeks. "I don't care how *slow* and *easy* you are. Keep your hands off my tits and don't come near me again!"

There was no warning signal in Toots's eyes before she slammed the back of her right hand against Anjanette's jaw—a stinging blow, a fire ripping through Anjanette's lower lip.

As Anjanette's head flew back, Toots leapt toward her, wrapping her hands around her neck. Anjanette tripped on the slippery rocks and fell on her back in the water. Toots fell on top of her, driving Anjanette's head under the water as her fingers pressed into her neck, pinching off her wind.

Anjanette thrashed, panicking as the back of her head was ground against the rocks and the water washed over her face.

She looked up through her own bursting air bubbles to see Toots's face pinched with fury just above the surface, teeth gritted. She ground her knees into Anjanette's chest and ribs and dug her fingertips into her throat, as though trying to claw out her windpipe.

Anjanette, choking on water, flailed with clawed hands, but Toots, grinning maniacally, tipped her head back out of reach. Feeling as though her lungs were about to explode, Anjanette raised her right leg and pushed off the river bottom with every ounce of her remaining strength.

Toots flew to the side, splashed into the river. At the same time, Anjanette bounded up, water flying off her body, sucking air down her battered throat between choking coughs, her nose burning. She'd barely gotten up when Toots was on her again, rising up out of the river and throwing her head into Anjanette's belly.

Again they went down, but this time Anjanette twisted, punching her right fist against Toots's cheek so hard that Anjanette's own knuckles barked painfully. The

big woman screamed and tumbled sideways. As she
lifted her head once more, Anjanette staggered toward
her across the rocks, water splashing up around her legs,
and jabbed her again with her other fist.

Toots screamed as her head flew back, and one arm
dropped in the water. When she turned toward Anjanette
again, the left side of her bottom lip hung down like a
bloody leech.

Fire flashed in Toots's eyes. With a great rumbling
shriek rising from deep in her chest, she leapt toward
Anjanette.

They went down together, rolled, struggled back to
their feet, shared slaps and punches, grunting and
yelling. As Anjanette turned to parry another in a series
of vicious blows, she glimpsed the rest of the gang,
which had dwindled to only seven or eight men, gathered
along the shore in various states of dress.

Behind the webbing curtain of fog, they hooted and
yipped and clapped. A couple of them, including Toots's
brother, Tomas, were shaking hands as though a bet had
been placed. Considine stood before a willow snag in
only his long underwear, boots, and cartridge belt, fists
on his hips, grinning bemusedly around a cold cigar.

Anjanette turned back toward Toots as the big woman
lurched forward and gave Anjanette's right breast a
savage twist. Anjanette cursed sharply. Laughter and ap-
plause rose on the riverbank.

Made lucid by fury, Anjanette ducked a haymaker,
then brought her right fist up hard into Toots's plump
belly. Toots spat out a Spanish epithet and dropped to her
knees, then lurched forward and pulled Anjanette's feet

out from under her. Anjanette hit the rocks hard. Knowing how fast Toots could move in spite of her size, Anjanette quickly regained her knees, but somehow Toots had wrapped her arms around the back of Anjanette's neck.

Snaking her hand under Toots's arms, Anjanette dropped her head and slung the big woman over her right shoulder.

"Ahhh!" Toots screamed, hitting the river on her side and sending up an enormous, thundering splash.

Again sucking air down her battered windpipe, Anjanette scrambled to her feet. Toots pushed onto her hands and knees, hanging her head with exhaustion, bleeding from the half dozen cuts and scrapes on her face, arms, and knuckles.

Anjanette staggered before her, grabbed her under her arms, hoisted her up.

Toots's dark, dazed eyes met Anjanette's.

"If you know what's good for you"—Anjanette head-butted the big woman so hard that Toots's eyes rolled back in her head and she went limp in Anjanette's arms—"you'll stay the hell away from me, bitch!"

Anjanette dropped her arms. Toots fell into the river, lolled on her back, arms and legs spreading out around her in the current. Covering her breasts with her arms, already feeling one of her eyes swell and licking blood from her split lips, Anjanette headed for shore.

The men standing on the bank were exchanging money. Considine held her blanket out while Mad Dog stood beside him, grinning and squinting through puffs of cigarette smoke.

"I'm impressed, Chiquita," Considine said. "Not many men, let alone women, have ever beaten Toots in a fair fight."

Anjanette grabbed the blanket out of his hands, wrapped it around herself and under her arms, folding it closed. She sneered at Considine and Mad Dog, then stooped to gather her clothes and stalked off through the trees.

When Considine had pocketed the twenty dollars he'd won from Mad Dog, he turned and began walking back toward the ruins and Anjanette. Nothing got him randier than two women fighting naked.

He'd moved only a couple of yards before a Mexican-accented voice called, "Hey, Boss. Look there!"

Considine turned. Toots's brother, Tomas, was out in the river helping his sister to shore. He'd stopped several yards from the bank and, holding the big woman with one arm, pointed toward the opposite side of the river.

Three horses stood at the edge of the water, staring toward Considine. The other men had begun dispersing and heading back to their morning coffee fires before Tomas had yelled. Considine stared at the horses. At first he didn't think they were carrying riders, but he saw now that he was wrong. They were carrying riders, all right—the riders were sitting backward on the saddles, and they were lying belly down across their cantles.

Unless the fog was creating some sort of illusion . . .

Considine threw his cheroot into the river. He glanced at Mad Dog, then moved into the river, heedless of the water rising over his boots and climbing past his knees and thighs. He took long strides against the stream, swinging his arms, frowning at the three horses watching him warily, snorting, twitching their ears and flicking their tails.

The water dropped back down Considine's legs as he approached the opposite shore. Mad Dog and the other men spread out to his left and slightly behind—all except Tomas, who stood with Toots on the opposite shore, staring across the sliding, fog-shrouded stream at the horses—two duns and a claybank.

Considine stopped several feet in front of the clay belonging to Latigo Hayes and ran his gaze across the horse's saddle. His beard bristled and his face warmed.

Latigo Hayes sat the saddle backward, leaning forward so that his face was pressed against the horse's spotted ass. Latigo's hands and ankles were tied under the horse's belly; his face was turned toward Considine, tongue protruding slightly, sightless eyes half open and staring at something downstream. He wore no hat, and his blond hair was ruffled by the morning breeze.

Considine moved around behind the clay. The other men were moving up around the front of the horses, water sluicing off their underwear bottoms or denims, frowning as they cast their gazes across the three horses' grisly cargoes.

Yasi and the black outlaw, Ben Towers, both sat their own saddles the way Latigo sat his—backward and dead.

Considine looked at Mad Dog staring at him over the ass of Tower's dun gelding. He didn't say anything, but his half-grizzled face looked even more grizzled than usual, the mottled skin drawn tighter across the bone, the right eye narrowed to a slit.

"Banditos?" Considine said, his voice trembling with rage.

"That'd be my guess," Mad Dog said. "They seen us carryin' the gold, trailed us here. They're tryin' to pick us off a little at a time until there's nothin' left but the gold."

"I reckon it's time we all mounted up and got after 'em," said one of the other riders, holding the bridle of Hayes's paint.

Considine turned and stared up the low hills rising away from the river, toward the surrounding blue mountains growing more and more distinct as the sun rose.

He shook his head. "That's what they want. So they can run us to a frazzle and bushwhack us somewhere off in them mountains."

He shuttled his gaze this way and that. Anger was burning in him. Anger and the emotion he enjoyed least—fear. Someone was toying with him, playing a nettling little game of cat and mouse. The stalker hadn't yet gotten the gold, but the fact that they'd wiped out nearly half his gain—so quickly and cunningly—meant that they were winning.

Eventually, they'd get the gold.

The idea of him being whipped like this, by an unknown enemy, was enough to blow the top of his head off.

He gritted his teeth so hard they cracked. "We'll stay right here. Let them come to *us*."

"I reckon that's the best." Mad Dog glanced at the others standing around the horses before following

Considine's gaze toward the mountains. "Though I sure would like to run those jaspers down. Teach 'em you don't mess with the Thunder Riders."

Considine looked around, counting the men they had left. Including Tomas, on the other side of the stream, there were seven.

Considine's eyes darted up toward the ruined mud shacks climbing the canyon's southern wall. "Hey, who's supposed to be guarding the gold?"

The other six men glanced at each other. Finally, the half-breed Sioux, Quint Broken Bow, turned to Joolie "clubfoot" Hale.

"I . . . I reckon I was," Hale said, running a gloved hand through his shaggy beard. "I just come down to see what all the commotion in the river was about."

Mad Dog's cheek dimpled. "You mean that gold is sittin' up there in them ruins *unprotected*?"

Hale backed away toward the river, shuttling his sheepish gaze between Considine and Mad Dog, hemming and hawing and wringing his hands.

"Haul ass, fool!" Considine shouted.

Hale jumped with a start and stumbled into the river, heading for the other shore.

Considine turned to the half-breed. "Go with him, Quint. From now on I want two men guarding the strongbox at all times!"

He looked again at the three dead men and made a sour expression, eyes narrowed. "I can't *wait* to meet the smart sonsabitches who done this! I just can't *wait*!"

Chapter 20

Yakima woke at midnight. He lifted his head from his saddle, threw his blankets back, reached over in the cold darkness, and jerked Patchen's left boot. The marshal gave a startled grunt and snapped his head up, a hand dropping to the holster on his hip.

"Time to move," Yakima said quietly.

Patchen froze, glanced at Yakima, then turned and nudged Speares, lying a few feet away. The sheriff, too, woke with a start, looking around wildly until he realized he wasn't about to have his throat cut by the Thunder Riders.

It was dark as tar in the hollow where they'd cold-camped, and Yakima began rolling up his blankets and gathering his gear mostly by feel. Yawning and grumbling but not saying anything, the lawmen followed suit, and in a few minutes all three horses were rigged and ready. The men swung into their saddles, the creaking of the leather sounding dangerously loud in the quiet, frosty night. Low clouds sharpened the slightest sound, but the

absence of moon and stars would make Yakima's job in
the canyon easier.

He and the lawmen rode southwest. Because of the
darkness, they had to hold their horses to a trot. An hour
after they'd left the camp, the giant stone walls of an ancient Spanish cathedral rose on a low mesa before them,
glowing as though from a faint light within the crumbling, vine-shrouded stone.

At the cathedral's east end, Speares and Patchen
checked their horses down among the rubble of the collapsed ceiling and the giant, cracked pillars.

Yakima merely slowed the buckskin as he continued
southwest. "I'll try to lead them this way. Stay alert."

He batted his heels against his mount's ribs, continuing on across the sloping mesa.

"There he goes again," Speares complained, leaning
forward on his saddle horn.

"You can take it up with him after we've got the gold,"
Patchen said, swinging down from his saddle. "After
we've kicked the rest of that gang out with a cold shovel."

Speares dug in his shirt pocket for his makings sack.
"Shit, if that crazy half-breed can sneak into that canyon,
find the gold and the girl *and* lead that crew into our rifle
sights, I might just give him my badge."

Chuckling softly, Patchen led his horse off. "What
makes you think he'd want it?"

Yakima had spent his whole life drifting around the
American West and Old Mexico, where he'd done some
prospecting a few years ago. He knew that every ride
took longer than expected.

Still, the ride back to the warm-river canyon, which he remembered the Yaquis called the Canyon of Lost Souls, was frustratingly long. The ridge before him rose with teeth-gnashing sluggishness, like a curtain of black velvet inching above the pale fog to stand high and jagged peaked against the clouds.

He skirted the canyon's center, where a previous scouting mission had told him the desperadoes were camped, and crossed the river at a rocky ford a good mile east of the ancient ruins. A few days ago, he'd spotted a notch in the canyon wall—a talus-strewn chimney—and this he and the buckskin negotiated slowly, carefully. The slope was steep, the talus unstable.

Halfway up the ridge, Yakima dismounted and led the horse, wincing at every clatter of falling rock behind him. The desperadoes probably had no pickets this far from the main camp, as they'd lost too many men for such an extravagant precaution, but this was desperado and Yaqui country. It was said that few Indios ventured into the canyon, which was supposedly filled with evil spirits, but it was a known hideout for Yanqui and less superstitious Mexican bandits.

At the top of the ridge, Yakima ripped the blanket and bridle off the horse, turned it south down the slanting ridge crest, and slapped its rump. As the horse trotted away in the darkness, Yakima swung his rifle over his shoulder by its rope lanyard and began making his way east, staying well back from the canyon.

When he'd walked a good mile and found himself staring down the steep canyon wall at three fires shivering in the rocks on his side of the fog-capped river, he sat down and removed his boots and socks. He hadn't been able to get close enough to study the ridge wall in the daylight, so he picked a route now in the darkness and hoped that luck and whatever dark gods remained in the canyon chose to either smile on him or ignore him.

Hoisting himself over the lip, he crabbed down the wall, grinding his fingers and toes into any dimples or fissures he could find. A couple of times, holds gave way and he found himself hanging by one hand and a foot or, in one case, only the first two fingers of his left hand until he swung back toward the wall and ground his big toe into a crack.

The toe rubbed against something at once leathery, furry, and prickly, something that apparently made its home in the crack. The bat shot out from under Yakima's foot, screeching. Gritting his teeth, he dug his fingers and toes into the wall and hung there until his heart slowed.

Continuing to spider down the wall, he glanced below. The dark smudge of an ancient mud roof rose slowly toward him. A couple of viga poles protruded from one wall, while a chimney—or what remained of a chimney—climbed the one opposite.

His fingers and toes were leaving blood on the wall behind him by the time he dropped to the mud roof. He bent his knees and hunkered low, praying that the roof would hold. It did. He looked around, hearing nothing but the wind shunting against the stone, the rattle of a falling pebble, and the occasional screech and sinewy flap of a bat somewhere above.

Tossing his sweaty hair back from his face and swinging his Winchester behind his shoulder, he stole over to the edge of the roof and crept down a crumbling stone stairway. Avoiding caved-in floors and fallen walls, occasional storage pits and cisterns now home to only snakes, rats, and insects, he made his way down the ruins. Occasionally he used a ladder, testing it first to make sure it would support him.

He was nearly to ground level when he moved across a crumbling ceiling, dropped slowly down a short, inside staircase dank with spring water, and hoisted himself over a stone wall. He dropped his bare feet to the mud-and-grass ceiling below, testing its weight carefully.

It seemed solid until he began to stride across it. With a lurch and a crack, the floor suddenly disappeared beneath his feet, and he plummeted straight down through darkness. He grunted sharply when his feet hit the ground, then again when his back slammed against the hovel's earthen floor. He lay blinking against the ancient mud and grass tumbling down around him.

When the rain of debris ceased, he spat grit from his mouth and blinked up at the hole he'd fallen through—a ragged opening about four feet in diameter. He squinted up at it, steeling himself for a complete cave-in.

There were a couple of creaks and groans, and a mud clump fell in a corner with a thump, but the rest of the ceiling held.

Yakima shook the debris off his legs and belly as he turned onto his side. Planting his knees, he was about to rise when a low voice sounded outside.

He froze, listening.

Boots ground gravel and spurs rang softly, growing louder until Yakima could hear the labored breathing of two men approaching from his right. Moving slowly, he grabbed his rifle and crawled to the wall facing the canyon. He hunkered down in a dark corner, opposite the hovel's low, narrow door, and drew his knees to his chest. Hoping that he would blend in with the wall shadows, he held the Yellowboy low, so no light would reflect off the brass receiver.

He stared at the door, little more than an opal smudge in the darkness, on the other side of the low mound of ceiling rubble. The footsteps approached, the two men now setting their feet down slowly, carefully. Yakima drew a deep breath, held it.

Outside, whispers.

A minute passed, and then a shadow moved in the gray doorway, almost indistinguishable from the shadows around it. The shadow stopped. There was the high, soft whistle of air drawn through a nose. The musty air of the hovel mixed with the smell of sweat and fresh gun oil.

Yakima's throat grew dry as stove wood as he stared at the stationary shadow in the shape of a man's head and shoulders. If he had to fire a shot, he'd have the entire gang on him in seconds.

Go on, he silently urged. *No one's here.*

After a few beats, the man in the doorway cleared his throat and turned back out through the door. From a ways off, another man called, "Anything over there?"

"Looks like another ceiling fell in. We best get back to the strongbox."

Yakima waited, listening as the footsteps receded. He let his breath out slowly, and rose, hefting his rifle. Wincing at the ache in his lower back and left hip, he crossed to the door and stared out.

A couple of fires fluttered down the hill toward the river. More ruins humped around him in the darkness, in various shades of brown and gray.

Yakima stole down the slope, his bare feet moving silently across the sand and gravel. He held his rifle high, a fresh round seated, the hammer cocked. Several times, dropping down the slope toward the river, he stopped, listening, his eyes searching close about, then farther out, then farther still.

The canyon was eerily quiet, the ruins like grave-stones. Occasionally a mouse moved in the brush. Above the canyon, where the clouds had thinned, a meteor arced across the sky, trailing sparks. To his right and left, low fires flickered. He cat-footed down the slope between the fires, then worked his way downstream through the brush.

First he would find Wolf and get the stallion ready to ride. Then he'd look for Anjanette. The gold was a pe-ripheral concern. Once he'd led the desperadoes out of the canyon and into an ambush, Speares and Patchen could come back for the strongbox.

When he'd moved a hundred yards downstream, Yakima stopped suddenly and dropped to one knee behind shrubs. A figure stood twenty yards before him, between a stand of willows and the stream. A young woman in a long skirt and a man's shirt. Long black hair hung down her back. Her arms were crossed on her chest as she stared out over the fog-shrouded water.

Anjanette . . .

Yakima looked around, then rose to a crouch, began to move around the shrubs. The sound of a spur ching froze him. Another figure, taller, materialized in the darkness beyond Anjanette, heading toward her.

Yakima dropped back down behind the shrubs, peering through the branches. The tall man, wearing a low-crowned, silver-trimmed hat and drooping mustache and carrying a Winchester over his right shoulder, sidled up to Anjanette. He wrapped an arm around her, leaned his head close to hers. She shrank away slightly.

He could hear the man's smooth voice, but he couldn't make out the words. Yakima frowned through the shrubs as the man drew Anjanette close, muttered something, then slowly lowered his head and kissed her forehead. She put her hand on his chest and said something too softly, intimately, for Yakima to pick up, then rose up on her toes and kissed the man on the lips. They both chuckled softly, turned together, and walked through the poplars and willows and up the slope toward the fires.

Yakima sat hunkered down behind the shrubs, frowning. Gradually the befuddlement cleared until the picture swam into focus.

Anjanette and Considine.

Anger stabbed him, sharp as a Yaqui spear. He ran the

back of his hand across his mouth, ground the Yellow-boy's butt into the sand. After a time, kneeling there, his head swimming, he chuckled, rose slowly, and continued upstream.

He'd gone fifty more yards when he heard a soft nicker on his left. He climbed a natural levee and walked slowly through cottonwoods toward a patch of manzanita grass. Before him, seven or eight horses were tied to a picket rope strung between two trees. Moving up to the horses slowly, cooing softly to placate the skittish beasts, Yakima raked his eyes across each.

There was no black in the bunch.

Where was Wolf?

His stomach churned with dread. Having been trained to carry only Yakima, Wolf would have been a contrary mount. Considine or one of the other gang members might have shot him.

Yakima stepped wide of the horses, looking around for both Wolf and a possible guard. He'd taken only a couple more steps when a voice rose on his right, from about ten yards away.

"Hey!"

Yakima turned, froze. A man's hatted silhouette stood between two cottonwoods. He wore an old Confederate greatcoat and hat, and he was crouched over a carbine. Behind him, the foggy river slid by.

The man moved toward him slowly, keeping the rifle leveled on Yakima while shifting his head slowly from right to left and back again. No doubt looking for others.

"One move, and I'll drill you." He moved closer, still swinging his head. "Drop that iron."

Yakima crouched to lean the Yellowboy against a tree bole. The armed man moved up on his right, prodded his side with the carbine's barrel. He was a little shorter than Yakima, thick-bearded, with long hair falling over his shoulders. His coat was open, revealing revolvers on both hips, positioned for the cross draw. He reeked of tequila. He must have left the horses to take a piss.

He kept his voice low, pitched with caution. "You alone, amigo?"

Yakima grinned. "Only a fool would come alone, amigo."

"Where's your friends?"

Just then, a horse whinnied somewhere off in the darkness. It was a shrill call, a plea. The man turned his head toward it. Yakima leapt toward him, nudged the rifle wide, and slammed his right fist into the man's jaw—a savage blow that knocked the man straight back, off his feet, with a groan.

He landed on his back, cracking branches. Lifting his head, he brought the rifle back around, but Yakima pinned his arm to the ground with his bare left foot, then bent down and drove his fist into the man's face. When the man's head bounced off the ground, Yakima punched him again, then again, until he'd smashed his face to a bloody pulp and the man lay limp at the base of a cottonwood.

Wheeling, Yakima grabbed the Henry and dropped to a knee, holding the Henry straight up and down in his hands as he snapped his head around, peering into the darkness, listening. Behind him, the horse snorted and whinnied softly.

Wolf.

Deciding that none of the outlaws were headed this way, Yakima rose and strode back into the darkness. He stopped. Before him stood the black stallion, two ropes looped around his neck, tying him taut to a tree on each side.

"Easy, boy, it's me." Yakima moved slowly forward, noting the rawhide hobbles on the horse's feet. "Shh. That's it. Quiet."

He ran his hand along the horse's back as he walked up beside him. Moving toward his head, he saw the gunnysack draped over Wolf's snout. No holes had been cut for his nostrils. The burlap dimpled as the stallion breathed, sucking air through the tightly woven fabric.

Tied, hobbled, and blinded! Yakima set his rifle down, reached up, and slowly peeled the sack down over the horse's long, fine snout. "You must have raised holy hob with those bastards!"

The black's molasses eyes stared back at Yakima, the pupils expanding and contracting quickly as he bobbed his head with joy, snorting happily.

"Easy, easy," Yakima said, running his hands down the horse's snout, feeling the six- or seven-inch gashes. They'd partially healed over, but some of the cuts still oozed blood and pus. When he probed one such spot with his fingers, Wolf jerked his head up sharply.

"It's all right, boy. Easy. I'm not gonna hurt you.

What'd those bastards do to you, anyway? They'll soon wish they hadn't tangled with either—"

A voice rose behind him. "Yakima?" He spun around, snagging his .44 from its holster and thumbing the hammer back.

But the voice had been familiar. And a familiar figure stood before him now, ten feet away.

Anjanette stared at him through the darkness, her long black hair framing her face, the silver crucifix winking softly between her high, proud breasts.

Chapter 21

Yakima's finger closed over the trigger, and the gun quivered slightly in his clenched fist. Anjanette stared at the gun pointed at her chest, then at him. She held his saddle by the horn, his blanket, bridle, and saddlebags draped over it. Her breathing was ragged.

She slung the gear forward, dropped it in the dust at Yakima's feet. "Figured you'd need these."

Yakima looked around. "Where's Considine?"

"He headed off to powwow with Mad Dog."

Yakima kept the .44 aimed at her. "Any of your compadres know I'm here?"

She stared at him coolly, then, unable to hold his gaze, looked down. "Only me. When I heard Wolf, I figured you'd come." She looked up at him. "How did you know—"

"I saw you with Considine."

Absently, she lifted a hand to one of the many bruises on her face. "I made a mistake. It wasn't the first one. Probably won't be the last." She stepped forward, placed her hand on his forearm. "Take me with you."

Before he knew what he'd done, he'd slapped her with the back of his right hand. Her head flew sideways, and her hat tumbled off her shoulder.

Yakima's voice was tight. "Between here and Saber Creek, there's anywhere between twenty and thirty men dead because of you and them."

She shook her hair back from her face and stared up at Yakima, her dark eyes bright with tears. "I didn't know what he was like. I didn't know what *any of it* would be like!"

"So, now you know, and you want to run home to your grandfather, just like nothing happened?" Yakima grabbed the bridle and turned to Wolf. "Well, I'm not your ticket. If you want to go home, you'll have to find your own damn way."

"Please!" She sobbed as Yakima slipped the bridle bit through Wolf's teeth, then draped the harness straps over his ears. "I'm scared, Yakima. Considine's crazy. They're *all* crazy!"

Yakima spread the blanket over Wolf's back, followed it with the saddle. "Killers usually are."

When he'd cinched the latigo under Wolf's belly and slung his saddlebags over the horse's rear, Anjanette wrapped her arms around Yakima's waist, pressed her head against his back.

"We shared a night together, Yakima," she whispered. "Doesn't that count for anything?"

Yakima spun around, his jaw taut, and grabbed her by one arm and the back of her neck. He ran her into the willows and was about to heave her into the river when a voice sounded up the bank behind him—clear and conversational in the quiet night.

"I'm relievin' ya, Jimbo. Go on and . . ."

Yakima froze, then whipped his head to see a shadow standing atop the dark bank on the other side of Wolf. The shadow jerked suddenly, bringing a rifle up. "Who's there?"

Yakima released Anjanette's arm and slipped his revolver from its holster. He loosed two quick shots over Wolf's back. Bounding forward, he leapt into the stallion's saddle. A rifle cracked to his right, the slug curling the air along the back of his neck.

Holding the black's reins taut with his left hand, Yakima loosed two more shots up the bank. He gigged the horse toward Anjanette, then reined the horse in a tight circle.

"Climb up, goddamn it!" He fired two more rounds into the inky darkness.

Anjanette leapt forward, grabbed Yakima's hand, and swung up behind him as the rifle on the hill flashed and boomed twice, the slugs plunking into the willows behind Yakima.

"Hold on!" Yakima shouted, reining the sure-footed stallion in another tight circle, then giving him his head. They galloped downstream, the black stallion chewing up the damp shoreline with his long, plunging stride. The horse laid his ears flat against his head, snorting with every breath, leaping driftwood logs and dodging boulders.

Behind, the man on the bank squeezed off two more shots, both rounds plunking into the river to the left and behind Yakima and Anjanette. Shouts rose from the ruins.

The man behind yelled, "Rider headed downstream with the girl! Cut him off!"

As if on command, a gun flashed ahead and to the right, from just above a rocky knob. The boom made Wolf tense his shoulder muscles. The slug whistled over Yakima's head and splashed into the river.

Yakima tightened his jaw. He'd wanted to reach a shallow ford another thirty yards downstream, but the shooter on his right stood above the rocky knob, aiming a Winchester. Yakima swung the black into the river at the same time the desperado triggered another shot. The slug plunked into the water just off Wolf's right shoulder.

The horse whinnied. Her arms wrapped tightly around Yakima's belly, Anjanette cursed.

Yakima hunkered low and batted his heels against the stallion's flanks, urging him into the fog. "Move, boy!"

Rifles and revolvers clattered behind them, punctuated by angry shouts and the scuff of heels on rock.

Someone shouted, "He's straight out in the water, fer chrissakes! *Shoot* the bastard!"

A slug barked into a rock just right of the long-striding stallion. Wolf gave a start, and there was the angry scrape and splash of a shod hoof slipping on a half-submerged rock. The horse leaned sharply right, his head swinging left. Yakima reached for the saddle horn too late. He and Anjanette slid down Wolf's right side, taking the saddle with them.

Anjanette screamed as she followed Yakima into the river, the horse plunging onto his side and trapping

Yakima's right leg underneath. Yakima winced against
the sharp pain of a half ton of horse grinding his leg into
the rocks and sand under three feet of water. But before
he'd fully realized what had happened, Wolf was pulling
his hooves back beneath him, slipping and sliding on the
slick rocks, lifting a wild whinny.

Heedless of the sharp pain in his right hip and knee,
Yakima rose, pulled Anjanette up by one arm, and swung
her back behind him. Guns flashed and popped on the
opposite shore, the slugs whistling around Yakima's
head, splashing into the river.

As Wolf gained his feet, the saddle hanging down his
right side, Yakima grabbed his Winchester from where it
had fallen between two rocks and quickly raked a fresh
shell into the chamber.

"Lead the horse to shore!" he shouted to Anjanette,
spreading his legs and firing the Yellowboy from his
right hip.

He continued peppering the desperadoes' shoreline,
hot cartridges arcing and sizzling into the river behind
him, until the Winchester clicked empty. He slung the
rifle over his shoulder and, stepping straight back in the
water, grabbed his revolver from its holster and fired two
more rounds. He'd try to hold as many shooters at bay as
he could until Anjanette and Wolf had made the opposite
shore.

He stumbled backward, shooting at darting shadows,
flinching at occasional gunfire on the bank before him.
Glancing behind, he saw the girl and Wolf topping the
brow of a hill on the opposite shore.

Yakima fired the last two rounds in his six-shooter as

two slugs ripped into the river around his ankles, then turned and ran to the opposite bank. Water sluicing down his denims and sand clinging to his bare, wet feet, he bulled through willows and ironwood shrubs, climbing the bank and diving over the ridge just before three slugs tore up gravel and sand behind him.

He scrambled on down the bank to where Anjanette held fast to Wolf's reins, the stallion snorting and starting at the gunfire.

"Easy, boy, easy!" Yakima said, slinging the rifle over his shoulder again.

"You go on ahead," Anjanette said, breathless, holding the stallion's reins in both hands, her wet hair hanging limp on her shoulders. "They'll be after you now. I'll only slow you down."

"Don't tempt me." Yakima righted the saddle and reached under Wolf's belly to tighten the latigo strap. "Now they'll kill you for sure."

Thumbing cartridges from his belt loops into his Winchester's receiver, he climbed back up the bank and took a cautious look over the lip. The river gurgled between its fog-shrouded banks. None of the desperadoes were wading across. But yells and shouts rose from the direction of the horses, upstream about sixty yards.

They were saddling up, preparing to give chase. Three were just now galloping along the opposite shore— jostling shadows within the fog—riding downstream toward the ford.

Yakima slung his rifle behind his shoulder, then plucked his Colt from its holster and thumbed open the loading gate. Except for his finding out Anjanette's ugly secret, all was going according to plan. He just had to make sure the desperadoes stayed on his trail till it led them to Patchen's and Speares's ambush.

When he'd filled the Colt's six cylinders, he triggered two shots over the lip of the bank, in the direction of the three riders now splashing across the river ford to his left, then turned and ran down the bank, grabbed the reins out of Anjanette's hands, and swung into the saddle.

"What were the shots for?" she asked as he slung her up behind him.

"Wouldn't want to lose your friends."

She tightened her arms around his waist as he gigged the horse up the opposite hill and down the other side, racing into the gradually rising northern hills. Keeping the horse to a moderate gallop and glancing back to make sure the desperadoes' shadows were still behind him, he angled east, in the direction of the cathedral ruins.

He hoped he could follow his own back trail in the dark. The Thunder Riders were coiled up and rattling, and he'd need the lawmen's help to take them down.

Wolf wanted to run full out, but Yakima checked him down, not wanting to lose the horse to a chuckhole or rock or one of the many narrow, deep gullies that scarred this high Mexican desert. He also didn't want to lose the Thunder Riders, though several glances behind gave him no reason to worry. The bouncing shadows snaked out through the darkness about a hundred yards away, moving fast and showing no sign of slowing down. As the gang passed before a pale rock wall below him, Yakima was able to count seven riders.

Staring down the ridge, Yakima said, "Nabbing you piss-burned him good. I don't think he even left anyone with the gold."

Anjanette turned toward Yakima. "Is that why you took me? For bait?"

It was only half the reason, but Yakima said, "Why else?"

He turned the black away from the ridge crest and heeled him up a narrow pass between jagged rock walls sheathed in creosote and sycamores. The cloud cover had thinned, and the stars and a sickle moon cast a ghostly illumination onto the trail, which was probably an old Spanish smuggling route.

The better light allowed the gang to push their horses harder. When the jumbled cathedral ruins rose on the mesa ahead of Yakima, the desperadoes were probably only seventy yards behind him—close enough that he could hear their shouts and the occasional chuffs and blows of their mounts.

Yakima loped the horse on past the ruins, looking around but seeing no sign of Patchen or Spears—they were probably snugged down among the crumbling rock and adobe, waiting. Fifty yards beyond the ruins, Yakima turned Wolf off the trail and behind a steep shelf of sandstone rising like a ship's prow above the chaparral.

"Stay here," he told Anjanette as he swung his right foot over the saddle horn and dropped to the ground, slinging the reins over a cedar. He slipped his rifle off his shoulder and rammed a shell into the chamber.

"Yakima," she called as he climbed the steep, stone-scaled rise.

He paused to glance back at her. She'd moved up into his saddle and regarded him over her shoulder. Wolf was contentedly cropping galetta grass.

"Be careful," Anjanette said softly.

He studied the rocky ledge before him, thoughtful. Shucking his revolver from its holster, he turned back. "Catch." He tossed the gun down to her, and she caught it with both hands in the air above her head. "You might need that."

He hoisted himself over the lip of the rise, gained his feet, and jogged back in the direction they'd come from, weaving through the cedars, creosote, and Spanish bayonet, staying left of the trail. When he saw the cathedral ruins cropping up ahead, he ducked into a boulder snag and wedged himself into the cracks, with a good view from forty yards away.

The trail passed between him and the ruins.

He stared along his back trail, his own shod hoofprints limned by the light from the moon and stars. In an arch of the ruined church, he picked out a man-shaped shadow. Either Patchen or Speares, waiting.

Yakima turned back up the trail. The gang should have arrived at the church by now. Back in the direction of the canyon, nothing moved. A heavy silence weighed upon the desert. Not even the lonely yammer of a coyote or the sinewy flap of a bat's wings.

"Breed," Speares called from the shadows of the ruins.

Yakima's gut tightened. *"Shhhh!"*

"They follow you?"

Somewhere behind Yakima a twig snapped.

As he turned to look, a horse whinnied on the far side of the cathedral. He turned back to the church as two rifles spoke, one after another, echoing inside the ruins.

Speares shouted, "They're behind us!"

Three more rifle shots exploded across the night.

Men shouted. Horses screamed.

Chapter 22

At the same time that rifles and revolvers barked in the direction of the hulking church ruins, hoof thuds rose in the dark scrub behind Yakima. He whipped around. Guns flashed in the scrub, bullets barking off the rocks around him, peppering his face with sand and gravel.

He scrambled onto his heels, dove right as two more slugs tore into the rocks where he'd been crouched. He brought the Winchester up as two riders burst out of the brush—a dun horse on his right, a cream on his left. Starlight reflected off trace chains and gun iron.

Yakima rolled onto his right shoulder and levered the Winchester until five smoking casings lay in the gravel behind him and both riders had tumbled back or side-ways from the saddles of their screaming horses.

One horse bounded past Yakima, and the other swerved so sharply right that it fell in the loose gravel. It scrambled to its feet and galloped away. Behind it, dust sifted and gun smoke webbed. The fallen desperadoes thrashed and groaned. The nearest one heaved onto a knee and clawed a revolver from a shoulder holster.

Yakima stood and drilled a round through the man's chest, punching him back in the dust with a clipped grunt. He fired two more rounds into the other man, stilling him as well.

Hearing guns popping in the ruins behind him, Yakima dropped to a knee and began reloading the Winchester from his cartridge belt. He'd risen and turned toward the ruins when the rake of a sharp breath rose on his left.

As the clouds scudded away from the moon, casting a pale radiance across the night, he jerked his head around. A big man with long black hair leapt off a boulder, gritting his teeth as he plunged toward Yakima, a revolver in one hand, a wide-bladed bowie in the other. Knowing he had no time to bring the Yellowboy to bear, Yakima dropped the rifle and threw his hands up.

The revolver in the man's right fist barked. The slug tore across the top of Yakima's right shoulder. At the same time, Yakima grabbed the man's left wrist, jerking the knife wide.

Yakima fell straight back. The man—a half-breed by the look of him—fell on top of him. He released the revolver and hammered Yakima's face with his left fist, then wrenched his knife hand free of Yakima's grip. As he raised the knife for a killing stab, Yakima plunged his flattened hand, palm down, fingers out, wrist-deep into the man's gut. He angled it up toward the heart.

Unlike the Chinaman who'd taught him the maneuver, Yakima had never been able to snatch the beating heart from a man's chest. But his own hand was nearly as effective. The big half-breed raked a hoarse breath through gritted teeth and froze, eyes nearly popping out of their sockets. His fingers uncoiled around the knife handle.

As the bowie hit the ground near Yakima's shoulder, Yakima slid his .44 from its holster, rammed the barrel into the half-breed's gut, and fired twice.

The man sagged forward. Yakima shoved him aside and got to his feet. He picked up the Henry and looked around the moonlit scrub as he thumbed more shells into the rifle's loading gate. His chest rose and fell sharply, and his breath puffed visibly in the air before his face.

Behind him more shots rose from the other side of the ruins.

With one more glance around the quiet scrub, he wheeled and sprinted across the trail toward the cathedral, following the erratic reports to the north front corner of the hulking ruins.

Thirty feet beyond lay a low adobe wall. Two men crouched on Yakima's side of the wall about fifteen feet apart, triggering rifles over the wall's lip and into the small cemetery beyond.

As a gun barked among the silhouetted shrines and crosses limned by the milky moonlight, one of the men behind the wall cursed and sucked air through his teeth. "Son of a bitch damn near took my ear off," Speares yelled.

To his left, Patchen triggered his Henry repeater over the wall, then ducked down and glanced at the sheriff. "What did you think they were gonna do—shower you with roses?"

He jerked up again and triggered two more quick

shots, eliciting a sharp curse from deep in the cemetery's shadows.

Yakima ran crouching toward the wall, announcing himself to the lawmen. He ducked behind the wall between them, pressing his back against the crumbling adobe bricks.

"Shit," Speares said, thumbing fresh shells into his Winchester's breech. "I figured you was dead." The shells clicked on the rifle's loading gate as the sheriff stared at Yakima. "You find my girl?"

Yakima glanced at him, lips parted, hesitating. He was glad when Patchen cut in: "You kill all them sons-abitches on that side of the church, Yakima, or do we gotta watch our backsides?"

"I killed all the ones that tried to kill me," Yakima said, pausing to return a shot from the cemetery with three from his Yellowboy. When the shells had clattered into the dust behind him, smoking, he levered another fresh round. "That isn't to say I got 'em *all*."

"We accounted for two over here," Speares said, reloading his Winchester as Patchen fired behind Yakima. "But three more pinned 'emselves down in a stable yonder."

Yakima thumbed the last of his .44 shells into his Yellowboy and squatted on his haunches, looking up and down the wall. "I'll try to swing around behind—"

A man called from the shadows, cutting him off. "Hey, assholes!"

Patchen chuckled. "Speares, I think you're being summoned."

"Funny." Speares edged a glance over the wall's lip,

toward a ruined stable hulking up at the far end of the cemetery. "Are *you* assholes ready to give up?"

"Don't count on it, friend," the desperado yelled. "But we *are* tired of hunkering down out here like greaser cowards, using up all our ammo. What do you say we all show ourselves like real men, finish this thing out in the open?"

Yakima turned toward Patchen, who was crouched behind the wall, his hat off, staring toward Yakima. Yakima looked at Speares. The sheriff shouldered up to the wall, rammed a fresh shell into his Winchester.

Yakima edged a look over the wall toward the stable. The pearl moonlight angled over the thatch roof, silhouetting the two small windows. "No one starts shooting until we're all out in the open?"

"Square's square," rose the reply.

"Hey, Yakima," Patchen said. "You got a couple extra .44 shells?"

Crouching, keeping his head just below the wall's lip, Yakima moved down to where Patchen sat in the dust, his back against the wall, his hat on the ground beside him. A bullet had burned a bloody line across his right cheek.

Yakima ejected two shells from his Yellowboy. He held them out to the marshal, who plucked them off the palm of his gloved hand, then shoved the first shell into the Henry's loading tube.

He squinted one eye. "Sorry about the misunderstanding at Saber Creek, huh?"

Yakima glanced over the wall, spying a couple of

moving shadows near the stable. "Just don't be late with that Henry."

He stood, stared across the cemetery. The three men were moving out from the stable, one with his rifle barrel resting on his shoulder. The other two carried their rifles at port arms.

Yakima swung a leg over the crumbling wall. To his right, Speares followed suit, moved up beside Yakima. Patchen stepped up on his left.

Moving out, the three matched their strides to those of the three desperadoes walking toward them, the moonlight dropping down over the outlaws' hat brims to limn their unshaven faces and deep-set eyes. The one on the left wore an eye patch and bowler hat, and had two pistols strapped low on his thighs. The man in the middle had long hair and silver hoops hanging from his ears. The right side of his face was badly scarred, that eye as white as the moonlight pooling on his broad hat brim.

As the three moved to within twenty feet, the short man on the right passed under a leafless sycamore, and the moonlight angled across his hatless head to reveal a Mexican woman's plump, round face and her flaccid breasts jiggling behind her heavy tasseled poncho.

Her expression was as hard as any man's, and she carried a carbine repeater in her gloved hands.

"Just my luck," Speares grumbled. "I been wantin' nothin' more than to drill a pill through Jack Considine's forehead, and here I am facing a *woman*."

"That's no woman," Yakima said. "That's a killer."

When the desperadoes were about fifteen feet away, the man facing Patchen stopped suddenly, jerked his rifle up, and swung the barrel forward. The man with the hoop earrings stopped and crouched a half second later, grinning savagely as he spread his feet and snapped his Winchester toward Yakima.

As the man with the bowler fired at the marshal, smoke and flames stabbing from his rifle, Yakima snugged the Yellowboy to his right hip and fired, the Winchester leaping in his hands. The man with the hoop rings fired his own Winchester twice in the time it took Yakima to squeeze off three rounds.

As the woman shrieked and hurled Spanish epithets amid the gunfire that she and Patchen exchanged, Yakima fired two more shots at the man with the hoop rings. Concentrating solely on his own target, he continued striding forward through the smoke and echoing reports and gun flashes.

The man with the hoop rings shrieked and dropped to one knee, firing his own rifle one-handed, the bullet plunking into the ground three feet in front of Yakima. The gun flash revealed bloodstains in his torn duster and a gushing wound in his right cheek.

As Yakima moved forward, his rifle clicked. Calmly, he set the empty Yellowboy down against a wooden cross, then, hearing shouts and rifle reports behind him, slid his Colt from its holster and thumbed back the hammer.

The man with the hoop rings fired another errant shot, pushed to his feet, and ran staggering off toward the stable, his bloody duster flapping like wings around his legs.

"Turn around," Yakima said.

Behind him, Speares yelled above the sporadic shots behind him, "Why won't you die, you *bitch*?"

The man with the hoop rings dropped his rifle and continued past the stable. Near a cluster of pecan trees, he dropped to his knees, facing away. Suddenly, he spun, aiming a revolver.

Yakima continued walking toward him, firing once, twice, three times. The outlaw jerked with each shot, triggering his own revolver skyward. Yakima's last shot blew the top of the man's head off.

He fell on his side, kicking for a long time before he lay still.

Holding his pistol straight down at his side, Yakima turned. The shooting had stopped. A couple of figures were slumped amid the stones and crosses. Striding back through the cemetery, he saw the woman lying on her side to his left. To his right, the man with the bowler hat lay slumped forward over a gravestone.

Continuing forward, he found Speares lying on his side, clutching his chest with one hand, his upper left thigh with the other. His hat was off and his hair flopped in his eyes.

"Bitch *shot* me!"

Yakima knelt beside him, ripped the sheriff's neckerchief off his neck, and wadded it up. As he stuffed the cloth into the hole in Speares's chest, footsteps rose on his right. He turned to see Patchen staggering toward him. Blood shone on the marshal's forehead, above the previous bullet burn. He cradled his left forearm across his chest, wincing, sucking air through his teeth.

The marshal glanced at Speares. "How bad he hit?"

"Can't tell," Yakima told him.

Patchen looked down at Yakima. "How is it you always make it out o' these scrapes clean as a whistle?"

"Not this time." Yakima closed his hand over the throbbing wound in his upper right arm. He had several more burns—one along his side, another along his neck—but the shoulder wound needed tending first or he'd bleed to death.

Wincing and squeezing the wound, he looked around, listening, wondering if any desperadoes were still alive and lurking.

As if in reply to his silent question, a horse whinnied shrilly somewhere off in the darkness. Yakima whipped his head around, trying to get his bearings. As he did, another scream lifted. A girl's scream.

Anjanette.

Yakima wheeled, stumbled over a gravestone. Shoving the pain in his arm to the back of his mind, he hobbled and skipped over the graves, making his way toward the adobe wall. As he leapt the wall, a revolver popped in the distant hills, and the horse screamed shrilly.

His gut tightening, Yakima sprinted west around the cathedral, striding through the chaparral, heading back toward the shelf where he'd left the horse and the girl. As he ran, he levered the Winchester, but the magazine was empty. He dropped his hand to his cartridge belt, but all the loops were empty as well.

He paused to set the rifle down against a boulder, then, grabbing his revolver from his holster, continued to sprint through the chaparral, leaping cacti and rocks and deadfall branches. When he came to the shelf where

Anjanette and Wolf had been, he stopped and aimed the revolver straight out from his shoulder.

Only rocks and gravel and the several gnarled piñons.

A horse snorted to his left. Yakima bounded that way, leaping an ocotillo. He stopped suddenly. A long black shape lay in the galleta grass before him. Yakima felt as though a lance had pierced his ribs.

Wolf was down, his sleek black coat glistening in the starlight. The horse was on his side, breathing hard, the right stirrup rising and falling rapidly. As Wolf's eyes rolled back toward Yakima, Yakima spied the dark fluid gleaming behind the horse's ear.

Yakima moved forward slowly, suddenly feeling as though his moccasins were filled with lead. The horse snorted again, jerked his head as though trying to lift it. Blood gushed from the wound behind his ear.

"Easy, boy," Yakima whispered.

The horse stared up at Yakima, beseeching, sliding one hoof forward, but slowly the lids began to fall.

Yakima held out his hand, knees trembling as he crouched down beside the black. A revolver popped ahead, the flash puncturing the darkness about fifty yards away and up a slight rise. A girl groaned.

A man yelled, "Sorry about the horse, but he's been trouble since the day we met! I don't know how you ever put up with such a contrary beast!" The mocking laugh died suddenly. "If you want the girl, you're gonna have to come and get her."

Anjanette gave a clipped, anguished cry.

Yakima straightened and peered up the rise. Two shadows stood side by side against the stars. As Yakima strode toward them, leaving the dying horse behind him, unable to put Wolf out of his misery, rage fueled a strange calm inside him. Keeping his eyes on the pair at the top of the rise—Anjanette and a man in a funnel-brimmed Stetson decorated with silver conchos—he picked his way through the brush.

In his right hand he squeezed the stag grips of his .44, keeping the barrel aimed at the ground.

Anjanette's voice trembled. "Don't come any closer, Yakima. He'll kill you."

Yakima moved slowly up the slope, the two figures growing and sharpening before him. One arm crooked around the girl's neck, aiming a revolver at her temple, the man was grinning, white teeth gleaming beneath his mustache.

A handsome, dimple-cheeked devil in a string tie, checked vest, and gaudily stitched deerskin coat: Jack Considine.

As Yakima topped the rise and closed the gap between himself and the desperado and Anjanette, the man's eyes narrowed nervously. He shuffled straight back, pulling Anjanette along with him. Her boot clipped a stone, and she stumbled, but Considine held her tight against him, pressing the barrel of his revolver against her right temple.

She stared at Yakima, her eyes bright, teeth gritted. The silver crucifix nestled in her cleavage winked in the starlight.

As Yakima stopped ten feet from Considine and the girl, the desperado's smile grew cold. He looked Yakima up and down, spat to one side. "So you're the bastard after my gold and my woman."

Yakima gripped the Colt so hard his knuckles throbbed. He no longer felt the wound in his left arm. "The woman and the horse. I have no use for the gold."

Considine's right eye narrowed slightly, then both eyes dropped to the gun in Yakima's fist. "Drop the gun and I'll turn her loose. *Don't* drop the gun and I'll kill her."

"Her life for mine?"

"That's right. Hold on to that gun, and you'll *both* die."

Anjanette snarled a curse as she struggled against Considine's arm, curled taut around her neck. Tears welled from her eyes, dribbled down her bruised, dusty cheeks. "Don't do it, Yakima."

Yakima held Considine's gaze with an implacable one of his own. He squeezed the Colt's grips, slid his index finger back and forth across the trigger. Hot blood coursed through him. Several times, standing there, he felt his hand begin to lift the revolver, and in his mind's eye he aimed at Considine's head and pulled the trigger.

He looked at Anjanette, her chest heaving as she stared back at him.

Considine slowly uncoiled his left arm from around her neck and shoved her out in front of him, holding the revolver behind her back. He extended his left hand toward Yakima, palm up, and dipped his chin slightly. The corners of his mouth lifted, the dimples in his cheeks deepening.

Yakima wanted to lift his hand and turn over the gun.

But he kept seeing Wolf lying dead in the grass behind him. His grip on the revolver wouldn't loosen. Before he knew what he was doing, he'd jerked the Colt up. He aimed straight at Considine's head, thumbed back the hammer, and squeezed the trigger.

Click!

He glanced at the aimed Colt in horror.

He'd fired all six shots. His eyes flicked back toward Considine. The desperado's lips bunched with fury, eyes blazing.

There was a bark, and as the revolver flashed and smoked behind Anjanette, she jerked as though struck by lightning, her eyes snapping wide. The bullet opened her shirt and flung the crucifix straight up in the air as it hammered out of her chest and nipped Yakima's right arm before careening into the darkness behind him.

"No!" Yakima shouted.

As the girl was punched forward and off to Yakima's right, crumpling, Yakima leapt toward Considine. He grabbed the wrist of the desperado's gun hand, shoved the revolver out to his left as Considine tripped the trigger. The pistol's bark was still echoing as Yakima bulled the outlaw straight back and down, ramming his fists blindly at the desperado's face.

The hill dropped sharply behind them, and Yakima found himself, his own limbs entangled with Considine's, rolling down the hill through sand, gravel, and sage, cacti nipping at his arms and legs and shoulders. Halfway down the hill they bounced off a boulder, separated, and continued rolling down side by side until both piled up at the bottom, at the edge of a dry creek bed.

Blood oozing from cuts and scrapes, his head swimming from the fall, Yakima gained a knee and peered along the bank. Considine struggled to his own knees, grunting and wheezing. He reached down toward his right boot, straightened with a pistol in his hand.

There was a ratcheting click as he thumbed the hammer back.

Considine's shoulders rose and fell as he caught his breath, and his lips stretched, perfect teeth flashing. He straightened and turned to face Yakima, raising his gun hand heavily.

Hoofbeats sounded suddenly, quickly growing louder. The ground trembled beneath Yakima's knees. He and Considine glanced toward the hill. An enormous ink-black figure plunged off the side of the hill like a tidal wave.

Considine screamed and raised an arm above his head. With a bone-chilling shriek, the black stallion bulled into Considine, lifting the outlaw two feet straight up and then punching him back into the riverbed, hat and revolver flying in opposite directions.

"*Aaghhhhh!*" Considine groaned as he smacked the dry creek bed's rocks with a thunderous thump, then rolled as the horse's scissoring hooves kicked and dragged the outlaw into the middle of the wash.

"No!" the outlaw screamed as Wolf galloped toward the opposite bank, then spun and headed back toward the writhing desperado.

Considine lifted his head and ground his heels into the rocks, trying to crab backward on his butt. "Call him off! Call him *off*!"

Wolf pitched with an enraged scream, wide eyes glowing with reflected starlight, mane buffeting wildly. He drove his front hooves into the man's gut and chest and groin, then bounded up on his back legs to repeat the maneuver until Considine's shrieks subsided to guttural sobs and then, finally, silence.

Holding his right hand over his wounded arm to stem the blood flow, Yakima gained his feet and moved to the edge of the streambed. Wolf continued pitching, snorting, and blowing, shaking his head wildly, mercilessly pummeling the outlaw with his front hooves.

On the rocks, Considine looked like a smashed scarecrow, half stripped, broken, and bloody. He moved only when the horse's hooves hammered him, his dead body bouncing up and down and rolling among the rocks.

Yakima walked into the streambed, placed his hands on the horse's neck. Wolf, about to bound off his front hooves once more, froze. He turned his head toward Yakima, pupils expanding and contracting, vapor jetting from his nostrils, ears twitching. Blood matted the top of his head, rippling down the white blaze on his snout.

"Easy, boy," Yakima said, running his hand up the horse's sweat-lathered neck toward his head. "You nailed him, pard."

He held Wolf's head still as he inspected the wound behind his ear. There was a lot of blood, but it appeared the bullet had ricocheted off the horse's skull.

Yakima chuckled as he probed the inch-wide gash with his fingers, holding the horse's snorting head still between his arms. "That hard head of yours saved your life, you stubborn son of a bitch."

He grabbed the reins, adjusted the saddle, and swung heavily into the leather. He gigged the black back up the hill, plodding slowly. When he saw the dark figure in the grass, he stepped down from Wolf's back and knelt beside Anjanette. She lay twisted on one side, her face in the grass, hair fanned out around her head.

The wound in the middle of her slender back had made a large black stain. He placed his hand on her shoulder, about to turn her over, but stopped. Instead, he lowered his hand to her lush hair, caressed the back of her neck.

Footsteps down the hill jerked his head up.

When Patchen announced himself, Yakima rose slowly, removed his neckerchief and wrapped it around his arm. Stooping, he snaked his arms under the dead girl, then straightened and laid her body facedown across his saddle.

Patchen moved up on his right, glancing at the body. "Who killed the girl?"

Yakima began leading the horse down the hill toward the ruins. "I reckon I did."

Epilogue

Yakima and the lawmen built a fire in a ravine half a mile from the ruins, trying to avoid desperadoes, Indians, and other predators possibly summoned by the gunfire and the smell of fresh carrion.

Patchen and Yakima dug the bullets out of each other's hides and sutured the wounds. Because Patchen had lost the most blood and was thus the shakiest—he'd been wounded twice and had lost a finger—Yakima set to the task of sterilizing his skinning knife and digging the three rounds out of Speares's neck, thigh, and upper right chest.

Sitting against his saddle, Speares guzzled whiskey and cursed every time the knife point penetrated a bloody, ragged wound.

"Shit, breed," he rasped as Yakima stitched the neck wound closed. Firelight flashed off the bloody needle. "I believe you're enjoying this!"

Yakima grunted and shoved the needle through another pinch of bloody skin. Speares groaned and threw the bottle back.

The next morning, Yakima tended Wolf's head with mud and whiskey, then buried Anjanette on the ravine's lip, arranging rocks over the grave and erecting a small oak cross. He saw no reason why the others should know that she'd thrown in with the Thunder Riders, so he kept the fact to himself, tucking it back with his guilt at not having turned his gun over to Considine and thus causing her death.

Knowing that Considine probably would have killed them both did little to temper the pain. And knowing that she'd gone willingly with Considine did little to lessen his sorrow that he would never hear her raspy, husky voice again, or glimpse the devilish, earthy glint in her wide brown eyes.

He and the men, having secured the strongbox and the mule they'd need to haul it back across the border, spent three days wallowing in the warm, healing waters cleaving the Canyon of Lost Souls. Wolf ran loose, staying close to Yakima but taking frequent rolls in the stream and, to relieve his growing boredom with the bivouac, bedeviled the men with his attempted shoulder nips.

Yakima and Patchen built a travois for Speares, who couldn't yet ride astraddle. At sunset of their third day in the foggy canyon, they harnessed the travois to the mule and started northward. They rode at night to avoid banditos, rurales, *federales*, and Indians. Not wanting to risk a gunshot, Yakima hunted rabbits and prairie chickens with his Jesus stick and snares. It was a slow, tedious trek, but by the time they reached the border Speares was able to ride his own horse.

They pulled into Saber Creek around two o'clock on

a pitch-black morning, the town's dark buildings falling in around them, a dog growling from an alley mouth. The main street was as still as that of a ghost town, though a torch burned on the porch post of one of the brothels and a piano's faint tinkle came from the second story.

"As soon as I secure the strongbox, I know where I'm headin'," Speares said as he angled his horse toward the stone jailhouse. "Anyone wanna join me? Miss Colette's girls are a mite flat-chested, but they please right fine."

"No, thanks," Patchen said. He dismounted in front of the jailhouse to help Speares with the strongbox. "I think I'll bed down over to the hotel. See you in about three days."

Speares glanced at Yakima. The swelling had gone out of the sheriff's broken nose, though the bridge was lumpy. The sutures in his neck wound stood up above his collar on the right side of the neck, where Toots's bullet had come within centimeters of trimming his wick. "What about you, Yakima? I don't think Miss Colette's got any rules against half-breeds."

Yakima began to rein Wolf up the street. "Maybe next time. I'll bed down in the livery barn, pick up my supplies in the morning, and start back to my cabin."

"There's probably a reward for hauling in the gold," Patchen said. "We'll split it three ways."

Yakima walked Wolf up the dark street. "I don't have time to wait around for it. Gotta see if the Apaches left me a cabin."

"Hold on," Speares said. Clutching his wounded side, he climbed heavily out of the leather and reached into one of his saddlebags. He turned, tossed something up to Yakima, who caught it against his chest.

He opened his hand. A deputy sheriff's star.

Yakima peered over the star at the sheriff.

Speares said, "I done lost all my deputies. The pay ain't bad, and it's steady."

Shaking his head, Yakima lowered his hand to toss the badge back to the sheriff but stopped when Speares held up his hand. "Now, I knew you'd balk. But hold on to that star for a while. Just see how it feels. If it don't feel right in a few days, toss it into the woods."

Yakima dropped the star in his shirt pocket. "It's a waste of good tin, but have it your way."

He pinched his hat brim to the men standing under the jailhouse's brush arbor, then gigged Wolf up the street toward the livery barn.

He spent that night in the same stable as Wolf, then started back north the next morning, riding Wolf and leading his paint horse burdened with twenty-six dollars' worth of dry goods and a couple bottles of whiskey— enough to sustain his quiet life in the mountains for a good long time.

As he jogged the horses up a rise in the rolling desert, he felt the badge against his chest. He plucked it from his pocket, glanced at it.

DEPUTY SHERIFF.

He gave a wry snort. Clutching the star between the thumb and index finger of his right hand, he drew his arm back, intending to toss the badge into a mesquite snag about thirty yards off the trail.

He stopped, pulled his hand down, and opened it.

Lifting his gaze from the nickel's worth of tin, he saw Wolf craning his neck to stare back at him, eyes wide, vaguely curious.

"What?" Yakima grunted. "I'm supposed to swap lead with Apaches the rest of my life?"

He glanced at the star once more, then dropped it into his pocket, buttoned the flap, and heeled the stallion into a jog through the chaparral, gradually climbing the lonely slopes rising toward Bailey Peak.

Ride the trail with Frank Leslie . . .

The Wild Breed

Coming from Signet in March 2008

Read on for a special sneak preview

Looking around cautiously, jaws set grimly, Yakima Henry climbed a low rise stippled with crumbling volcanic rock and palo verde shrubs, and reined in his sweaty, dusty mustang—a blaze-faced, coal black stallion with the fire of the chase in its eyes.

Brush snapped and rustled ahead and left, and the half-breed touched his pistol grips. A mangy brush wolf bounded up a nearby knoll, a charcoal-colored jack hanging limp from its jaws. The coyote turned an owly, proprietary glance over its shoulder, then dashed over the rise and disappeared in a mesquite-choked arroyo.

Tall and broad-shouldered, his muscular frame sheathed in a sweat-stained buckskin tunic, blue denims, brush-scarred chaps, and a leather necklace strung with large, curved grizzly teeth, Yakima dropped his hand from the stag-horn grips of his .44. He shifted his gaze under his flat-brimmed, dust-caked plainsman hat to the horse tracks dropping down the rise and disappearing in the chaparral.

Four horseback riders herding five unshod mustangs toward the town lying a good half mile away—a handful of log and adobe dwellings and cow pens clustered in the vast, rolling desert, bordered distantly on all sides by bald crags of isolated mountain ranges.

Beyond Saber Creek, the ridges rippled away like ocean waves, foreshortening into the misty, blue-green reaches of Old Mexico.

Yakima shucked his Winchester Yellowboy from the saddle boot under his right thigh. The mustangs belonged to him. The rustlers had taken them out of his corral when he'd been off hunting wild horses to break and sell to the army. They'd hazed them through the slopes and arroyos, dropping down and away from his small, shotgun ranch nestled at the base of Bailey Peak, no doubt intending to sell them south of the border.

Yakima levered a fresh shell into the Yellowboy's chamber, off-cocked the hammer, set the barrel across his saddle bows, and booted the horse off the ridge, his shoulder-length black hair winnowing out behind him in the hot breeze.

A few minutes later, horse and rider gained the stage road, followed it past the first cow pens and horse corrals of Saber Creek, then across the dry creek bed the town was named for, and into the sun-baked little village, somnolent and sweltering in the late-afternoon heat.

Buildings of whip-sawed cottonwood, sandstone blocks, and adobe brick lined the narrow Main Street, over which a lone ranch wagon clattered, heading toward the opposite end of town. Chickens pecked along the boardwalks. Dogs lazed in shade patches. Few people were about, but Yakima noticed a couple of silhouettes peering at him through sashed windows.

Cicadas whined, a goat bleated unseen in the distance, and the faint tinkling of a piano rode the breeze, drowned by the occasional screech of a shingle chain.

Yakima turned the stallion right and angled it around the town's cobbled square, which was surrounded by old Mexican adobes and a sandstone church with a frayed rope hanging from the boxlike bell tower, and drew rein before a stout log blacksmith shop.

He stared at the nine horses tied to the hitchrack fronting the Saquaro Inn Saloon and Hotel on the right side of the street, just ahead. The horses stood hangheaded in the shade of the brush arbor—all nine dust-streaked and sweat-foamed. Only four were saddled. The rifle boots tied to the saddles were empty.

Yakima booted the black up to the hitchrack, dismounted, and dropped the reins in the ankle-deep dust and manure. "Stay here and don't start no fights."

Patting the horse's slick neck and resting his rifle on his shoulder, he stepped onto the boardwalk. He raked his jade green eyes—which to some seemed startlingly incongruent in his otherwise dark, Indian-featured face— across the five barebacked, unshod mustangs. Then, chaps flapping about his legs, sweat streaking the broad, flat plains of his dust-caked face, he wheeled from the street and pushed through the batwings.

He paused in the cool shadows just inside the door, letting his eyes adjust as he took in the room—the ornate mahogany bar and backbar mirror running along the wall to his right, the dozen or so tables to his left, the stairs at the back. A little man with spats and close-cropped gray hair played a piano—a slow, Southern ballad that might have been recognizable had it been played in the right key—against the far wall below the stairs. Near him, four hard-faced hombres in ratty, dusty trail garb played cards, Winchester and Sharps rifles leaning against their table or resting across empty chairs nearby.

One of the two men facing him wore a couple of big pistols in shoulder holsters, revealed by the thrown-back flaps of his spruce green duster.

To Yakima's left, a girl's voice said, "Well, look what the cat dragged in! Did Mr. Henry get tired of taming horses and come to town to see what *else* needs tamin'?"

Yakima turned to see a small, pale-skinned brunette clad in a low-cut, knee-length red dress sitting alone at a table, her bare knees crossed. The dress was so sheer he could see her small pear-shaped breasts through it, and nearly all other aspects of the pretty girl's delicate anatomy, including a mole on the inside of her right thigh. A strap hung off her skinny shoulder.

She smiled up at him, showing a missing eyetooth and wagging a dirty, slender foot, the red paint on her toenails as chipped and scaled as the siding on an old barn.

An empty shot glass and a half-empty beer mug sat on the table before her. Her admiring gaze ranged across Yakima's broad chest and yokelike shoulders before climbing back to his face.

She twirled a finger in a lock of her curled hair.

He nodded. "Rose."

"*Yakima?*" The bartender—a stringbean with wide-set eyes, thick pomaded hair, and a pronounced overbite—rose suddenly from behind the bar. Floyd Sanchez scowled savagely. "What the hell are *you* doin' here? I thought the sheriff done banned you from town, for breakin' up my place and every *other* place in Saber Creek!"

"Go back to work, Floyd," Yakima growled, barely favoring the man with a glance.

He sauntered forward, his spurs chinging on the rough puncheons, the barrel of his Yellowboy repeater still resting on his shoulder as he approached the table before which the four saddle tramps played cards. One of the men facing him—the man with the dust and the double-rigged holster filled with matched Smith & Wessons—glanced up at him, a stogie in his teeth, five cards fanned out in his left hand. He was a hulking hellion with a freckled, sunburned face and a thick red beard still slick with sweat and coated with seeds and trail dust. He smelled like horses, mesquite smoke, piss, and rancid tobacco.

"Hey, lookee here," he sneered around the stogie, elbowing the round-faced Mexican beside him, "we got us a newcomer."

The Mexican glanced up, black eyes rheumy from drink. He, like all the others, had looked toward Yakima when he'd first pushed through the batwings, but he, like the red-bearded, double-rigged gent, feigned surprise at seeing him at their table. He grinned, showing chipped crooked teeth, including one of gold, inside his thin black beard. "You want in, amigo? Always room for one more if you got money and not just matchsticks, huh?"

One of the two with his back to Yakima glanced behind him and ran his slit-eyed gaze up and down Yakima's tall, rugged frame. He turned back to the table, tossed some coins into the pile before him. "I don't care if he's packin' gold ingots fresh from El Dorado, I don't play with half-breeds."

The red-bearded gent leaned toward him, canting his head toward the round-faced Mexican. "You play with greasers, but you don't play with half-breeds? Where the hell's the logic in that?"

Suddenly, the piano fell silent, and the little gray-haired piano player swung his head toward the room.

The Mexican grinned, chuckling through his teeth, as he stared glassy-eyed at Yakima. A corn-husk cigarette smoldered in the ashtray beside him, near a big Colt Navy, its brass casing glistening in a shaft of sunlight from a window behind him.

Yakima's voice betrayed a hard note of irritation, matter-of-fact contempt for losing two days' work by having to chase stolen horses—horses he'd worked damn hard for the past three weeks to break and ready for the remount sergeant at Fort Huachucha. "You boys can play with yourselves. I'm here for those green-broke mustangs you stole outta my corral. And I'm here to make sure it don't happen again. Get my drift?"

"Ah, shit," the bartender complained behind Yakima. "Mitch, fetch Speares!"

The little man rose from the piano bench, adjusted his spats, and came slowly down the room as though skirting an uncaged lion, shuttling his fearful blue-eyed gaze between the card players and Yakima. When he was past the table, he broke into a run and bolted through the batwings like a bull calf who'd just been steered, his running footfalls fading in the distance.

"Breed," said the big hombre with the shaggy red beard, a dirty black Stetson tipped back on his red curls, "You ain't callin' us *horse thieves*, now, are ya?"

"Since you spoke English, I naturally assumed you could understand it."

"Them horses—they are not branded," said the Mexican, canting his head toward the batwings. In his left eye, he had a BB-sized white spot just to the side of his inky black pupil, and it seemed to expand and contract at will. "How you can prove they're yours, huh?" He shrugged his shoulders, as if deeply perplexed by his own question.

"I didn't brand 'em because the U.S. cavalry generally likes to do that themselves. But I don't need to prove anything to you coulee-doggin' sonsabitches. I tracked *them* and *you* here, and I'm takin' those horses back with me. But I'm willing to wait for the sheriff, so we can all sit down and discuss it, civilized-like, over a drink." Yakima quirked a challenging grin. "That is, if you are."

The red-bearded hombre cut his eyes around the table. The Mexican poked his tongue between his teeth and hissed a chuckle.

One of the men with his back to Yakima half-turned his thick neck and long-nosed face and grumbled, "Me, I personally don't like bein' accused of long-loopin. Not by no half-breed, 'specially."

The gent next to him—square-built and wearing a fancily stitched doeskin vest with a rabbit-fur collar, said in quickly rising octaves, "Especially one that smells as bad and looks as *ugly* as fresh dog shit on a parson's *porch*!"

He'd barely gotten that last out before he snapped sideways in his chair, a silver-chased revolver maw appearing under his right armpit, angled up toward Yakima. Yakima stepped quickly left, snapped his rifle down, back, and forward, smashing the octagonal maw against the side of the man's head, just above his ear.